I0595809

reign OR SHINE

ROSAVIA ROYALS

BOOK 2

HJ WELCH

REIGN OR SHINE

Chapter One

MATTY

"I can do this," Matty Doyle muttered to himself as he stepped from the airplane onto foreign soil for the very first time in his life. He clung to the small hand currently gripping his own like a vise, and looked down at the top of his niece's previously neatly-braided black hair.

After a dozen hours flying, it was sticking out all over the place. She was staring straight ahead as they and the other passengers thanked the crew and crowded down the gangway into the capital city of the tiny European nation of Rosavia. Matty swallowed down the panic that threatened to crawl up his throat and took a long, shaky breath. "I can *do* this."

A woman with two children swinging from her hands smiled kindly at him as the kids shrieked and hopped about. She had tight, natural curls and a backpack crammed full of juice boxes and wet wipes that indicated she knew what the hell she was doing. She didn't seem fazed as she deliberately caught Matty's eye. "You sound like you've come from a lot further than London," she said with a British accent.

Ordinarily, Matty avoided chit-chat with strangers like the plague, as would any true New Yorker. He'd thought it was a kindred trait his city shared with England's capital, but perhaps this family was from the suburbs. Besides, they weren't escaping this throng pouring into Alpina International Airport any time soon, and the lady seemed kind enough. A bit of distraction might be just what Matty needed from his bone-crushing dread.

"Yeah." He nodded and squeezed Finley's hand gently. He looked down to see her look up in trepidation with blue eyes that matched his own. "We transferred through there from JFK. It'll be nice to breathe un-recycled air again."

The woman laughed as the crowd finally emerged from the plane's gangway into a glass-walled corridor. "Agreed. I swear these two are made of farts."

The kids giggled and blew raspberries at her. Matty was shocked, but the woman seemed unbothered. Apparently, that was something kids did? Did Finley do that? He should have asked his sister, Reghan, a few more questions before they'd left home.

"First time in Rosavia?"

Matty blinked as he looked back at the woman, who was smiling and seemed unruffled by the travel, the noise of the airport, the kids' raucous behavior, all of it. "Uh," stammered Matty. "First time anywhere," he admitted sheepishly. Hell, he'd had to get his first-ever passport rushed through for this.

He was a *long* way from Queens.

The woman's face broke into a delighted smile. "Oh, you and your daughter will *love* Alpina. All of Rosavia, really. It's like a bloody fairy tale. We're here for the rest of the summer. My sister moved here and we come over here all the time, don't we?"

The boy and girl attached to her started babbling over one another about rose-flavored ice cream, a royal maze garden, and a lakeside waterpark, but Matty zoned out a little bit. He hadn't slept in twenty-four hours, and had consumed nothing but peanuts and energy drinks in that time. He'd noticed the woman's mistake, but didn't have the energy to correct her.

But of course Finley did, and that was the moment she decided to pipe up.

"Uncle Matty isn't my daddy," she said in a rush to the woman with wide eyes. "I don't have a daddy. My mommies had to stay home, because Mama got really sick, so Mommy has to take care of her, so Uncle Matty came all the way to Europe with me, and now we're finally here, and I thought it would be greener."

She took a deep breath, then bit her lip, her eyes shining with tears as they often did these past few weeks. The kid was a trooper, really, but there was only so much an eight-year-old could carry on her shoulders.

That was what Matty was for.

So before he could let his fears run away with him – that this woman might sneer at Finley for having two moms, or think that Matty wasn't really her 'uncle' and report him – all the usual shit his brain came up with in a panic – he plastered the biggest smile on his face. Because that was what Finley needed.

"Yep," he said brightly. "We're going on an adventure."

Of course the woman just smiled back. He had nothing to worry about. "How fun!" she said sincerely, yanking up the boy who almost tripped over his feet before he smacked into the linoleum. Matty assumed she was the pair's mother, and admired her A+ parenting skills. Maybe one day, he wouldn't be so terrified of being left alone with Finley, or even a kid of his own.

Unfortunately, having not let his mind go down the panic rabbit hole, it decided this was the moment to tumble down the melancholy one instead. The voice in the back of his head unhelpfully reminded him that before thinking about kids, he wanted to get married first. *And that wasn't happening now, was it?*

Matty gritted his teeth and willed the voice to shut up, instead focusing on keeping his smile in place, but not so forced that he looked like a crazy person. Everything would be better once they got their luggage and got to the hotel. He could sleep and maybe have a cry in the shower, shake all these worries off, and be the damn adult in the room.

Finley was counting on him.

"Oh, look," said the British woman, pointing with her chin and managing to twist the kids so they were pointing in the same direction. "That's our carousel. Why don't you go get us a trolly, Double Trouble?"

The kids raced off, arguing about who would get to push the luggage cart. Matty exhaled as the throng from the plane began to mercifully disperse as they circled the carousel. He suspected the woman had announced where their luggage was going to come out from for his benefit, and he was fucking grateful. He didn't mind being mollycoddled in the *slightest.* In fact, if anyone else could jump in and take charge right now, he'd kiss them.

Well…almost anyone else. Jeremy could go fuck himself. It had taken Matty a while to realize that there was a difference between someone loving and caring for you…and a controlling, manipulative asshole.

Sadly, Super-Mom here wasn't his type, but he still beamed at her as they arrived at the moving belt. "How do you keep up with them?" he asked with a laugh.

She tapped her chin and hummed. "Mostly wine," she said sagely with a wink.

As the two other kids came hurtling back, Finley tugged on Matty's hand eagerly, smiling brightly for the first time in what felt like weeks to him. "Is my bow gonna come out soon?" she whispered excitedly.

The British woman lifted her eyebrows in surprise before attempting to school her expression. But she'd heard correctly, and Finley didn't mean the kind of bow that went in her long, black hair.

"Finley's a championship archer," he said proudly. "She qualified for an elite training program here in the city."

To his own surprise, the two British kids became suddenly still, staring at Finley with open mouths. "You know how to fire a *bow and arrow?*" the boy demanded.

"Like Meri-Mera…like in *Brave?*" the younger girl asked in awe.

It was like a lightbulb flicking on. Finley suddenly stepped out from behind Matty's legs and started talking non-stop about her number one passion, waving her arms around as she described the bows she'd owned and the training she'd had.

The woman chuckled. "Can I hire her as a babysitter?" she joked. "I haven't seen them that still since Animal Crossing came out."

Matty watched his niece, overwhelmed with pride for a moment. Not just for Finley, even though it was a huge relief to see her acting like her old self again, but for himself. *I can do this,* he firmly reminded himself. He wasn't going to fuck this up. He could be responsible and capable and all those other things people in charge of kids had to be.

So what if Jeremy had dumped him just when his sister's cancer had come back? So what if he'd called Matty selfish for prioritizing his family over his boyfriend? Yes, the universe could be a real dick sometimes, but Matty was a capable adult. He had to be, for Finley's sake.

"She's hoping to make the Olympics someday," Matty murmured. She was so young to have such motivation. She definitely got that from her birth mom – his sister, Reghan. Determined and ferocious, the both of them. It made Matty rethink his ambitions, of which he had startlingly few.

Reghan would *also* be fine. Matty just needed to make sure this trip for Finley went as smoothly as possible, so his sister could focus on restarting her chemo with her wife by her side. Simple. One step at a time. All he had to do was collect their bags, find the Uber pick-up point, then check in at the hotel. Just because Jeremy had obsessively taken charge of all those kinds of things when he and Matty travelled out of state didn't mean Matty couldn't cope now.

And he *refused* to wish that douchebag was here. Matty

might have wanted someone else to take the reins for him, but not *that* badly. Besides, he was getting a small kick from knowing that he'd managed to get himself and his niece all the way to Europe in one piece. His sister would be proud of him.

One step at a time. I can do this.

"Well," said the British woman, sounding apologetic. She hefted a case from the conveyer belt, then stacked it alongside the other big one she'd already retrieved and the smaller carry-on bags already on the cart. "That's us done. Come on, kids. Good luck with your archery," she added, beaming down at Finley.

"Can we go watch Finley's tournament, Mum?" the little boy asked, clutching his hands together. "She said we could! It's in two weeks."

The woman smiled and nodded at Matty. "Maybe. We'll see," she said neutrally. Then she held a hand out to shake. "I'm Shommie," she said.

"Matty," he replied.

"Uhh, sorry," said Finley in her adorably bossy voice. At least, it was *usually* adorable. "But Uncle Matty's gay."

Matty and Shommie spluttered, but at least Shommie also laughed. "And I'm married," she assured Finley, wiggling her ring finger at her. "But sometimes grown-ups make friends, too." Finley nodded, apparently satisfied. Shommie just smiled and shook her head, fishing out a business card from her pocket. "If you do ever want to grab a glass of wine, though, my sister and I would be happy to show you one of the good-but-cheap bars in town."

Matty took the card, a little dumbfounded. Did people really do that in real life? Make friends so easily?

Suddenly, the thought of having a kind face during the next two weeks was overwhelmingly comforting. "Thank you," he spluttered. "I might just take you up on that."

Shommie grinned, then snapped her head down, looking at where her kids had begun hanging off the luggage cart and pretending they were medieval knights. "All right, you horrible lot!" she cried, pointing toward the exit. "Into battle!"

They tore off, and with a final smile, she left Matty and Finley by the luggage carousel.

Only then did Matty realize that a lot of other people had left from their flight as well.

He frowned and turned his attention back to the moving belt, scanning the bags that were still trundling around. But, no, none of them were his or Finley's. He'd tied rainbow ribbons around all of them, just in case he didn't recognize any of the cases he'd borrowed from Reghan and her wife, Lola. Finley's precious bow case had several attached to it, as well as a whole sheet of unicorn stickers plastered all over, just to make it extra identifiable. The case, the bow, and the sheath of arrows inside were worth a lot of money.

"Uncle Matty?" Finley said, her voice strained, no doubt starting to worry what Matty was already thinking.

Where the fuck was their stuff?

But Matty smiled down at her. "Don't worry," he said cheer-fully. "I bet ours will be the last off, as they've come *all* the way from New York. Here, why don't you help me look?" He picked her up, even though she was slightly too big for that now, and balanced her on his hip. She wrapped her legs around his waist and held her hand above her eyes, like a scout looking over the sea from the crow's nest of a ship.

There were only a few people left now, and unhelpfully, they were looking as anxious as Matty felt. But there were still a couple of bags circling the belt, and he made himself breathe slowly in and out. *Nothing to worry about, they just had to be patient, and…*

The carousel juddered and ground to a halt with a dull squeal.

In his arms, Finley went rigid as undoubtedly the fear rushed through her as fast as it did Matty.

All their clothes. Their toiletries. Finley's irreplaceable bow. *Where were they?*

"Uncle Matty?" Finley whispered, her lower lip trembling.

"It's okay," he said. "Everything's going to be *okay.*"

But he was starting to think he'd been wrong. He could *not*, in fact, do this.

He was pretty sure he was totally screwed.

Chapter Two

CAS

Prince Cassander Fabian Ivor van Rosavia was a grown man of twenty-nine. Some might even say that he was an extremely capable and well-educated grown man, one who took on *too much* responsibility and was *too* mature for his own good.

And yet, there were still two words that could flood him with guilt and make him cringe. Especially, when they were spoken by a certain fiery red-headed woman.

"Your Highness?" Valentina Roth called down the corridor sweetly. Her words bounced off the palace's marble corridor as much as the click-clacking of her pencil-thin high heels. Cas grimaced, attempting to plaster a not-guilty smile on his face as he turned around to face his approaching valet.

He loved the woman, he genuinely did. But the truth was he'd been caught red-handed, and they both knew it.

"Hi," he said, attempting to use the voice he usually reserved for addressing international dignitaries. Instead, it came out as a sort of squeak.

Valentina's red lips twitched as she peered over her black glasses. She came to a halt in front of Cas. She was a good foot shorter than him, but he stared meekly down at her all the same. She was resting a slim leather portfolio on her hip like a baby, its front embossed with the royal crest. She rested her hand on the other hip and tilted her head, making her large red curls bounce.

"Your Highness," she said pleasantly. "I thought I'd find you here."

Of course she did. The woman knew everything. Cas sighed and slipped his hands into his old, faded school hoodie that he'd never normally dare be seen in, glancing around the deserted corridor that was tucked near the back of the palace walls. Not many people came down here. Usually.

"I was just…" Cas began, scrambling around for an excuse. But Valentina had already slipped out a sheet of paper, resting it on top of the leather portfolio, and produced a fountain pen from within her perfectly fitted suit jacket.

"I'll just need your signature on these. Some of them are for Leo, but you know how it is." Cas did. It was easier for Cas to simply take care of it rather than try and track down his older brother.

"Of course," he said, seeing his plans vanishing before his eyes as he began signing. What other calamities would he have to cover for his brothers?

But Valentina smiled as he handed the documents back. "Excellent. Then you can go."

Cas blinked at her, then glanced down the corridor that would eventually lead to one of the palace's lesser known exits where his car was parked waiting for him. No driver, of course. Just a packed bag in the trunk.

"I can?" he asked with a frown. "Go, I mean?" Normally she fought him harder than this.

He honestly wasn't sure when it had started. Some time in the past five years, probably? All Cas knew was that every now and again, he just *had* to escape this madness, even just for a little while.

He knew it was irresponsible to sneak off without even letting anyone know where he was going. But Valentina and his security detail always seemed to be aware of where he was in the city, and anyway, nothing had ever happened. It was amazing how just putting on casual wear could make the citizens of Rosavia look straight through him.

Because from time to time, that was *all* he craved. He was tired of being the responsible one and observing every tiny detail of his brothers' madcap lives. Because then he inevitably tried to *fix* everything. And enough was enough.

"I talked to Leo after he skipped out on that damned dinner," Cas said as he rubbed his eyes. He *refused* to feel guilty about this, but apparently his churning stomach hadn't gotten the memo. "I'm not doing him any favors. He has to stand on his own two feet for once. It doesn't matter if he thinks I'm better suited, I'm *not* the one who's going to be king someday."

And honestly, that was absolutely fine by Cas. Just because he was sure he'd do a decent job didn't mean he wanted the crown in the slightest. In fact, what he was craving now was completely the opposite.

"I know," said Valentina smugly. He really shouldn't be surprised by her after all this time, but still, he raised his eyebrows ever so slightly.

"You do?"

She nodded. "I had your apartment cleaned this morning and a fresh delivery of groceries should be waiting for you when you get there." She scanned the several sheets of paper inside the portfolio before sliding one out that Cas hadn't signed yet, presenting it to him on the leather with the pen once more poised for his signature. "Your parents were delighted to hear you're now a supporter of the Junior Archery Association. They *completely* understand that you'll be very busy over the next couple of weeks."

"I will?" Cas asked dubiously. Then he realized what she meant. "Of course. The anniversary ball." There was no escaping the country's celebrations for their five-hundredth anniversary in two weeks' time. But Cas had honestly been hoping for a little break.

However, Valentina winked. "Oh, no, Your Highness. You've put in the lion's share of work for the ball up until now. It's time for other people to step up. Your parents have approved you taking some time to support this sporting organization and…" She took the signed slip of paper back with a sly smile. "…the Junior Archery Association is thrilled that you'll be there to judge their graduation tournament in two weeks' time, and have *no need* to see you until then."

Cas exhaled, understanding, and flooded with gratitude. She was unofficially giving him a two-week vacation. He'd kiss her if a) she was his type and b) he wasn't so scared of the pint-sized valet. God bless her.

"I'm always happy to be of service," he said as she filed away the document.

Valentina snapped the portfolio closed and took back her pen, replacing the cap with a loud *click*. "That, Your Highness, is the whole problem."

He watched with a faint smile as she *clip-clopped* away.

She was right. It *was* the whole problem. Cas liked being needed. He was *good* at being needed. There was a certain calmness like no other that came from knowing he'd solved a problem and eased another person's burden. But a line had to be drawn.

His brothers – in fact, this whole household – was using him as a crutch. It wasn't that Cas didn't get satisfaction from problem-solving. But it wasn't enough. He couldn't explain exactly how, but it had become hollow in recent years.

Him jumping in and fixing every little hiccup wasn't doing his brothers any favors. Especially Leo, who needed to stop playing up to this rebellious bad boy image he'd fashioned for himself and start acting like the heir of Rosavia. The only way Cas saw to make a clean break from this pattern of behavior was to remove himself from the vicinity for a little while.

He could have visited the Zasfer castle where the family vineyard had stood for centuries. It was peaceful there and only ran on a skeleton staff, but Cas needed more of a break than that.

He needed to be someone else, if only for a short time. Even though he really shouldn't be indulging in this dangerous habit any more than he had been. The eyes of the country were on the palace in the runup to the ball, especially from the press and the likes of that vile reporter Ida von Tarr. She was always looking for any excuse to tear the royal family down, and Cas was being irresponsible by running off and playing commoner. He should be scaling back his secret trips into the city, not planning on a solid two weeks immersed in civilian life. But it was like a drug.

Here, he was Sander, the brother who had all the answers. To the people of Rosavia, he was Prince Cassander, currently second in line to the throne (until Leo started producing heirs, in any case). And to the world...he wasn't really anyone. Their neighbors, like Grechzen and Thedes, knew who they were, but most other countries had barely heard of their small European state. They certainly wouldn't recognize anyone from the royal family apart from King Alphonse, and even that would be a long shot.

It had been that realization that had first given Cas the confidence to go out into the city and see if he could get away with being just that – simply 'Cas.' Sure enough, he hardly *ever* got recognized in a hoodie and sneakers.

It was bliss.

But he kind of thought he'd been getting away with it. He suspected Valentina might have known, but they'd never actually discussed it until just now. Of course she knew about his secret apartment. He'd been foolish to think otherwise. Was it really sensible for him to go out like this?

Cas chewed his lip, but decided not to look a gift horse in the mouth. He'd been banking on having clothes at the apartment he rented in the city, but of course Valentina had suspected his plan, and now it was fully cleaned and stocked as well.

He was good to go on vacation.

Well, not really. He'd come back the second he was needed for anything, and with the country's five-hundredth anniversary ball looming, he had no doubt he'd be pinging back and forth like a yo-yo. But for now, he was just like any other ordinary guy.

And he was going to make the most of it.

He had a little routine now. A secret series of rituals that helped him morph from Prince Cassander into plain old Cas. By the time he'd let himself into his moderately-sized but still very nice apartment, dropped off his bag, checked the place over, then taken a stroll around the block, he was starting to feel like a totally normal guy. He ordered his usual cappuccino with a blueberry muffin from his favorite café, thrilled when the server recognized him and called him Cas. He resisted the urge to say 'That's me!' in response. Instead, he snuck a ten-Euro tip into the jar, then slipped outside to enjoy the sunshine.

He should have known better.

When scanning the small seating area outside the café, he did a double take at a guy sitting opposite a free chair at a two-person table. "Typical," Cas muttered with a smile.

His younger brother, Benedict, waggled his eyebrows as Cas took the seat opposite him. "Why hello, Cas," he said, his voice amused. "Fancy seeing you here."

Cas sighed, accepting his fate. Ben was the only one in his family as observant as he was, by a long shot. They were similar in a lot of ways, with their generally calm demeanor and fast-thinking problem solving. But where Cas had technically qualified as a child for the country's spy agency, run by their aunt Geraldine, he'd been too valuable as the spare to the throne. Ben, on the other hand, had outdone Cas's scores, and he'd been set early on for a thrilling life of espionage.

As much as Cas worried for him, he also knew Ben loved his work. At least, he usually did. There had been a sadness in his eyes these past few months that Cas couldn't quite figure out.

He shook himself mentally and smiled at Ben. The fact that his brother had called him Cas and not Sander meant he knew exactly what Cas was doing; hiding out in the real world for a short spell.

It also meant he supported it.

Cas smiled fondly at Ben. Not quite the baby of the family, but Ben being seven years younger than him meant that Cas still felt a protective urge stir through him, despite the fact his little brother dodged bullets for a living.

Not that anyone else in the family knew that, of course. Aside from Aunt Geraldine, who ran the damn agency. God, this family had so many secrets. Cas wished he didn't know quite so many of them.

At least it meant he and Ben were close. It stopped Cas from going out of his mind some days, worrying about all and sunder.

"How long are you on leave this time?" he asked, taking a sip from his coffee. He watched his brother take a toothpick from a rose-shaped pot on the wrought iron table, slipping it between his lips to delicately chew on.

"You know how it goes," Ben replied. "They say two weeks, then call me back up without a moment's notice like there's some kind of emergency."

"Almost like you're in the Army," Cas said dryly.

The rest of their brothers genuinely thought Ben was in the armed forces. Cas didn't know much more than that he *wasn't*, but he liked to give Ben the chance to talk as much as he was able to when he was on leave. If he was honest, he kind of loved that the two of them had this exciting little secret about his double life. Cas spent so much time fussing over Leo, Jules, and Wren, he didn't always feel so close with them. With Ben, even though his life was shrouded in mystery, Cas actually felt their relationship was closer and more authentic than he had with almost anyone else at the palace.

"How about you?" Benedict deflected, discarding the tooth-pick on an empty plate. "It's not like we're having lunch in the palace. Why are we out here doing this?"

Cas narrowed his eyes. So, Ben knew that Cas liked to slip out and play commoner, but did he really not know why? Or did he have an inkling and was fishing for more?

"It's important to understand what life is like for the people of our country," Cas said, repeating the stock answer he'd composed long ago in case anyone ever caught on to what he was doing. "How can we do that from inside the palace?"

However, like Valentina, Cas was pretty sure Ben was not only aware of what he'd been up to, but supportive of it. It was funny they should both approach him on the same day about it.

Perhaps his brothers were finally starting to listen to him and his vow not to save their asses all the damn time.

"I'm never going to be Head Kitty," Cas said, using the ridiculous codename they'd come up with a while back for their father, the current reigning king of Rosavia. Their baby brother, Wren, had a thing about cats, and one day it had just stuck. "I don't *want* to be Head Kitty. It's kinder to let Leo flounder on his own now and work things out." He bit his lip and absently pushed some sugar packets around. "I should have done it years ago."

He looked up to see Ben staring into the middle distance.

Cas arched an eyebrow, mostly in amusement, but also in slight annoyance. This was kind of a big deal for him, forcing himself to stop enabling his other brothers' behavior.

"Are you even listening?" he asked with a sigh.

"I'm always listening," Ben said wryly, just as his phone buzzed from his pants pocket. "Hold on."

Cas took a sip of coffee, then tried to quash the sliver of dread that snaked through his guts. Benedict was a grown man and fully trained spy. Cas had to let him do his job and trust him not to get in serious trouble.

Much like Cas was asking Ben to do for him, in a different way.

Still, he was allowed to worry, just a *little*.

"Let me guess," said Cas. "They want to cancel your leave?

What even do you do in the Army that's so important?" They both knew when he said 'the Army,' he meant the intelligence agency. But Cas genuinely was curious as to what Ben was doing already. He was only twenty-two, after all.

Ben's expression was pure devilment. "Oh, you know. Suck the brass. Their egos are very fragile. They need a lot of sucking."

"Up," Cas corrected, despite knowing his brother wouldn't listen.

Sure enough, Ben just smirked as he read the message and typed out a quick response. Then he made a spectacle of rolling his eyes and letting out a big sigh. "Sorry," he said, not sounding the least bit sorry as he pushed his chair back and stood up. "It looks like you're right about my leave being cancelled. Apparently I have more sucking to do."

"*Up*," Cas insisted, feeling his mouth twitch in amusement. Ben knew teasing him would make Cas worry a little less as to why Ben was suddenly being recalled. "Sucking *up*."

"Sure. If you insist." Ben blew a kiss, but his flippant attitude hadn't squashed Cas's fears entirely. He couldn't help but stand up to embrace his little brother tightly, silently urging him to keep safe.

So Ben's words to him were slightly unexpected as he actually returned Cas's hug for once. "Be careful, okay?"

Cas leaned back and frowned. "About what?"

"Everything." Ben winked at him as he stepped away, infuriatingly vague as usual, then vanished into the crowd of people wandering down the street, enjoying Rosavia's summer sunshine.

Cas sighed and sat himself back down. By the time he'd finished his coffee, he was less rattled. The whole point of this little 'real-world' sabbatical was to *stop* fretting over his brothers. So, what would he have done if he hadn't run into Ben?

He tapped his fingernail on the side of his empty cup, a smile creeping onto his face.

Typical Valentina.

Cas had not once expressed an interest in archery, let alone a children's program. But now he was enthralled by the idea. Rosavia was so goddamned obsessed with lacrosse, Cas had long grown weary of it. He'd been forced to play at school, and everything else seemed to stop for lacrosse season over the summer. The streets would be packed with celebrations for the Grand Championships come October, but Cas could never seem to muster the enthusiasm he had as a child.

But archery? That was romantic, noble. He'd had no idea that Rosavia was hosting this elite training program.

He found himself wanting to know more.

Dutifully, he picked up the empty crockery and took it back inside. The server smiled fondly when she caught him doing it. "I told you, you don't have to do that, Cas," she said with only a slight sigh.

Cas saluted her as he left. "I can't help it, Elina. Have a nice day!"

With his sunglasses on he felt like he was on another planet as he strolled down Alpina's bustling streets. He was invisible, and it was glorious.

It wasn't until he'd gotten older and learned to become a different version of himself that he'd been able to appreciate the beauty of his country and home city. Official duties had brought him to many nations over the years, but there was definitely something that made Alpina *Alpina*. As Rosavia was so small, and this was its biggest city, for Cas it showed off the best of his homeland.

Since becoming Cas, rather than Sander, he'd been able to appreciate all the beauty around him through fresh eyes. The mountains rising inland to the north, the gorgeous alpine lake to the south, and wild roses in the rugged, green heathland in between. Cas breathed deep and smiled to himself, pretending he was a tourist, out for his first exploration of a brand-new city.

After wandering for a while (and getting an ice cream to follow up his muffin lunch, because he was an *adult)*, he found himself on Coniston Street, Alpina's premier shopping district. Ordinarily, Cas would think of this place as hell on earth during a hot summer's day. But he was free, master of his own time, with nowhere to be and no one to please. So he strolled along, rolling up the sleeves of his hoodie, but keeping it on just for that added layer of anonymity. He nimbly sidestepped families of tourists, friends with dozens of box-shaped bags walking arm-in-arm, and harassed-looking suited people, no doubt office workers, most of them frantically talking or texting on their phones.

This was living. Not being pampered in a palace. Cas felt giddy, taking in all the sights like a kid in a candy store.

Then he spotted it. A sporting goods store on the corner of Coniston and Lowther.

And they had an archery sale on.

Not questioning it and following his feet, Cas sauntered into one of the only stores he'd purposely avoided since beginning his secret jaunts into the city. He touched his nose in phantom pain just looking at the lacrosse supplies. But almost immediately, he was drawn to an archery section that looked suspiciously new and shiny. There were posters for the graduation tournament that he was going to be attending, and advice pamphlets on beginner's technique and local classes.

But Cas only took those details in superficially. Because he wasn't the only one currently examining the mechanical-looking bows hanging from the wall.

"Can you see anything that looks any good, honey?" a man around Cas's age asked a small girl by his side. The guy might have been a few years younger than Cas, actually, and Cas used his extensive knowledge of children to put the kid somewhere between five and fifteen years old. They both had jet-black hair, pale skin, and the man had spoken English with an American accent.

Something immediately drew Cas closer, but not so close he was intruding. At least he hoped not. Really, he should keep walking, as these two were clearly having a slightly stressful moment, judging by their tense body language and the way the guy's eyes kept darting over the price tags of the half-sized bows. But Cas's heart sped up, and he pretended to inspect a set of arrows.

The little girl gave a shaky sigh. "Uncle Matty," she said, sounding very close to tears. "I think…I've been thinking we should just go home. I need *my* bow. I can't…"

A lump rose in Cas's throat as this girl almost started sobbing right there and then. Cas glanced over and saw the guy – had she said 'Matty'? – look down at the girl as if he was going to bawl too. Then he plastered a big smile on his face, blinked a couple of times, and scooped the kid up in his arms even though she was almost half his size.

"Hey, kiddo. No way, all right?" Cas was trying not to obviously stare, but he tried to keep watching them out of the corner of his eye. He could sense people's upset a mile off, and these two were radiating it. "You *earned* your place at that fancy-schmancy academy. The airline spoke to Heathrow Airport – you remember, where we changed planes in London? They *definitely* have our stuff. It's just gonna take a little while to get it back to us, as they have a lot of other people's stuff, too, and we all flew off to different countries. We just need something to get you through tomorrow, and um…"

His gaze lingered on what Cas had already surmised was the cheapest bow available…and his whole body visibly trembled.

"Sweetheart? I'm going to speak to the nice lady at the checkout and see if they rent any bows, okay? But everything is *fine*. Uncle Matty is gonna make sure you're all set for class tomorrow, so you can show all those instructors what a star you are!"

He carefully set the girl down, bit his lip, and turned away to walk toward the cashier.

And somehow, Cas found himself stepping away from the display to block the guy's path.

For a second, they just stared at each other. And…dear *lord*… Cas hadn't even been looking properly before. Not by half. He'd completely missed the sharp square jaw and piercing blue eyes that bore through him like plunging into the ocean. Matty's hair was a mess of tousled curls that he'd definitely been running his fingers through due to stress.

Cas's hands itched to do the same, but for far more pleasurable reasons.

They were still staring at each other.

Cas cleared his throat and flashed his best crowd-pleasing and reassuring smile. "I'm so sorry," he said, easily switching into English. He spoke several languages, after all, but English was undoubtedly the one he used most aside from Rosavian. "I couldn't help but overhear your predicament, and I was wondering if I could help?"

Matty blinked slowly, taking a few seconds to glance down at the girl, then back up at Cas. "You...want to help us?" he asked. "How?"

Cas almost snorted a laugh. How would he help this caring, gorgeous man and adorable kid?

Any way he could.

Chapter Three

MATTY

Matty's new friend, Shommie, had described Rosavia as a fairy tale back at the airport. And now Matty had to question if he hadn't fallen into some kind of wonderland.

He risked taking a glance over at the guy – *Cas* – who was currently driving him and Finley from the shopping district to the fancy boarding school on the outskirts of the city. Finley was due for registration to start her training tomorrow. Cas, who had not only bought Finley a bow to tide her over until her beloved one came back to them – *bought*, not rented – but he'd suggested they visit a clothing store, and purchased them both a clean outfit to keep them going until their bags returned. He'd also insisted they go to a drug store to get the essentials like toothpaste and deodorant.

Matty would have slummed it. But thanks to the kindness of a stranger, Finley didn't have to arrive at her first day of archery academy feeling like a swamp monster.

"Honestly, it's my pleasure," Cas had insisted more than

once, especially at the cash registers. Matty had promised to pay him back, but Cas kept insisting he had a wealthy family and "more money than I know what to do with." He made it sound as if Matty and Finley were the ones doing *him* a favor, not the other way around.

What the hell was this place Rosavia?

Well, from the view out of the windows, he could tell it was a stunning country to look at. Breathtaking land-scapes seemed to stalk them wherever they turned, especially once they ventured beyond the city limits. Picturesque mountains peeked up in the distance from fields of lush green grass, until they passed through a forest where the foliage seemed to run wild in a way that suggested it was protecting a sleeping princess from a terrible curse.

In his jet lagged state, Matty finally dragged his eyes away from the window long enough to glance at Finley in the back seat. She was sleeping, again, and Matty was almost painfully envious. She needed the rest, no doubt, but if Matty didn't put his head down soon he was going to start hallucinating. If he wasn't already.

He looked over at their mysterious charitable benefactor, half wondering if he was just a figment of Matty's imagination. Surely no one was that handsome *and* kind? But his divine aftershave certainly smelled real enough, and when they'd shaken hands earlier after introductions had been made, Matty was sure he'd felt flesh and blood.

Had Matty made the right decision to trust a total stranger, though? He'd been so overwhelmed and desperate for help, he'd clung to the first offer that had come along like a barnacle. But what if this guy wasn't what he seemed? What if he was a serial killer or something?

Matty rolled his eyes at himself. That was *ridiculous*. But he couldn't help but notice that Cas wasn't using any kind of map to get them to the school, and in Matty's sleep-deprived state, that suddenly seemed suspicious. Cas could be taking them *anywhere*. Had Matty let himself be conned by a pretty face in a foreign country, only to end up in serious trouble? Wasn't this how several Liam Neeson films started?

Cas caught him staring, and Matty blushed. "Uh," he said uncertainly as they continued to speed along the twisty, turny highway. "You're, um, not using a map?" he eventually managed to stammer.

Cas laughed and smiled briefly at Matty before gluing his eyes back on the road, despite there being very few other cars around now they'd left the city. "I did say earlier," Cas reminded him gently, "Elm Willows was my old boarding school. I spent seven years there. I know this route like the back of my hand, I swear. You've got nothing to worry about."

He bit his lip, letting it drag slowly between his teeth, making Matty practically whimper. *Damn*. He hadn't lusted after any guy like this in a long time. He blamed the jet lag for it, as well as his complete blip on recalling Cas talking about this being his school.

"Oh, cool," Matty said when he realized Cas was probably waiting on a response from him.

Cas looked briefly over at Matty, though, with a slightly concerned expression. "But if you're anxious, please feel free to follow along using your own navigation. If your network doesn't cover you here, you can hotspot off my own phone, it's fine."

Matty studied Cas's side profile as the other man kept his beautiful brown eyes diligently on the road. His skin was tanned a light coppery brown, and the hair on his head and jaw was dark, with a hint of auburn when the sunlight hit it.

Okay, Matty could admit it. There was a chance he'd said yes to a serial killer, just because he was drop-dead-fucking-*gorgeous*.

But every bone in his body was telling him that Mr. Cas NoLastName was on the level. Which was probably the first ticket to Liam Neeson-ville, but Matty was only human. There was *also* a chance that Cas was just a nice guy, and Matty was lucky enough to get to spend even just a little bit of time with him.

"N-no, that's cool. I trust you," Matty stammered. *Moron.* "Is it much further?"

Cas flashed that smile again, and Matty's heart flipped. "Not long now, I promise."

And Matty believed him. Which he shouldn't. Because handsome men who said 'I promise' were lying liars who *lied*. Matty pushed his tongue against the back of his teeth until it got painful.

Jeremy had made a lot of promises. He'd seemed so *right*. Like Matty might have found The One. They'd had fun, the sex had been good, and Jeremy had been employed at a decent firm in the city, so he had that all-important stability Matty always craved. But when push came to shove, Jeremy had laughed at Matty for thinking they were truly serious (after two fucking years, thank you very much) and vanished quicker than a tear on a rainy day.

Because Matty's sister having her cancer relapse was "just, like, way too much right now, baby."

Asshole.

So Matty chewed his lip and stared out at the scenery that looked like it belonged on the top of a chocolate box. *Jeremy is a long, LONG, way away from Rosavia,* he reminded himself. Cas was not Jeremy, as evident by him taking two seconds to look beyond his own needs.

"Do you have a job?" Matty blurted, apropos of nothing. He clutched the edge of the leather seat of the beautiful, very sleek and fancy car Cas apparently owned, and felt his face burn. *So smooth.* "Sorry. I mean, uh, I've lost track of what day it is, but I work shifts myself, and I was suddenly worried we'd pulled you from your job, and, uh…"

Cas grinned at Matty's sleep-deprived attempt at small talk. "I do have a job," he said in a measured voice that sounded pretty much British to Matty's ears, but had a lilt over the odd syllable every now and again. "Although I'm very flexible, and on something of a vacation right now. I'm genuinely honored to introduce a couple of travelers to the wonders of Coniston Street." He winked at Matty. "So *wild* and *exotic,*" he teased.

Matty wasn't used to being teased. A little part of his brain worried that Cas was mocking him. Looking back on it, Jeremy used to love making Matty feel dumb and foolish. But the rest of Matty's brain, along with his belly and his cock, were tingling with the gentle ribbing, basking in the attention.

"You've been very kind," Matty mumbled, mortified at the wetness that prickled at the back of his eyes. "I mean, uhh… above and beyond, really."

He and Cas glanced over at each other at the exact same time, their eyes locking for a second that seemed to want to stop Matty's heart. But then they looked away just as quickly. Cas flicked his eyes toward Finley in the back, whose mouth was hanging open as she very gently snored.

"It seems like you've been through a bit of a time," Cas said softly.

To his horror, Matty sniffed, swallowing down a whole sob as those tears threatened to spill again. "Uh, sorry," he stammered, hastily rubbing at his eyes. "Yeah, it's been a bit of a shit show. I've literally never left the country before, and to lose our luggage? Urgh. I wasn't even supposed to *be* on this trip." He scrubbed at his face, staring doggedly out of the window. But of course Cas still asked.

"What happened?"

Matty inhaled another shuddery breath. Cas was an almost total stranger, but Matty didn't have Jeremy to talk to anymore (not that he'd ever given a shit anyway, apparently) so why not offload for a second? Cas was offering, after all.

"My big sister – Finley's mom. She had breast cancer. We thought it was all gone, but a couple of weeks ago it reared its ugly head again." He swallowed and bit his tongue, determined not to cry. "Her friends were amazing, and started a crowdfunding campaign in days, and she's already started treatment. She's still got a real fighting chance, but…"

He trailed off, looking at sleeping Finley in the back seat.

"But traveling was too much," Cas supplied. "So brilliant Uncle Matty stepped up to the plate, and saved the day."

Matty offered Cas a sheepish smile, trying not to let his warm words into his heart, because Matty didn't deserve them. "I lost our luggage," he whispered.

Cas raised a very stern eyebrow at Matty, which made his insides squirm for more reasons than one. "You did, huh? Personally? You jumped off at Heathrow and mucked around the loading bays, throwing your bags into the dumpster?"

Matty went weak thinking of their stuff in the trash, but then he realized Cas was obviously kidding. "Uh, yeah," he said weakly. "I totally did. You caught me."

Cas snorted and grinned over at him as they took another curve through the seemingly never-ending countryside. "Just as I suspected," he said, like he'd caught a thief in a cheesy mystery show. "I can see why you're taking all this guilt on yourself."

"All right, shut up," Matty mumbled, lightly slapping at Cas's thigh…which was a mistake, because *dear god* those muscles. He snatched his hand back and cleared his throat. "Okay, I've never left the country before. I've never looked after Finley for more than an evening of babysitting while Reghan and Lola went out for dinner or whatever. I am *so* in over my head, and that was before we lost the uber-duber expensive bow and arrows and their case. Then you swoop in and save the day… I just really need you to understand what this means for us, I guess?"

Cas licked his lips – which really didn't help the developing situation in Matty's jeans – and glanced over at him for just a second. "You're *very* welcome," Cas said in a velvety voice that made Matty want to curl up and cry with longing.

This guy was going to kill him before he was done rescuing him.

Okay, Matty had to admit it.

He was jealous.

"Nibblet!" he admonished. "You never told me you were going to *Hogwarts* for this thing!"

"I didn't know," Finley whispered back.

They both stared up in awe at the old reddish building and all its cream towers and turrets. The enormous square structure was surrounded by lush green grass and woodland, with birds tweeting and the sun shining down. A clock tower stood in the middle of the school's front, and as Matty and Finley gaped up, it chimed the quarter hour. The bells resonated through Matty's bones, and he suddenly felt a part of something much larger than himself.

For him, high school had been a terrible endurance test to simply survive. But looking at this place, he felt like he was a part of history, even though he wasn't even going to be attending. But Finley was. Even if it was just a couple of weeks. This was going to be epic for her.

"You really went to school here?" Matty asked Cas. They were standing beside his sleek BMW, and Matty had Finley's shopping bags and new bow case in hand. Cas raised his eyebrows.

"I really did," he said faintly. Then he rubbed the back of his neck and cleared his throat. "I'd love to walk down memory lane with you both, but I remembered I have to make a work call in about five minutes." Then he turned those smoldering brown eyes on Matty and quirked his lips. "But I can wait for you out here, Matty?"

Matty forgot how words worked for a second. What reality had he stepped into, where this super-hot guy was sounding almost *anxious* for Matty to come back to him?

"Uh, sure," Matty managed to utter.

Cas beamed, then crouched down to address Finley directly. "It was wonderful meeting you, young lady. I hope you have the most amazing time and learn loads of cool things."

Finley bit her lip, then rocked on her toes. "I'm going to be the best one there!" she announced, as if she couldn't believe her own daring. "I'll do it for Mama and Mommy, and Matty, and you too, Cas, for being so nice. I promise!"

Cas smiled at her and squeezed her skinny shoulder. "Just so long as you do your best, I know your family is going to be so proud of you."

She grinned, showing off the gap from the last tooth she'd lost near the back. Matty's heart ached to see her smiling like that again. "And will you look after Uncle Matty?" she asked Cas sincerely. "He doesn't know anyone here apart from our airport friends, but they might be busy."

Oh, shit! Danger! Danger!

Matty was mortified at the idea that Cas might feel obliged to do any more for them. He'd already been so kind.

But Matty knew what he was really terrified of was the idea of spending any time with Cas without having Finley there as a buffer. He was stunning, and Matty was…not. They'd run out of conversation in two minutes flat. Nope, it was just a very bad idea that Matty needed to squash immediately.

"Oh, well," Matty spluttered, shaking his head. "That's not – I mean – uh…" He took a breath and smiled at her. "Why don't we get you registered and settled in, okay? I'll be fine." He threw an apologetic look at Cas, who just smiled faintly.

"Okay," said Finley, rolling her eyes. "You don't have to be weird about it."

She skipped off, leaving Matty with his cheeks flaming. When he looked over at Cas again, though, he just smiled brighter. "I'll be here," he said with a nod.

Matty readjusted her bags and the bow he was carrying, nodded once in understanding, then fled. He jogged from the parking lot to catch up with Finley. "Do you know where we're going?" he asked, consciously changing the subject and scanning the area as they approached the school.

He realized belatedly he shouldn't ask her that kind of thing. As the adult, he should just know or find out. But Finley pointed to a temporary sign up ahead with *Junior Archery Association – Registration This Way* written on it.

"That looks good!" she proclaimed, skipping along the path. "Cas is nice."

Matty hummed, trying to look for any more signs.

"And he's pretty."

"Men aren't pretty," said Matty automatically, then he winced, realizing he'd been parroting his dad.

Sure enough, Finley stopped walking and jammed her hands on her hips with a huff and a scowl. "My mommies say that guys can be pretty if they want! And ladies can be handsome!"

Matty rubbed his eyes, suitably scolded by an eight-year-old. God, he was jet lagged and rattled by Cas, if that old nonsense had come out so easily.

He hadn't thought about his parents for so long. It had been years since they'd talked to him or his sister, since they'd both come out together in solidarity. Turned out, they'd needed it when their folks had kicked them out of the house, cut all contact with them, and refused to attend Reghan's wedding. *Fuck them.* Reghan, Lola, and Finley were his family now.

"You're right, Nibblet," he said contritely. "Sorry. Cas is very kind, for sure." And apparently, Matty didn't want to talk about him so badly he'd resorted to the first nastiness from his old man that had fallen out of his mouth.

"Oh totally, he's nice." Finley crossed her arms, a dangerously smug look on her face. *"And* handsome-pretty?"

Matty urged her to get walking again with a hand on her back. It was perhaps best not to say anything at all right now.

Mercifully, they were soon distracted as they found the court-yard where registration was taking place, and several very friendly staff members were coordinating the arriving kids efficiently. They seemed perfectly fine as he explained their luggage situation and handed over Finley's shopping bags and bow case. Logically, Matty felt confident leaving his niece with the chaperones, despite his irrational fears trying to tell him that if he let her out of his sight, the school was definitely going to get attacked by a pack of wild lions or be flattened by a tornado.

He bit his tongue and told his brain to shut up as he hugged Finley goodbye for the third time. Then he double-checked that she had the cell phone Reghan had bought her especially for this trip, as well as the charger and European adapter that had thankfully also been in her carry-on bag.

"I'll text as soon as we get our bags back," he promised. "And you text me and your moms with everything that's going on. If you have any questions, no matter how silly, you ask these nice people here, okay?"

Finley giggled and shooed at him. "Oh my god. I know, all right? I know! Cas is waiting for you. Now go!"

Matty opened and closed his mouth, determined to tell her that he wasn't thinking about Cas at *all*. But another kid arrived for registration, and Finley excitedly spun around and ran to introduce herself.

There was nothing left for Matty to do but as he'd been told, and head off.

Back to Cas.

He licked his lips and caught the nearest staff member's eye. "Thank you again," he said.

"Don't worry, Mr. Doyle," said the old guy kindly, in that same almost British accent that Cas had. "We'll take good care of your niece. Have a lovely time in Rosavia."

"Right, sure," Matty muttered to himself as he began traipsing back through the school towards Cas's car.

He really wanted to call his sister, but it was still a little early back in New York, and the last he'd heard from Lola was that Reghan was feeling pretty damn rough after her first chemo session. So he'd promised to only text for now and wait for her to be well enough to call him.

He'd let her know there was a hiccup with the luggage once he'd heard from Heathrow and found out they had it all and would be forwarding it on to them, so there was no reason to worry. He texted again now as he walked back through the school, to tell both Finley's moms that she was settled at Elm Willows, but his finger paused on the send button.

The urge to ask his big sis for advice was strong. She'd always looked after him. He supported her, of course, but she was the strong one of the two of them. Now she needed him to be strong, and his silly fears were completely benign when compared to her health.

But the truth was, he hadn't actually thought this far ahead. Hadn't researched a single tourist spot or anything. He was only *just* keeping his head above water back home, waiting tables in a pizza place and taking ticket stubs at a small theater. He'd been able to fly out here with Reghan and Lola's help after they managed to get a partial refund on their own bookings. Then together, they had just about been able to scrape together enough money for his stay. But playing tourist? He absolutely didn't have the cash lying around for dinners out or for visiting any attractions or anything.

So it was all well and good, Finley telling Cas to look after him, but Matty was terrified Cas was soon going to realize that Matty was a broke loser, if he hadn't figured that out already. He must have, otherwise why would he have insisted on buying all that emergency stuff for them? Humiliation layered itself over Matty's jet lag, washing nausea through him.

He *really* didn't want Cas to think he was a loser. Even if they never saw each other again after today, the idea made Matty cringe. Cas was a dream. Was it too much to believe that he might like Matty more than just for a pity party?

He shook his head as he reemerged from the front of the building. First things first, he *desperately* needed to check into his hotel, have a scalding hot shower, then maybe sleep for two days straight. He'd *done* it. He'd gotten Finley here. That was all that mattered. Now he could relax.

Not that he'd done it alone, he reminded himself as he approached the car. Cas was still talking on the phone, and looked up as Matty got closer.

His smile was enough to stop traffic. And he directed it at Matty.

Damn. If he really turned out to be a serial killer, at least Matty wasn't going to blame himself too much. Who could resist this guy?

Lord only knew why he'd paid a second of attention to Matty, but it had meant Finley had made it to her training with a bow and everything. So Matty refused to question his good fortune any more than he already had, and decided to at least *try* and enjoy the drive back to Alpina with this gorgeous near-stranger.

"Hey," he said as he approached and Cas closed his call. "Everything okay?"

Cas appeared to be confused for just a second, then he looked at his phone. "With work? Oh, yes. Same old, same old. Did everything go smoothly with Finley?"

Matty chuckled and came to a stop in front of Cas. He wasn't too much taller than Matty, but he was certainly broader and more muscular. He crossed his legs out in front of him as he leaned on his car, looking like a tall drink of water.

Focus, Matty told himself.

"Great," he said brightly. "She barely even looked back at me. Practically shooed me off." He placed his hand mournfully over his heart. "I'm already yesterday's news."

Cas laughed, a deep rumbling sound that went straight to Matty's balls. *Damn.* He needed to get laid, desperately. Since Reghan had received her diagnosis and Jeremy had fucked off, Matty honestly hadn't even thought about sex. But it had been weeks now since he'd even taken himself in hand, and suddenly, with Cas right in front of him, he was acutely aware of how much his dick needed tending to.

Soon, he promised himself. He'd have plenty of time at the hotel. Maybe in that hot shower he'd been fantasizing about.

"So," said Cas, pushing himself off the car and walking around to the driver's side. "You ready to head back to the city?"

Matty nodded, barreling through the wave of exhaustion that threatened to engulf him. He only had about forty-five minutes left with this stunning guy, then he'd probably never see him again. He needed to make the most of it.

"Absolutely," he said cheerfully. "I have the address of my hotel, or do you know that by heart, too?" he added with a smirk.

Cas grinned. "Sadly, I'm not an A to Z of Alpina. But I promise to get you there safely."

Again, Matty was foolish enough to believe that he'd be safe with Cas *wherever* he was.

For a while, they drove in companionable silence. Cas had the radio on low, playing a mixture of songs that Matty knew from back home and others that were brand new to him.

"Did you know," he said suddenly, already laughing at himself, "that the *only* reason I'd heard of Rosavia before now was because of Eurovision."

Belatedly, Matty realized that by bringing up Eurovision, he was essentially announcing he was gay. But maybe that was what his subconscious wanted. To test the waters with Cas in a relatively safe way.

He didn't even have time to hold his breath and see how Cas would respond. "Oh, *no*," said Cas right away, visibly cringing as he also laughed. "I didn't think you watched that in the States."

"There's a bar I go to that screens it," Matty confessed. He'd almost said 'a gay bar' so he was being absolutely clear, but he chickened out, hoping that the inference was enough. "It's a riot."

Cas shook his head. "We always send really weird songs to compete! That's so embarrassing. Please don't judge my whole country on that one guy with the panpipes and bird costume. Or the grannies dancing around the cauldron."

"Oh, I *forgot* that one," Matty said, giggling. Cas's enthusiasm was a good sign regarding his sexuality, and Matty allowed himself to feel the thrill of that for just a moment. Nothing would obviously happen between them, but just knowing that Cas could be queer was heady. "And wasn't the song itself about space aliens or something?"

"Mercy, I beg you," Cas said in mock pleading. "We can be cool, I promise! Just last month they filmed a whole car chase here for the new James Bond film."

"Oh, that *is* cool," Matty said, turning slightly in his seat to look at Cas better. He was still ridiculously handsome, but Matty liked how animated he was when he talked, even with his hands on the wheel and his eyes on the road.

For most of the rest of the drive they chatted easily about films and music, and even the latest play Matty had done front of house on back in New York. When Cas stopped the car, Matty had hardly even noticed they'd reentered the city. He almost asked why Cas had killed the engine.

Then he realized with a drop of his stomach that meant they were at his hotel.

It was time to say goodbye.

"Oh," said Matty faintly after Cas announced they'd arrived. "Wow, that was so fast. Um, thank you."

Cas turned his head to look at Matty. He narrowed his eyes and licked his lips. For the briefest second, Matty felt like he was going to be devoured, and *fucking hell* he was okay with that.

"So…" Cas began, arching an eyebrow. "Finley said I should look after you."

Matty spluttered in horror. "Yeah, well, you know kids." He laughed shrilly. "They say all kinds of crazy things."

Cas frowned slightly. "So you wouldn't want that?"

Matty blinked. "Want…what?"

"A local tour guide."

Matty stopped breathing. Was Cas serious? Was this impossibly hot, kind, thoughtful guy really offering to look after Matty, the biggest bumpkin Queens had to offer? "You'd want to hang out?" Matty asked, making sure he really understood.

Cas's expression softened as he smiled again. "Yeah," he said, nodding. "Like I said, I'm kind of a loser. I like showing off my city. Let me inflict all my useless trivia on you."

It was almost comical that Cas thought he could be a loser. He was *heavenly.* And he wanted to spend time with Matty.

So why was Matty's first instinct to run a mile?

His heart caught in his throat, and he frantically raced through several thoughts. He was still raw from Jeremy. He wasn't sure he could take investing in another guy just yet. How could Cas be paying him so much attention when they were in such different leagues? Was he *flirting?*

But just as Cas's smile began to falter, Matty exhaled and told his brain to shut the fuck up. He was so used to his ex-boyfriends and his parents dumping him on his ass, the thought of Cas doing the same was horrifying. But Matty was *only* here for two weeks, and Cas was *only* offering to show him some monuments or whatever. He wasn't asking for a lifetime commitment, for crying out loud.

"I'd *love* that," Matty blurted before Cas's face could fall any further, thrilled when it immediately perked up again. "But, um, I am broke. So free and cheap stuff would be great, if that's okay?" He admitted it fast, like ripping off a Band-Aid.

Cas gave him a strange look. "Of course it's okay," he said with a lopsided smile that was a different kind of gorgeous than the full one. "Alpina has all kinds of things to offer. But promise me one thing."

Matty's insides squirmed. Those words seemed so *intimate*. "Uh, sure," he said. "What?"

Cas tilted his head ever so slightly. "Let me spoil you at least *once*. Okay?"

Matty's jaw dropped as his vision went slightly dizzy and his cock fucking *throbbed* in his jeans.

Cas couldn't have possibly said those words to him, could he? Except, yes, he had, and he was looking at Matty through his eyelashes, waiting for an answer.

What else could Matty say but, "O-okay"?

Chapter Four

CAS

This was new.

Cas had never, *ever* allowed himself to flirt with a civilian on one of these secret excursions before. The risk was just too huge. What if the guy was to kiss-and-tell? What if he got hounded by someone like that vile royal correspondent, Ida von Tarr? What if he turned out to be some gold digger after the Crown Jewels?

And yet, Cas had almost tripped over himself to be Matty Doyle's own personal tour guide.

The more personal, the better.

Damn. Cas rubbed his freshly-shaved jaw as he waited in his car outside the hotel. He couldn't ever remember a man getting under his skin like this before. But this was *exactly* what he needed, and hadn't been getting from fussing and clucking after all his brothers for all these years. He didn't want to fret over someone. He wanted to *care* for them, and make sure their every need was being met.

Seeing the way Matty was agonizing over looking after his family and going to such extraordinary lengths had shown Cas what kind of man he was right away. The kind of man Cas just *had* to get to know better, and possibly spend a little time looking after. Even if only for a day.

It didn't have to be anything more than friendly. Maybe a little flirting. But Matty was only going to be around for a couple of weeks, so as long as Cas was careful, there wouldn't be any danger for either of them, surely? Unless Matty was a master actor, Cas was sure he wasn't faking it for money or a story, and Cas knew how to be vigilant. Besides, Cas had approached Matty, so there was very little chance of that. Von Tarr hadn't managed to catch him out with her snooping yet, and she wasn't about to now.

What better way to truly go on vacation than to have a little fling with a guy who thought that Cas was just ordinary? Maybe he thought Cas was kind of rich, sure, but not a fucking prince. Not like all those other dukes and dignitaries and ambassador's sons Cas had fooled around with in the past. There was always a worry that they were just interested in Cas for the power he had over Rosavia.

Matty didn't know about any of that. He'd agreed to spend the day together just because he liked Cas for himself.

Well…maybe for his money, but damn it, what was the point of being rich if you couldn't spoil a gorgeous guy once in a while?

Cas bit his lip, and tried not to follow his rambling thoughts. But with someone like Matty – no – with *Matty* – he could imagine what having a boyfriend might actually feel like. Cas had tried a relationship at school, but it hadn't worked out and he'd not bothered again since. Everything was so impossible when you were a prince. Even more so when you were trying to hold the heir of the throne together and stop your other brothers from getting into even more trouble.

But that was Sander. As Cas, he was free to ask an impossibly cute tourist out for a day of fun. And, *oh*, his blush when Cas had asked to spoil him? Yeah, Cas had liked that a *lot*.

Enough to make up for the white lies that were piling up. But they wouldn't cause any harm, surely? Matty never needed to know who Cas really was. It was okay to be vague about his family and job. Pretending to make a work call when he'd really just caught up with Jules for a while didn't feel great, but Cas reminded himself again that what Matty didn't know, wouldn't hurt him. After all, he couldn't very well have walked back into Elm Willows yesterday and risked bumping into a former teacher who would have addressed him as Your Highness.

Besides, as much as Cas had promised himself not to meddle in his brothers' affairs during the next couple of weeks, Jules had been a little flustered as he'd told Cas that Prince Dante of Thedes was coming to stay, possibly even attending the Royal Ball. Those two had been thick as thieves their whole lives, but then, four years ago it was as if they'd drifted apart after university and never spoken again. Cas hoped Jules knew what he was doing.

But that was Jules's business, not Cas's, so he ensured the worrying stopped there. Cas wasn't doing any of his brothers any favors by trying to stop every disaster before it happened. Jules – like Leo and Wren – needed to start trying to avert their own catastrophes.

Was that what Cas was doing right now, though? Walking into a situation he really should be steered away from? He huffed and shook his head to himself in the car. Like his brothers, he needed to live a little and stop trying to control every little thing. Life was messy, and Cas should embrace that more.

It was just…Cas wasn't sure what he'd hate more. His little make-believe bubble with Matty being burst…or Matty finding out that Cas had lied to him.

But neither of those things had happened, nor were they *going* to happen. So Cas made himself relax as he waited outside of Matty's hotel to begin their day of fun. It was a narrow building nestled between two other independently run hotels, all in the lower three-star range, but more than likely perfectly clean in this area of town. Just basic.

Cas itched to get Matty an upgrade. He'd agreed to let Cas spoil him once, and that could very well have been with a five-star penthouse. But there was something slightly seedy in organizing a hotel room to Cas's mind. Like Matty might think Cas expected to be invited back with him that night.

So, no, Cas had resisted. Instead, he'd planned a day of wandering between some of his favorite sights and a simple lunch. Then he'd booked his favorite sushi restaurant for the evening, along with a play he'd been dying to see that he hoped Matty would love too, followed by drinks at an exclusive rooftop bar. Cas wanted Matty's first full day in Alpina to be utterly unforgettable.

After that, Cas had promised himself he wouldn't push Matty. He might not want to hang out again, preferring to see the city by himself. And Cas would respect that.

But he kind of hoped Matty would want to spend a few more days together…and if there were any nights, Cas was absolutely not going to say no. He'd never invited anyone back to his secret apartment in the city before, mostly due to security concerns. But now, he felt like he might break his own rule.

Matty had that kind of effect on him.

Speaking of which, the man in question came walking out of the hotel doors, then smiled and waved when he saw Cas waiting in the car. Cas was surprised how far his heart lurched in his chest. He hadn't even known Matty a day. That was a little too much enthusiasm, surely, especially when he was attempting to play this cool. There was still a slim chance this could blow back in his face if he wasn't careful.

He just really hoped it didn't.

Matty looked positively edible in the clothes Cas had bought for him yesterday. Just a fresh T-shirt, but *damn*. There was also underwear that he couldn't see, but very much liked thinking about.

A strange feeling of possessiveness crawled over Cas's chest as he watched Matty jog towards him. He didn't really understand *why* he loved seeing Matty in the clothes they'd picked out together and Cas had paid for, but it was kind of making him hard. Rather than think it over too much, he decided to just enjoy it. That was kind of the whole theme for this vacation. To *stop* worrying.

"Hey," Matty said breathlessly as he opened the car door and dropped into the seat. "Sorry I'm late."

Cas shook his head. "You're right on time," he assured him. "Since we didn't swap numbers, I wanted to be early."

"Oh," said Matty as a little blush crept onto his cheeks. "Well, um, did you want to?"

Cas blinked. "Want to what?" he asked gently.

Matty squirmed, and Cas tried not to think too much about the ass currently wiggling on his leather. "Swap numbers?" Matty elaborated nervously.

There were protocols for this. The palace had to keep a very strict and confidential list of who had any of the princes' phone numbers. It was a huge security risk.

So naturally, Cas just fished his phone out from his pocket and beamed at Matty. Because while his upstairs brain had been fussing over whether or not Matty could screw him over, his downstairs brain was apparently occupied with a completely different kind of screwing, and wanted to make sure Matty didn't disappear on him without a trace.

"Sure," he said. "That makes sense in case anything happens." *In case I want to see you again,* he thought to himself. Protocol be damned. This was only for a couple of weeks at most. What could really go wrong?

Within moments they had traded digits, and Matty had an adorable, slightly giddy smile on his face. Cas wanted to keep it there all day. "So, where would you like to start?" Cas asked. He might have had a plan, but he could change it all if Matty had his heart set on something else.

But Matty hummed as he clicked his seatbelt on. "Wherever you like," he said sweetly. "I'm in your hands."

Oh. Cas really hoped that might literally be the case. Maybe later.

"Okay, then," he said with a nod. "Let's go!"

Matty had arrived in Rosavia at a good time. The weather wasn't too hot, but the sun was shining gloriously, making everywhere look its best. There were plenty of pop-up stalls out in one of the more touristy areas by the bend in the river Urden, so Cas parked his car in a secure lot he'd used before. His small personal security team were undoubtedly close by, out of sight and making sure he stayed out of harm's way, but to Cas, it felt like he and Matty were all on their own in a sea of strangers. It was glorious.

He walked with Matty to buy them some breakfast from one of the outdoor markets. Little stalls were lined up along the flowing river selling freshly made food and hand-crafted wares. A sweet and tangy scent filled the air with the snow-topped mountains looming over the city from far in the distance.

"Uh, wow," Matty said uncertainly, reading the small menu written on a chalkboard hanging from the food truck. "You guys really like rose flavored stuff, huh? What does that even *taste* like?"

"Have you ever had real Turkish delight?" Cas asked. It was his standard response to that question, which almost all non-Rosavians asked in his experience.

But Matty shook his head. "I'll just have to try something, won't I?" he said with a happy shrug.

Cas swallowed down his rush of desire. *Fuck.* Matty looked a million times better for a decent night's sleep, and he'd looked good enough yesterday. The T-shirt clung to his surprisingly well-defined shoulders and biceps. Cas longed to run his hands over them, preferably without the T-shirt on.

Cas loved Matty's positivity and willingness to try something new, so he got them both an iced rose donut each. Matty apologetically asked for a regular coffee, but promised to try some of Cas's rose tea as well.

"Ooh," he said after taking a sip as they began walking along the riverbank. "It's…sort of sweet and floral, but not too much. I like it!"

He beamed at Cas as he handed back the disposable cup. Cas's plan to do anything to keep him smiling like that was apparently working.

"Actually," he said, beginning his Official Facts of Rosavia Presentation, which he really hoped Matty didn't get bored with, "our national food is the blueberry. That's everywhere all year around. We even have blueberry *pizza.*"

"No," said Matty, sounding scandalized.

Cas chuckled. "It's an acquired taste that some of us refuse to acquire." He winked at Matty. "Don't worry, I won't inflict that on you. You're lucky it's rose season, so you can try all the seasonal stuff that isn't around for the rest of the year."

Matty licked a bit of icing from his lips. "Lucky me," he said fondly.

No, lucky me, Cas thought.

"So, is it rose season because they're blooming or something?" Matty asked.

A warning sounded in Cas's head, but he ignored it. He wasn't going to waste the precious time he had with Matty second-guessing everything. Yes, discussing anything about royal life was a risk he hadn't intended on taking, but fuck it.

"They bloom for longer," he answered, "but for the next couple of weeks the gardens at the palace are open to the public. Each member of the royal family has a signature rose bred for them, and we have a dedicated cultivation program." He laughed. "Actually, my brother, Wren-"

The words died in his throat. He'd almost fucking *outed* himself! He couldn't tell Matty that Wren had been a real brat when he'd first been put in charge of running the rose program.

Luckily, most people didn't know that Prince Renford went by Wren at home, especially not Americans. But Cas cursed himself all the same. This lying by omission was getting harder and harder.

"Your brother?" Matty prompted during Cas's unnaturally long pause.

He shook his head. "My brother thinks flowers are lame," he saved himself. "But I think they're wonderful. Would you like to see the gardens?"

And he sure as *hell* hadn't intended on inviting Matty to his back yard. It was like his brain wasn't fully connected to his mouth right now. But when Matty smiled and nodded in delight, there was no way Cas was taking it back. He just had to hope no one recognized him in a casual button-down and jeans, especially if he kept his sunglasses on.

Cas decided to take Matty the scenic route to the gardens, so they continued strolling down the path by the river, past more stalls, street artists, and joggers. Cas pointed out several architectural features, such as the old Cherwell Theater and modern mayoral head offices. They visited one of Alpina's free museums to take a stroll through an exhibition on the city's medieval era, then took photos of Matty in front of the large peregrine falcon sculpture near Rosavia's parliament.

While Matty drank in the sights, Cas drank in Matty. His happiness and excitement made Cas deeply content. It was such a pure and simple feeling.

They jumped on one of the many tram lines that crisscrossed through the city, hopping off close to the palace. It was strange for Cas to approach his home this way – not via the private entrance on the other side – and he had to hurry Matty past more than one souvenir shop that was displaying mugs and dish towels with his damn face on them.

Luckily, Matty was easy enough to distract with food. Cas got them hot cheesy pastries and cold fizzy blueberry soda from a café, which they enjoyed as they wandered down the lane that led to the entrance of the gardens.

As Cas paid for the tickets, he saw Matty wince. Cas paused after he stepped away from the line. "We don't have to go in if you don't want to," he said, an unpleasant sickly sensation snaking through his guts. He'd thought that Matty was really eager to see the roses.

Matty gave him a sad half-smile. "It's just…I feel bad. You're paying for everything. I know you said to let you spoil me once, but I still feel a bit like a freeloader."

"Oh, no," Cas said earnestly. He was glad he'd finished his simple lunch already and thrown the trash away, so he had a free hand to reach out and squeeze Matty's arm. "It's totally fine, I promise. It's my treat, remember?"

Matty sighed and smiled up at him, but he still seemed reluctant. "You're very kind," he said quietly.

Damn. Had Cas misread this? Matty had mentioned he didn't have much money, so Cas thought he'd be excited for Cas to pay for everything. But Cas getting their tickets seemed to have been a step too far, and he wasn't sure why.

Cas licked his lips. He wasn't doing this as a favor or anything. "Matty," he said in what he hoped was a reassuring but also firm tone. "I'm having a wonderful time. Please don't worry. I don't mean to be a dick, but I really do come from a wealthy family. And, uh, I have a good job," he tacked on the end.

He didn't want Matty thinking he was a lazy trust fund brat. It was just difficult to get a paying job when you were second in line to the throne and spent all your time keeping the royal family and, in some ways, the whole country together. "I just want you to have a fun day."

Matty finally seemed to relax. "And I *am,*" he promised with a big smile. "I'm sorry. I shouldn't be rude. It's just…okay, my ex-boyfriend used to gloat a lot that without him we wouldn't be able to do anything fancy, because I spend all my money on rent. I didn't want to talk about him while we're having a lovely day, but then I got all bummed out and spoiled it anyway, but I didn't want you thinking it was because I wasn't having fun-"

"Hey, hey," Cas said firmly but kindly, smiling at Matty as he gave Matty's arm another squeeze before letting him go. "Not rude at all. Humble. Which is very sweet." Then he bumped their shoulders together, hoping to lighten the mood. "But shut up and let me be your sugar daddy for the day, okay?"

Matty burst out laughing. "All right, all right," he said,

throwing his hands up in defeat. "Just never say 'sugar daddy' again, please?"

Cas winked, hugely relieved to have dispelled the tension between them. Part of him was disappointed that Matty had been worrying about money, but the other part of him loved that Matty was so conscientious.

Definitely not a gold digger.

But as much as Cas was smiling, an ugly dark feeling curled around his heart thinking about Matty's shitty ex. It was mixed with a more pleasant feeling as he realized that Matty was indeed seeing today as a kind of date, just like Cas was, but fuck that guy. Who got off on gloating like that and making Matty feel small?

Cas wanted Matty to feel glorious. Special. It had only been twenty-four hours, but Cas was drawn to this sweet, caring American more than anybody he'd known before.

They strolled around the garden paths in the beaming sunshine, inspecting the dozens and dozens of different kinds of roses. Some were large, some were little more than tiny buds, and they came in every color of the rainbow. In fact, Cas knew that for Alpina Pride they dyed white roses in rainbow colors, but so far, they hadn't been able to grow them naturally. And Cas had never been able to experience Pride in the thick of it, only observing from afar.

Cas rattled off his silly trivia that his brothers usually teased him mercilessly for. Matty listened raptly, asking questions and genuinely seeming to care.

"Oh, *look*," he said excitedly. He was pointing to a specific rose up ahead, and dashed ahead to get a closer look.

Cas's stomach did a funny little flip when he realized which particular rose had seized Matty's attention.

It was *his* rose.

All members of the royal family were bestowed their own, distinct rose when they were born or married into the family. Their corsages at formal events and in official portraits were always that particular rose. And the one Matty was currently inspecting was the one Cas had known his entire life.

"I've never seen a *blue* rose before." Matty exhaled in awe, touching the petals with extreme care. They started at the base as a light sky blue and bled into a bright royal blue that Cas had to admit he loved. Not everyone felt a kinship with their assigned rose, but Cas had always adored his.

And now Matty had singled it out over hundreds of others as the one he appeared to admire most. It was like he was giving Cas approval without even knowing it. But that was stupid, wasn't it? It was just a rose. Still, Cas wished he could clip one off the bush and give it to Matty, but he didn't want to risk drawing any attention to them.

"Our breeding program is the envy of many countries," he said faintly, using facts to distract him from his feelings. "We have some of the foremost experts in horticulture in the world here."

Matty gave the blue roses one last look with a sigh. "They're really amazing," he said. Then he glanced up and saw a refreshment stand several feet away, and his eyes lit up like a small child's. "Oh! Do you want ice cream? *My* treat," he insisted with an impish grin.

Cas laughed. "Sure. Surprise me." Oh lord, he was already

feeling hopeless. Was there anything he wouldn't do to make Matty happy?

They enjoyed their rose and chocolate cones as they entered the greenhouse to see some of the other plant life the royal gardens had to offer. Cas distracted himself from the delectable sight of Matty's tongue licking up the creamy substance by babbling about flower shows from the past and the great scandal of '98 when two entrants had arrived with the exact same specimen, and there had to be a full investigation into who had stolen from who.

"It turned out they'd *both* been conned by the same guy selling off clippings and claiming they were exclusive," Cas said, rolling his eyes. "We get all the drama here, you see."

Matty bit his lip and grinned. "Sounds *very* exciting," he said teasingly.

Cas bumped their shoulders again. It was getting easier and easier to initiate these little touches between them. So natural and comfortable. "Not to a New Yorker, I bet. But it's kind of you to say."

Matty huffed. "I don't live in the city. Queens is more of a suburb where I just happened to grow up. I can't say I *love* it. But it's home. It's where my family is. Well, the family that counts." He scrunched up his nose but didn't elaborate, then caught a stray drip of ice cream with his mouth before it reached his fingers. Cas cleared his throat and tried to adjust himself in his pants without being too obvious. "I've always wanted to live somewhere else for a while," Matty continued, "just to see if I like it. But I doubt that'll happen now."

"Why not?" Cas asked. They were walking around the edge of a lush lily pond filled with colorful koi carp.

Matty shrugged and smiled sadly. "Money," he said with a laugh.

Cas was going to open his mouth to say something, but then he didn't know what. He'd never had to worry about money in his whole life. Logically, he understood that some people struggled, but it didn't seem fair that Matty should be held back from *anything* just because he didn't have the finances for it. In fact, it was down-right heart-breaking, and Cas felt like an ass for not understanding this earlier.

Matty might not see Cas paying for everything as a treat. He might see it as a slap in the face, a reminder of what he didn't have.

It was a stark wake-up call, reminding Cas that he was only *playing* at being a commoner. When Matty flew back to America, Cas would go back to the palace, and never want for anything.

The realization left him feeling pretty hollow.

I wanted 'real life,' he reminded himself. This was it.

So instead he opened his mouth to say something vague but encouraging rather than nothing, perhaps suggesting to Matty that he never knew where life might take him. But then they rounded a corner of thick, lush wisteria and almost bumped right into *her*.

Ida von Tarr. In the flesh.

Cas couldn't say he was particularly fond of any members of the press, especially not when they devoted their lives to snooping around the palace, just waiting to expose any little hiccup or hint of a scandal. But this harpy was one of the worst, resorting to flat out inventing lies about Cas and his brothers when she got too bored.

"Klaus, you *idiot,*" she was snarling at the guy towering over her. He had a camera with an enormous telephoto lens resting in his meaty hands, frowning as she smacked his shoulder. She had long red nails like bloody talons, and horn-rimmed tortoise shell sunglasses resting on the end of her pointy nose. Dirty-blonde hair was scraped back into such a severe ponytail, Cas had to wonder if it wasn't also giving her some sort of facelift. Or he would wonder if he wasn't so busy suddenly panicking. "What do you mean we missed them? They haven't been seen together in Rosavia in years – you're telling me your camera can't find them?"

She jabbed her hand toward the palace through the windows. They had a damned good view of the front entrance from here. Who had they been hoping to see? Maybe Jules and Dante, seeing as Dante was arriving from Thedes today? *Damn* von Tarr. Cas felt a flush of anger through his panic. She was probably trying to start up the dating rumors between the two princes again.

"Sorry, boss," the huge man, Klaus, mumbled. "If we'd gone to the train station-"

"We'd have the same boring shots as everyone else," von Tarr snapped, throwing up her red-taloned hands. "They were supposed to be *here.*"

Yep. Definitely Jules and Dante. But they seemed to have escaped her clutches, for now. Whereas Cas…

He appeared to have totally frozen. *This was bad, really bad!* Von Tarr might have been hoping to sneak up on Jules, and instead Cas had walked right into her by accident with an entirely different scoop if she cared to look hard enough.

He realized Matty was staring at him. "Uhh…" Cas said, scrambling to think of anything to say.

"You okay?" Matty asked, clearly concerned. He placed a hand on Cas's arm, warm and comforting through the cotton of his shirt. It grounded Cas. But he still had no idea how to get away from the terrible royal correspondent without alarming Matty. But von Tarr couldn't see him like this! All she had to do was turn around and they'd be face-to-face…

"Excuse me, sir," a blissfully familiar voice said. "I think you dropped this."

Both Cas and Matty turned to see the pint-sized Valentina offering Cas a pamphlet map of the gardens.

Matty frowned. "I don't think-" he began.

"Oh, yes, *thank you,*" Cas said meaningfully, plucking the map from his valet's fingers. "So kind of you, ma'am. Come on, Matty. Let's see where we are in the light over there." He immediately began walking them away from von Tarr.

As they made their way to a bright shaft of light streaming down from the skylight, he caught Valentina's faint words. "Good afternoon, Ms. von Tarr," she said pleasantly. "I wasn't aware you had an access pass for today."

Cas glanced up from the map to see von Tarr flick her ponytail imperiously. "It's a free country, isn't it?"

Cas hurried him and Matty out of sight, breathing easy again. Damn von Tarr. That had been too close.

He wasn't comfortable with the lies he was having to tell Matty, and he'd rather not be reminded of them so forcefully.

Sure enough, when Cas stopped looking frantically around, probably acting like a madman, he realized that Matty was staring at him with wide eyes. "Cas," he said seriously. "Is everything all right?"

Cas exhaled. "Yeah," he said, meaning it. "I'm great."

It had been a close call, but nothing had happened. They were fine. He could continue playing make-believe with his gorgeous American tourist. And although Valentina was obviously keeping close tabs on him, he trusted her not to get *too* close. She'd respect Cas's privacy if − or *when* − he needed it.

Matty gave him a tentative smile. "You're not getting bored playing tour guide?" he asked shyly. There was an anxious note to his words that Cas didn't miss, and immediately wanted to soothe away.

Cas scoffed, von Tarr completely forgotten. "No way," he said, folding up the map he didn't need to look at anyway. "You wait until you see what I've got planned for tonight."

"Oh?" said Matty, sweet excitement alive in his eyes. Cas's heart flipped at the sight, wanting to keep Matty happy, not worried. "What have you got up your sleeve?"

And just like that, all of Cas's fancy plans went out of the window.

What was he thinking? This was supposed to be a vacation from all that high brow stuff. All the glitzy fakeness of his usual life. Matty had fretted over Cas spending twenty euros in total on garden tickets. Would he *really* enjoy an exclusive restaurant, and box seats, and a bar when the cocktails cost an arm and a leg?

Cas was supposed to be stepping into *Matty's* world. Living like a real person, for once.

So, no. The fancy date had to go. Besides, almost walking into von Tarr had given him a wake-up call. Being around so many people just increased his chances of being recognized a hundred times over. He'd promised himself that he'd give Matty an unforgettable first day in Rosavia, and that didn't mean throwing money around.

It meant personal. Intimate.

He smiled and bit his lip, touching Matty's arm, loving how warm his pale skin was. "It's a surprise," he said, excitement bubbling through him as a new plan quickly began to take shape in his mind. "Do you trust me?"

Matty's eyes got a little wider. "Yeah," he said faintly. "I do. I trust you."

Cas loved those words a little too much – more than was probably sensible. But that was a Sander kind of problem. *Cas* loved that Matty trusted him already.

Now he just had to make sure he earned that trust.

Chapter Five

MATTY

Matty couldn't even blame the jet lag anymore.

He'd slept for close to fifteen hours the night before, then had a nap when Cas had dropped him back at his hotel after their day out in the city, promising to pick him up again at seven o'clock. And when Matty came back outside and saw Cas waiting for him again in his BMW, he had to face the fact that he was completely smitten with this guy.

His heart flipped and his tummy fluttered and his skin tingled with goosebumps. Just from looking at the damn man. He wasn't broken with exhaustion anymore. There was no external factor to blame this lust haze on now.

He was falling head over heels for a guy he'd only just met.

And, honestly, Matty couldn't *ever* remember feeling this strongly about stupid Jeremy or any of the other guys before him. It had always just been really nice with his previous boyfriends, until suddenly it wasn't. But this?

This was like a raging river flowing through him, a desperate need to fight his way through anything just to be near Cas.

A man who lived in another country, and whom Matty would never see again once his two-week vacation was over.

What the hell was he thinking?

He wasn't. That was the problem. His cock and his heart were definitely driving this train, with his brain nowhere in sight. There was no future with this man. Besides, Matty shouldn't even be thinking about his love life when his sister was sick, should he?

Cas hadn't noticed him yet. He was texting on his phone, looking fucking gorgeous in a different hoodie from the one he'd been wearing when they'd first met yesterday. He'd told Matty not to dress up, which was good, because Matty couldn't even if he wanted to. He still hadn't heard from the airline exactly when his and Finley's missing luggage was going to be delivered yet, so all he had was the new T-shirt that Cas had bought him yesterday. And the underwear, of course. That felt strangely intimate in a way that Matty was probably imagining, but he couldn't help it.

He loved wearing the simple briefs that Cas had bought for him, because they'd come from *Cas*.

Matty didn't get many presents, especially outside of his birthday or Christmas. It made him feel special. Important.

Urgh! He needed to get a grip, now! This wasn't anything, it couldn't be.

So why even bother going out tonight, if that was how he felt?

He ducked back into the hotel's small foyer and chewed his lip as he thought. Maybe this was *exactly* what he needed. Rather than obsessively calculating whether or not any guy he met was boyfriend material, he should just embrace the time limit that was imposed on him and Cas. He was just here for two weeks. He could have some fun, then go back to real life. There was no risk of falling in love or anything so stupid, because he simply wouldn't have the time. And was he really so much of an idiot that he'd pass up the opportunity to spend the evening with the stunning man-hunk currently waiting for him outside?

No. Matty still might not fully understand what miracle he'd performed to earn the attention of such a hot, sweet guy, but he had, and that was that.

Time to go enjoy the universe *not* being a douchebag to him, for once.

Allowing himself to smile, he jogged back out of the hotel and waved when he caught Cas's eye as he'd stopped texting. "Hey," Matty said as he opened the door. He smiled and did his best to relax. "Thank you for waiting," he said instead.

Cas grinned as Matty sat down and closed the door. But before he put his seatbelt on, Cas handed him a bundle of the softest material. It smelled like fresh rose-scented detergent that made Matty think of clear blue skies and rambling hills. "I thought you'd like to borrow this," Cas said as Matty tried not to rub the material too obviously. "So you don't get cold."

It was the hoodie Cas had been wearing yesterday. Matty suddenly realized that it had a faded Elm Willows logo on the front. In his jet lagged state, Matty hadn't recognized it when they'd visited the school yesterday, but now he tried not to gasp in surprise. He was so touched, though. This was Cas's personal school sweater that he was lending to Matty. Matty was pretty sure this was even *better* than the T-shirt Cas had bought for him. He tried not to grin too much as he shimmied his way into the enormous thing. It drowned him and the sleeves were far too long, and he *loved* it.

"It's perfect," he said, trying not to sound too eager. He might not be planning his wedding to Cas, but he didn't want to scare him off, either. He had that effect on men, it seemed.

But Cas didn't make him feel like that needy, insecure guy from New York. Matty was starting to suspect that a part of him always expected his boyfriends to leave, just like his parents had done.

So then they did.

But now, in this hoodie, he felt like he was wearing a costume. A disguise. If he bit his lip and shut off some of his noisy brain, he could imagine he was Cas's boyfriend, borrowing his too-big sweater. And Cas thought he was awesome, so he wasn't going to pull the rug out from underneath him in just two weeks, surely? Nope. Otherwise, why would they have hung out all day and were now going on *another* date tonight?

In the couple of seconds it took him to put on the hoodie, Matty drank in that confidence, channeling it to become a better version of himself.

He was…Vacation Matty. Yeah, that was it! And Vacation Matty didn't worry or second-guess everything. He lived in the moment.

So he squirmed a little in the super-soft hoodie and rubbed

his arms. "Definitely not going to get cold in this comfy cutie!" he announced. "Thanks so much."

Cas stared at him for a second before clearing his throat and starting the car ignition. "You're welcome," he said with a nod, pulling them away from the curb. That was a little strange, but Matty dug his fingernails into his palms and made himself promise not to forget his new resolve to be confident and carefree.

The evening was bright and the city alive with tourists going out to dinner and other amusements. Matty watched them walking through the streets as Cas drove by, the low music on the radio keeping them company again. It was easy to be quiet with Cas. Matty didn't feel the need to babble about nothing just to fill the awkward silence between them. He could just *be*, and that felt okay.

But when he realized they were heading out of the city, he felt confident enough to ask Cas again what he was planning.

"Are we going back to the school?" Matty asked, looking down at the hoodie he was wearing.

Cas chuckled. Matty *loved* the way that sound made him feel. "No, that's back that way somewhere," Cas said, jerking his thumb over his left shoulder. "We're going to a remote little spot where I used to hang out as a kid. My family has a log cabin out there." He frowned and flicked his gaze over at Matty. "Wow. Could I sound any more like a serial killer?"

Matty laughed, remembering his jet lagged thoughts from the day before. "It's okay. I trust you not to chop me up into little bits."

Cas snorted. "It's the full moon you should be worried

about." He waggled his eyebrows. "I'm a bit of a *beast* once the sun goes down."

Matty's cock very much liked the idea of Cas turning into some kind of wild animal at night. He giggled shyly and glanced out to see what kind of moon actually was shining faintly in the lavender-blue sky.

"Made you look," Cas teased him, fondness abundant in his words.

Matty wanted to ask what Cas intended for them to do once they got to his family's log cabin, but he was almost too afraid of the answer. He didn't want to break this magic spell between them. So he just tried to relax and promised himself that he'd go with the flow. This was Vacation Matty, who didn't have to declare his undying love just because a guy breathed in his direction. That was Regular Matty.

Vacation Matty could have a fling if he wanted to.

If that was what Cas was even intending. He might just want to genuinely watch Netflix or make a campfire or something.

As Matty's stomach grumbled, though, he wished he'd thought to ask if food was happening. Apparently, jet lag made you ravenous. Even though he'd been eating all day and had grabbed a burger from a cheap place near his hotel before his nap, he could still go for a decent meal right about now. But Cas was already being so generous and buying pretty much everything, and Matty didn't want to sound ungrateful or demanding, so he kept his mouth shut.

As much as he wanted to be all strong and independent, he couldn't deny that having Cas swoop in and solve all his problems, not to mention spoiling him rotten, was like some sort of dream. Did that make Matty a bad person? Or worse, weak? Relying on a man to take care of you wasn't particularly twenty-first century.

He bit his lip, the jolt of pain snapping him out of his spiral. That train of thought was too close to worrying. Vacation Matty didn't worry. Vacation Matty was allowed to bask in the attention of a hot rich guy and not feel like he had to get on his soapbox about it.

Speaking of which, when they rounded a bend and came across a lone log cabin, Matty had to say he was surprised. Considering how wealthy Cas's family appeared to be, he thought it would be one of those ultra-modern, glass-fronted cabins with two stories and a hot tub out back. But it was just a basic little cabin, with a pitched roof and wooden shutters. There was a small chimney and a short porch with a swing hanging next to the door, big enough for two people. From the size of the structure, Matty had to guess that it was just one room inside.

It was utterly adorable.

But honestly, it was nothing in comparison to the breathtaking scene that lay just to the left of the cabin as Cas pulled the car up. Matty gasped, craning his neck to try and see it all, but when Cas killed the engine, he just jumped out of the car instead.

He'd been aware that they'd been driving steadily upward, but it didn't feel that dramatic. Now, though, the evening vista showed Alpina far below in all its glittering glory, as well as the spectacular mountains beyond the forest behind them. The scent of pine was rich in the air and birds were chirping their dusk chorus.

But the pièce de résistance? The cabin was right by a small pond, complete with a little rushing waterfall and babbling brook that wound its way around the cabin. The pond was probably only sixty feet by ninety, with rocks to the left and a drop to the right, like a natural infinity pool. The water was a crystal-clear aquamarine, and bobbing on its surface at the end of a short dock was a rowboat.

Matty covered his mouth as he stared in awe, not quite convinced his jet lag hadn't returned and he wasn't hallucinating. This was so beautiful it seemed *impossible.*

With a jolt of surprise, he felt a touch on his hip and warm breath on the back of his neck. He hadn't even heard Cas get out of the car, and now he was standing behind him, his chest almost brushing against Matty's back.

"Good surprise?" he murmured, sending shivers down Matty's spine.

He nodded and swallowed, not trusting himself to speak for just a second.

"Yeah, yeah," he finally rasped. "Incredible surprise. I'm blown away. Thank you. I…this is really special."

Cas chuckled. "Good." He moved away, and Matty felt the loss against him keenly. Cas went into the trunk of the BMW to retrieve an honest-to-god picnic hamper and a folded blanket that he placed on top of the hamper. Then he reached out his free hand and waggled his fingers at Matty. "Come on," he said with a sweet smile that melted Matty's heart.

Not only was there food, but Cas had made them a full-blown, adorable picnic, and now he was leading Matty by the hand toward the cute little rowboat. His palm was warm and dry against Matty's and he held it firmly, like he was telling Matty everything would be just fine if he stuck with Cas.

Matty couldn't argue with that.

"Watch your step," Cas murmured, helping Matty to stand in the boat.

Cas then followed, sitting down and encouraging Matty to settle next to him. Then he placed the hamper on the floor in front of them, and draped the blanket over their laps. The sides of their legs were pressed together, and Matty could feel Cas's muscular thighs even more than he had when he'd lightly tapped his leg yesterday. He bit his lip, not trusting himself to speak. Cas didn't bother unmooring the boat, leaving them bobbing in the same spot, looking out at the incredible view with the waterfall splashing a dozen feet behind them.

"Do you like it?" Cas asked as he nudged Matty's shoulder. He'd been doing that more as the day went on, and Matty loved it. Much like the teasing, he'd initially felt a spike of apprehension that perhaps Cas was overbearing on him. But once he'd taken a moment to think about how he really felt, he loved it. Cas was crowding into his personal space, but gently and carefully in a way that made Matty feel safe, not threatened.

He responded by knocking their knees together under the blanket. "Hmm, it's all right, I suppose," he said, attempting a bit of his own teasing.

Cas burst out laughing, dropping his head back. "Oh, I see," he said through a big grin, bumping against Matty's whole body. They stared at each other for a second, and it was like all the air vanished from Matty's lungs. It was as if there was something palpable between them, and Matty was made of nothing but want.

Cas cleared his throat and smiled, this time softer, before reaching over to open the top of the hamper. Matty couldn't help but gasp. It was jam-packed with all kinds of yummy-looking nibbly food, as well as a bottle of fancy-looking sparkling wine and a hot drinks flask.

"I wasn't sure what you liked..." Cas began, raising his eyebrows.

"So you packed everything," Matty finished with a giggle. "Oh my goodness, this looks amazing. Thank you, I love it. Did you know that jet lag makes you *ravenous?*"

Cas laughed, nodding. "I did. Please, eat as much as you like. And I've got some rose tea, or-"

"Bubbly," Matty interjected enthusiastically. "I'm on vacation. Let's crack open the Champagne!"

"Good answer," Cas said approvingly. "Although this is actually Rosavian sparkling wine. It's called Zasfer. It's kind of like our Champagne or Prosecco. It's, um, produced by the royal vineyard. I hope you like it."

Matty licked his lips. "I'm sure I'll love it," he said sincerely, not sure why Cas would be hesitant about sharing that fact. Surely that just made it more awesome?

"I'll just have a small one," Cas said, "since I'm driving, then switch to tea to leave you the rest."

Matty almost protested. Did they have to drive back? Couldn't they stay in the cabin?

Together?

But that was way too forward for him, even with his resolution to be spontaneous Vacation Matty. He was much more comfortable having Cas take the wheel, so he would just go along with whatever he suggested.

Cas popped the cork and poured them each a glass. Then they picked at cured meats, tangy cheeses, juicy olives, sticky rice balls, some sort of blueberry paste on salty crackers (which worked surprisingly well despite Matty's initial hesitation), and lots of other delicious treats. The sun crept lower, turning evening into night, and Matty and Cas talked about a whole load of not-particularly-groundbreaking subjects that felt momentous to Matty.

This had possibly been the best day of his life.

And he realized with a horrible lurch that he was only here because his sister was deathly ill.

The thought sobered him up instantly, and he just sort of shut down, his gaze listless on the rippling water. He swallowed his last mouthful of food as a heavy lump rose in his throat, his fingertips going tingly and cold. Guilt flooded him, and he wasn't sure what to do.

"Matty?" He looked up to see Cas's concerned eyes staring back. "What is it?"

Matty bit his lip, the lump still lodged in his throat. "Sorry," he whispered. "I'm having such a lovely time, but then I remembered why I'm here, and I felt so selfish having fun when my sister is probably so scared right now."

"Hey." Cas frowned and set his tea flask down. Then he took Matty's drink from him and put it in the glass holder on the side of the hamper. He turned and held Matty's shoulders with both of his strong hands. "You are *not* selfish. You dropped everything to help your family. Worrying is natural, but doing it every single second won't help your sister, will it? And I thought you said they'd caught the relapse early, so she has really great odds?"

Matty sniffed and nodded. "Yeah, you're right," he said shakily. "Sorry, I didn't mean to spoil the evening."

Cas pulled a face and tilted his head. "You didn't spoil *anything*, sweetheart. I'm glad you feel comfortable to tell me things like that. I..." He bit his lip and laughed ruefully. "I'd like you to believe me when I say that I've never done anything like this before."

"Like this?" Matty asked.

Cas gave him that lopsided smile that made Matty's stomach squirm.

Then he wrapped his arm around Matty's shoulders, drawing him close.

"Spent a whole day with a gorgeous guy I just met," Cas elaborated. "I've certainly never brought anyone else up here to the cabin before."

"Oh," Matty said breathlessly. "That's...thank you. That's really nice."

Wow. Nice? Massive understatement. But Matty's tongue didn't seem to be working properly. Did Cas really mean that?

Matty wanted to ask what the hell Cas thought was so special about him, but he made himself stop. Vacation Matty didn't question things like that, did he? In fact, what *Vacation* Matty would do was lean in, just a little. His face was so close to Cas's already, and he was in his arms. Matty could feel Cas's breath ghosting over his lips and smell his spicy aftershave. If they just moved a fraction closer, their lips were only inches apart…

The shrill ringtone of Matty's phone almost scared him to death. He jerked violently, making the rowboat rock, sending ripples out over the previously peaceful water.

"Sorry, sorry!" he cried, wriggling to pull the phone from his pocket. Cas dropped his arms, his expression concerned.

Matty knew it wasn't Finley, Reghan, or her wife Lola, as he'd assigned them all their own ringtones. The number started with an international area code that Matty was almost sure was Rosavian. He jabbed the answer button and pressed the phone to his cold ear. "Hello?"

"Hello, is this Mr. Doyle?" the woman on the other end asked with a Rosavian accent. Matty confirmed it was. "Oh, excellent. I'm calling from Alpina International Airport. We have your luggage, Mr. Doyle. It just arrived. We're preparing to send it directly to your hotel now."

"Seriously!" Matty squeaked. Relief flooded through him so suddenly tears pricked in his eyes. "Thank you so much. That's amazing. Yes, I'll be there. *Thank you.*"

He wasn't a particularly materialistic person, but he did like his comfort. The thought of having all his clothes back and his own shampoo and all the silly little bits from home was a bit overwhelming. And Finley's bow! She was going to be so happy!

"Good news, I take it," Cas said once Matty closed the call.

He nodded and rubbed his eyes. "Our luggage just arrived. It's on its way to my hotel right now."

Cas smiled, but was it Matty's imagination, or was it slightly fixed? "Well, that's wonderful. Shall we head out?"

Matty blinked. "Now?"

Cas nodded and rubbed Matty's thigh. Despite his relief, the action still made his cock throb eagerly. "Don't you want your own pajamas to sleep in? Clean clothes for the morning? If we leave right away, we can have you back at the hotel with everything in less than an hour."

Matty opened his mouth. It was probably the Zasfer talking, but…*no.* He didn't really want that at all. He wanted to stay out here in this little slice of paradise. He wanted to go back to the moment just before the phone had rung and see if they really had just been about to kiss.

But he'd taken advantage of Cas's hospitality too much already. And if Cas was offering to drive him back to the hotel now, he'd probably make it in time to collect his things. Matty wouldn't have been so concerned if it was just his bag, but it was Finley's super expensive bow. His hotel was fine, but Matty didn't imagine it had any kind of decent security, and he'd never forgive himself if he'd been so close to getting Finley's beloved bow back only to lose it again at the last minute.

Even if it meant his magical day with Cas was over.

Apparently, Vacation Matty couldn't get his way all the time. He needed to be a grownup again, and do the responsible thing.

"If you don't mind, that would be amazing," he told Cas. "Thank you."

Cas licked his lips and rubbed Matty's back. "My pleasure," he murmured.

Matty groaned internally. Was it too late to take it back? He wanted to stay right here, in Cas's arms. Who knew if he'd ever get the chance again?

But all too soon, their picnic was packed up and they were on the road back into the city. Matty tried to tell himself that the day had still been perfect, and that he shouldn't want for more. But that was the trouble.

When it came to Cas, he was starting to worry he wanted *everything.*

Chapter Six

CAS

Cas should have known when his parents called him back for breakfast that morning, it hadn't been because they'd missed him over the past few days. Cas tried to squash down the flare of resentment that he couldn't even have a proper vacation without getting interrupted, because he was fully aware that his royal duties never really went away.

Besides, he'd needed a distraction when Matty hadn't replied to the two texts that Cas had sent him last night and when he'd woken up.

He'd tried assuring himself that everything was fine and that Matty was just sleeping. This was his first experience with jet lag, after all, and he'd stayed up late as Cas had insisted on driving him back to Elm Willows last night so he wouldn't have to waste money on a taxi to reunite Finley with her luggage. And, sure, Cas and Matty had enjoyed a glorious day yesterday playing tourist and strolling through Alpina, then the most magical picnic at one of the smallest, most secluded royal properties in the whole country. Just watching

Matty's smile as he relaxed, feeling his warmth as their bodies pressed together, and then leaning in for...

A kiss? Cas might never know.

But it was just a bit of fun, right? A bad idea from the start, best left alone now. What did Cas care if he didn't hear from Matty again?

A lot, apparently. He cared a damn lot, and it was driving him insane. He hated feeling vulnerable like this, so he hadn't cared much as to *why* his mother and father had asked him to grace them with his presence.

Until he'd discovered that his baby brother, Wren, was embroiled in some of the biggest trouble of his life, and apparently refused to see it.

Cas and his parents had tried to stage a gentle intervention to steer him back on the right path, lest he do something drastic in the run up to the ball. Cas didn't begrudge Wren having a romantic dalliance – even if it was *highly* unorthodox, with his damned valet, of all people – but they and their brothers had crown and country to consider. They always had and they always would.

It was foolish of Cas to think he could reason with Wren, but he found himself chasing his youngest brother through the palace, determined to try anyway. He didn't want to give up on him, even when he was being utterly impossible.

"Wren," Cas called out, getting his brother to stop his storming off.

Wren turned, and truly, his face did look miserable. Cas scrambled for something that might get through to him. He obviously fancied himself in love, but they and their brothers didn't have the same luxuries as other Rosavians had. They couldn't fall for just anybody they pleased. There were rules.

Something Cas would also do well to remember.

"I know it's hard thinking about the palace every time you want to date," he told Wren firmly. "But it *is* our duty."

Perhaps his own surge of bitterness was what made his words come out harsher than intended. But Wren didn't make things any easier when he smirked.

"Speaking from experience?" he needled.

Cas tried not to react, but something in his blasted expression must have given him away, because Wren's eyes widened. *Shit.* Cas couldn't let anyone find out about his little date yesterday, let alone Wren. He didn't have the experience of keeping his mouth shut that their other brothers did. The whole *point* was that no one was supposed to find out about Matty!

"That doesn't..." he spluttered, trying to finish the sentence without incriminating himself. But Wren was too quick. He'd sensed blood in the water, and no doubt the perfect excuse for him to deflect away from his own drama.

"So what about your date for the ball?" he asked accusingly. "Do we get to meet him, or are you hiding him away? Like I was *trying* to do with *my* plus-one?"

Cas growled out a huff and threw up his hands before changing his mind and shoving them in his pockets. He knew Wren was just fishing, and couldn't possibly have any clue how close he'd gotten to the truth, but he'd hit a sore spot all the same. Cas could only control his anger so far.

"I can't leave you guys alone for two minutes, can I?" he snapped.

He wasn't just thinking of Wren. Leo was running around with some damned librarian – a *male* librarian. No one had a problem if Leo was suddenly discovering a new side of his sexuality, but Cas had worked so hard with his parents on that damn list of suitable matches. If Leo had wanted to include men, Cas would have, without pause. But *nooo.* Leo had given them his usual 'fuck the rules' routine and was flouncing around with someone from the royal library rather than seriously considering his impending engagement announcement and the future of their country.

And goodness only knew what Prince Dante of Thedes was doing back in Rosavia after all this time. Cas had always worried about whatever had happened between him and his brother Jules to split them apart four years ago. Now he was consumed with what trouble they might cause in the days leading up to the ball.

Who knew what the hell Ben was up to…and then there was Wren, insisting that this was *love* he had with Thomas Pierce. Cas knew Wren had been acting differently these past few months and, honestly, it was a change for the better. But Pierce was almost two decades his senior and a member of *staff,* for crying out loud.

…and *wow,* there was Cas's snobbery showing again. The whole point of going and mingling among the commoners was to undo this hard-wired distance he had between the palace and the real world. Yet his knee-jerk reaction to both Leo and Wren dating regular guys was rejection and denial.

Possibly because he knew what he was feeling for his very

own commoner had no future, and was built on a dangerous lie.

Fuck.

Unfortunately for his youngest brother, the heir to the throne wasn't here. So Wren was suddenly the focus of all of Cas's pent-up frustration for being pulled back into all his brothers' drama after only a few days…but also for them holding up a mirror to all his own biggest fears right then.

"Jesus," he growled. "I don't know why we cut you so much slack, Wren."

But rather than get upset, Wren – the little *shit* – batted his lashes. "Because I'm adorable." He blew Cas a kiss. "Don't get caught. They'll have to call in Leo to tell *you* off."

Leo? That would be the day. But realizing that his older brother was just as responsibility shy as he'd ever been didn't improve Cas's mood one bit. That was his bloody fault, too. Rather than say something he'd regret, he decided to go back to his original plan, remove himself from this whole stupid situation, and allow his brothers to fend for themselves.

He spun on his heels and left Wren crowing to his back, refusing to concern himself any further.

And shame on his parents for drafting him back in to deal with this mess, quite frankly. Just because Cas *could* crisis manage didn't mean he should have to all the time.

Urgh. Wren was far cleverer than most people gave him credit for. He'd sensed Cas's own weakness, and gone for the jugular.

Don't get caught.

Letting down his family would be Cas's worst nightmare. Cas had no intention of allowing that harpy Ida von Tarr – or anyone else for that matter, *certainly* not his family – to get wind of the precious time he'd spent with Matty. But seeing Wren's botched intervention was a stark reminder of his own precarious position.

He was a *fool* to be messing around with a commoner. A blissfully ignorant tourist who had no idea who Cas really was, but a commoner nonetheless. That had been a big part of the appeal initially, Cas had to admit. But now he could see how dangerous it was, and how unfair it was to Matty. Matty wasn't choosing to get involved with something that could very well end in scandal, no matter how careful Cas was.

Maybe it would be for the best if Matty *had* lost his number.

The mere thought made pain twist in Cas's chest so badly he stopped walking down the corridor and rubbed above his heart.

Perhaps he should have listened better to Wren. These things weren't so simple, after all. Maybe Wren couldn't control his feelings any more than Cas could?

Except it was so difficult to be sympathetic to Wren when he switched on that bratty mode he apparently thought was so delightful. It drove Cas completely insane, and he'd been so relieved to see it less and less since Wren had turned nineteen and started working in the gardens at the start of the year. It finally felt like he'd been growing into his royal duties. But one argument, and it had all come flooding back.

And – *yet again* – it had been Cas that had to deal with the stinging barbs. Not Ben or Jules, and *certainly* not Leo. This had been exactly why he'd wanted a vacation from his whole life, not just the physical palace. But maybe he'd been playing with fire?

All these contradictory thoughts were so confusing. As Cas stormed down the palace halls, he tried not to look too visibly irked, in case any of the staff might see. But for the love of god, why was nothing ever simple? He'd thought going into the city would give him some distraction, but he'd ended up agreeing to come back to the palace to escape his messed-up feelings over Matty. Then Wren had unbelievably managed to find a way to throw *that* back in his face.

Maybe he should have followed Ben on his damned secret spy mission. That might have proved less of a headache.

Feeling distinctly put out, Cas put his head down and marched back to his suite. There was a difference between having responsibility and being used. He wasn't being selfish for putting his foot down and refusing to bail his brothers out any longer. He was practicing self-care.

So why did he feel so shitty?

He made a disgruntled noise and stopped by a portrait of one of his great uncles to pinch his nose and breathe for a few moments. Cas was doing *them* a favor, especially Leo. He had to grow up, fast, and take on the responsibility he'd been born into. Cas had inadvertently been hindering him and Wren with his good intentions.

No, it was the right thing for Cas to step back. He'd tried his best with Wren just now, but if his baby brother needed to make a spectacular mistake to grow the hell up, so be it. The same with Leo. He was old enough to deal with his own consequences. Cas had enough on his own plate to worry about.

That didn't mean he wasn't deeply concerned for his brothers' wellbeing, as well as the fate of the country, but what else could he do?

Feeling resolved, if not exactly happy, Cas continued walking. He ignored a particularly pointed stare from one of the less likable footmen, Archer. That man always seemed to be looking for drama, and Cas wasn't going to give it to him.

Cas banished the member of staff from his mind and tried again to focus on himself, something he was apparently not very good at. *Damn* Wren for being so observant and asking about Cas's date. He hadn't really intended on bringing anyone, even though he was expected to, and now he fancied it even less.

Because whoever he brought wouldn't be Matty.

For a brief second, he imagined what it might be like if he *could* bring Matty, but that was just a ridiculous fantasy. And acknowledging that just made him crankier. When had a little vacation fling gotten so complicated?

His turbulent thoughts paused momentarily as he let himself into his suite. As soon as he unlocked the door, there was a distinctive *thud*, and within seconds, an enormous silver ball of fluff waddled out from Cas's bedroom, no doubt where the hairball had been sleeping on Cas's silk sheets.

"Hello, bad girl," he murmured fondly as the fat cat bashed into his legs and wound her way around his shins. Then she rolled over, exposing her rounded belly. Unlike other cats, Bella loved having her tummy rubbed, and when Cas bent down to pet her, she clung to his arm like the sloth she thought she was. He sighed and grinned. "I suppose you've had a busy few days of sleeping, madam?"

She yawned, showing off her sharp teeth, and nuzzled her head against Cas's arm.

About four years ago, Wren had been asked to become the patron for a local animal shelter. After several (dozen) of the cats had mysteriously ended up inside the palace walls, it was discreetly suggested that perhaps it wasn't the best placement for the youngest prince. Still, it meant everyone had suddenly been gifted a new friend overnight, and Cas had to admit every single one of the roaming felines looked to be in the best shape of any cat in all of Rosavia.

Except maybe Bella, who refused to go on any kind of diet, and swanned around like the princess she was. When she was awake.

Cas sighed and disregarded all royal protocols by lying on the floor and cuddling with his kitty. There was no one else around to see, after all. Right then, he just needed some comfort. His anger at Wren softened as he petted the cat his little brother had found for him.

Cas *knew* he was playing with fire by getting closer to Matty, but he couldn't help it. They'd had such a magical day together. And then, since Matty had gotten the call that his luggage had arrived…nothing. He'd been quiet on the whole drive back to his hotel, and then to the school and back. Despite saying he'd text, there hadn't been a peep in response to Cas's couple of texts.

This was probably for the best. What was Cas hoping to get out of their time together, anyway? Sex? Yeah, that would have been nice. But what he was really enjoying was just Matty's company, and that wasn't going to work out. They couldn't be friends.

Because Matty didn't even have a clue who Cas really was. They were from completely different worlds.

This was more than likely the universe stepping in and doing him a favor by pulling them apart before anything more could happen. It was also showing Wren's current situation as a cautionary tale. But Cas felt like a small child throwing a tantrum as he lay on the carpet of his living room and scowled.

Couldn't he just have *one* thing that was his? Not something he had to do for crown or country or any of his damned brothers. Sometimes he felt like Lizzy Bennet in *Pride and Prejudice*, trying in vain to stop her family's car-crash decisions that were probably inevitable no matter what she did.

He rolled his eyes, focusing instead on the way Bella was purring pleasantly under his hand. Family was hard work and complicated, that was it. Like Matty and his sister and niece. You just did what you could, because you loved them. Cas honestly didn't resent his duties, and was always relieved to avert a crisis. But it had been so damned nice to have something that was all his with Matty. Something fun and exciting.

A swift knock on the door snapped Cas back to reality. Being born a prince meant yes, he was filthy rich. But he also had the weight of a whole country on his shoulders, and maybe reality was where he needed to come back to. Perhaps this vacation had been a terrible idea from the start?

He scrambled to his feet and brushed his clothes down. "Yes?" he called out, although from the specific knock, he had a feeling he knew who it would be anyway.

Sure enough, the door opened and Valentina stepped inside,

accompanied by her trusty leather-bound portfolio, as usual. "Your Highness," she said. Without blinking an eye, she opened a drawer in the table by the door, retrieved a clothes brush, and immediately got to work removing silver cat hair from his suit.

Cas stood still as he sighed and raised an eyebrow down at Bella, who licked her paws, her fat tummy still on display. "Troublemaker," he said fondly down at her.

"Indeed," said Valentina. For just a single word, it sure was heavy with accusation.

Cas sighed again as she stepped back and put the clothes brush away. He was pretty certain Valentina hadn't been agreeing that Bella was the troublemaker in the room. The thing was, did she mean Wren, or...?

"So..." he said.

"*So,*" Valentina repeated, "as far as I can tell, our favorite royal correspondent had no clue you were three feet away from her yesterday. But honestly, Your Highness *must* be more vigilant in the future. She's not the only ruthless vulture out there. If the press gets a hold of what you're doing, let alone the paparazzi-"

"I know, I know," Cas interrupted miserably. "I was an idiot. I knew it, I just..." He threw out his hands and shook his head. "I guess I was just being arrogant."

She frowned slightly. "Okay. A little dramatic, but I'm glad you're taking this seriously." She reached into her portfolio for a sheet of paper that at a glance looked to have a list written on it in her impossibly neat handwriting. "Here's a selection of palace-approved delivery outlets, and I took the liberty of sending a couple of other essential items to your apartment."

Cas frowned as he took the sheet of paper and read down the list. "These are..." he began, confused.

"Restaurants that offer takeout, yes," said Valentina, as if that was obvious. "As well as an independent supermarket that will deliver groceries. I took care of fresh flowers, and in the bedroom, you'll find some personal items." She waggled her eyebrows, apparently completely unfazed by whatever she'd purchased. "Prince Renford's valet, Pierce, advised me on the best establishment in town to get some *most* amusing things for you."

Cas spluttered, and he felt heat rising on his face. He did *not* want to be thinking about Wren and his valet right now, especially in the context of a sex shop. But was he really hearing his own valet clearly?

"W-what? I...I don't understand?"

Valentina blinked, as if Cas had lost his mind. "For you and your young man. So you can have a little more privacy. I know you're completely clueless how to date, but good call on cancelling that circus of an evening you'd originally planned. *Personal* is the way to go here."

Cas could feel his mouth hanging open. "I'm not clueless," he mumbled eventually.

The smile Valentina offered him was entirely patronizing. "Of course not, Your Highness."

Cas looked between her and the sheet of paper in his hands. "You...you're not mad at me for breaking palace protocol and fraternizing with a commoner?" After what Wren had just gone through, he felt guilty for even suggesting what he was doing was okay.

A muscle in Valentina's jaw twitched, like she would have preferred not to have heard those words spoken out loud, for plausible deniability's sake. But Cas was like a child again, needing permission to do something he really ought to have known better about.

He watched as his valet considered her words carefully. "Your Highness has been on exemplary behavior for the entire time I've known him." Which was pretty much his whole adult life. "You are a credit to your country and your family. No one here is talking about two weeks in Ibiza or Tijuana, getting off one's face on pills and booze."

Cas felt faint at the very notion. "No," he said carefully. "No one's suggesting that."

Valentina pursed her lips and looked down at her portfolio. "There's a fine line between what the crown expects, and what a young man should reasonably want from life, Your Highness. A secret little dalliance with a nice young man who may or may not have passed a background check with flying colors really shouldn't be that big of a deal." She looked up with a flick of a smile. "In that hypothetical situation, I'm merely suggesting that 'in is the new out.'"

Cas bit his lip, not quite sure what to make of this bizarre conversation. Was Valentina really encouraging him? Just when he'd been trying to talk himself out of his feelings for Matty?

"He's going back home in ten days," Cas said quietly, dropping all pretense. "The day after the ball."

Valentina tilted her head and offered him a sad smile. "And that's part of what makes it perfect. You don't want to wake up one day and wonder what on earth you did with your life. Live a little, Your Highness. It'll be okay."

Will it? he wanted to ask. But the only way to find out was to try, wasn't it?

He nodded once. "You make it sound so simple," he said with a weak chuckle. "But…you're usually right, so I should probably just listen to you."

She smirked, but there was fondness in her eyes. "I know, Your Highness. Now, I suggest you slip out the side entrance again before anyone else knows you're here and can start asking you any more inane questions." She glanced down at the ball of fluff still wrapped around Cas's foot. "I've been keeping a close eye on Her Highness, of course."

Cas managed a weak chuckle. "Thank you," he said again sincerely. "You're the best."

"*That* I definitely know," said Valentina with a wink. "Now go on, shoo."

The truth was, Cas wasn't sure her words of encouragement would make any difference if Matty had decided he didn't want to see Cas anymore. It was as much of a vacation fling for him as it was for Cas, too. Perhaps he'd decided Cas wasn't worth the effort, now he had all his things back and didn't need Cas to buy him stuff anymore? But honestly, Matty really hadn't felt like a gold digger. The exact opposite, in fact.

Cas couldn't control that. He could only control his own thoughts and actions. And he knew that deep down, despite all his reservations, if he didn't try again, Valentina would be right. He'd regret it.

So once he'd made it back down to his car without being spotted, he got out his phone and tapped out a message before he could change his mind.

Would you like to have dinner at my place tomorrow night? I'll cook.

He jabbed the send button, then pressed the side of the phone to his forehead, breathing carefully in and out. If Matty was worried about how much money Cas was spending on him, then a home-cooked meal might coax him out of his sudden silence. If not…

Well, then, Cas would just graciously accept that it wasn't meant to be and remember their couple of days together with warmth and fondness. He wasn't going to harass Matty, especially when he already had so much on his plate.

But he couldn't help the flicker of hope that sparked to life in his chest. Maybe, just *maybe*, he'd get to see Matty one last time.

Cas just had to leave it in the hands of fate and destiny now.

Chapter Seven

MATTY

"So let me get this straight," said Shommie as she swirled the Zasfer sparkling rosé in her glass and arched an eyebrow at her sister, Esosa. Then she fixed Matty with a stern glare. "This man saved your arse in a pinch, spoiled you rotten, took you on a super romantic date…and you're not sure if you should return his texts?"

Matty squirmed on the plastic café chair he was sitting on in the pretty little plaza, taking another gulp of his own wine. "Well, yeah, when you put it like that…" he mumbled.

"You sound mental?" Esosa suggested with a grin. She was the older of the two women, with braided hair and a deep rumbling laugh that made Matty feel immediately at ease. Or it had, until the sisters had started interrogating him over Cas, and Matty was starting to regret asking them if they wanted to meet up after all.

A nice cup of rose tea had quickly turned into a bottle of pink wine that was slipping down a little too easily, loosening

Matty's tongue, and before he'd known it, all his anxieties around Cas had come tumbling out. He hadn't wanted to burden his sister or her wife on their video call earlier, and it seemed Matty could only keep a lid on all his worries for so long.

Shommie patted his hand and offered a sympathetic smile. "So you really haven't messaged him back since he dropped you off?"

"No," said Matty with a sigh.

"But he's messaged you?" Esosa clarified.

Matty shrugged. "Yeah. He suggested dinner at his place tomorrow night. He, um, wants to cook."

He'd become aware that the sisters' mouths were hanging open. Then Esosa clicked her fingers and motioned with her hand. "I need your phone," she said firmly.

"Why?" Matty asked nervously.

Esosa grinned, her lip gloss shimmering in the afternoon sunshine. "Because you clearly can't be trusted with a good thing, and I need a new husband anyway."

Shommie snorted and elbowed her sister. "What she's *trying* to say, I'm sure, is that this bloke seems lovely. What's the hesitation?"

Matty opened his mouth to reply when Finley came running over to him, breathless and rosy cheeked. "Uncle Matty, can I have my water, please?"

He dutifully passed her glass over, remembering to take a big gulp of his own water. He didn't want to get too much of a buzz on while he was responsible for getting her back to her teachers shortly. Finley had been asleep when Matty (and Cas) had dropped her luggage off at Elm Willows the night before. Now the students were having an afternoon of free time in Alpina to see some culture before their training began in earnest, and those with family in town had been allowed to meet up with them.

Matty had jumped at the chance, eager to make up for their terrible start to the vacation. Finley was more interested in playing with Shommie and Esosa's kids, of course, but Matty was just pleased to spend any time with her. His sister was fretting a little that her baby girl was okay, so Matty had taken several selfies of the two of them to send to Reghan and Lola to reassure them that they were having fun in Rosavia.

The kids had been excitedly jumping up and down a hopscotch they'd drawn on the flagstones in chalk, leaving the grownups to talk. Matty was appreciative of the well-timed rescue. Naturally, it didn't last long.

Once Finley had run off again, Matty sighed and gestured toward her, unable to avoid the sisters' questions forever. "That's my hesitation. I have to make sure I don't screw this up. My sister is relying on me."

"You seem to be doing pretty good," said Shommie warmly, which Matty took to heart from such a competent parent.

"Besides," added Esosa with a raised eyebrow. "Isn't she going to be at that fancy school most of the time? What are you even planning on doing with yourself for the rest of the trip?"

Matty managed a grin as he lifted his wine glass. "More of this, probably."

The sisters shook their heads and traded a huff. "You can drink wine *with* this guy. Very nice wine, from the sounds of it!"

Matty bit his lip and placed the glass back on the plastic table covered with a rose-embroidered cloth. "That's just it. I did try, but it felt unbalanced. He was paying for everything."

Shommie frowned. "I don't see a problem."

Matty chuckled ruefully. "I *know* it sounds good on paper! But what can I offer him in return?"

Esosa tilted her head and gave him a fond but patient smile. "I know we've only just met, love, but you seem very likable. Is it so crazy to think your new fancy-man just wants to spend time with you and spoil you a little?"

Shommie poked him with a long, gelled nail. "It's *romantic,* you pillock."

"And he's been chasing you up!" Esosa added. "Men don't do that for just anybody. He's interested!"

Matty took another sip of wine. "What if he's only interested in..." He checked the kids were well out of earshot. "...S-E-X?"

Shommie blinked and turned to her sister. "I *still* don't see a problem."

Esosa laughed. "Babe. Do you fancy him?"

"Do you want to climb him like a tree?" Shommie asked, waggling her eyebrows.

"Oh my god," Matty hissed, covering his face as he felt himself blush furiously. "Um, yes. He's very hot. And I tried telling myself a vacation fling was okay, but it's so not *me*. I'm worried I'm falling for him and have real feelings and stuff. He's not going to want a clingy tourist. He'll be looking for wham, bam, thank you, ma'am."

He peeked out as the sisters cackled. "You're adorable," said Esosa, shaking her head.

But Shommie patted Matty's hand again. "So you're running away before anything happens?" she asked, a sadness to her words. "What if it's brilliant?"

"What if it's a disaster?" Matty countered.

Shommie shrugged her shoulders as she retracted her hand, a mischievous glint in her eye. "Bad decisions make great stories, babe," she said.

Matty chewed his lip, struggling to really listen to their words. They were being very kind, but they didn't really know him. Jeremy had known him and had dumped him in a flash.

And his parents...well. They had known him his entire life. And they'd taken away his choice to have a relationship with them, just for the way he'd been born. He didn't really feel like being messed around by Cas right now.

But what reason would the sisters have to lie? "He's just *gorgeous*," Matty protested weakly. "And kind, and rich, and I feel like I was lucky to spend one day with him. Why be greedy and ask for more?"

Shommie's expression became serious as she raised her perfectly-painted eyebrows. "Because, mate, life is too fucking short, as I think you're fully aware. Your sister isn't going to thank you for sitting in a beautiful foreign country just worrying about her."

Esosa pointed a finger at him. "She's going to want you to entertain her with lots of juicy gossip."

"For real, though," Shommie continued. "It's not greedy to want new experiences. And just because something isn't going to last forever doesn't mean you shouldn't go for it."

Esosa laughed and waved her left hand at him, the indentation where a couple of rings had evidently sat for many years clear on her finger. "And even when you think some things are going to last forever, they don't. There's no certainty in life. If you like this guy, stop self-sabotaging and *go* for it."

"He clearly likes you," said Shommie kindly. Then she topped up their glasses, finishing the bottle. Matty took another gulp, willing the alcohol to do its thing and help him loosen up for a goddamned minute.

This was why his ex-boyfriends had always gotten tired of him and left in the end. He was too highly strung, fretting about everything. Why couldn't he relax? Why couldn't he trust that Cas was genuinely interested in him without looking for the catch?

It seemed impossible to believe that Matty could have something fun and casual for a week, though, without getting attached. The truth was, he liked Cas so much that it scared him. He'd realized that in the moment they'd been about to kiss, and been interrupted by the phone call, which felt more and more like a signal from the universe to call it quits before Matty really got hurt.

Because, yes, he was still raw from Jeremy dumping him. But this felt like it could break him *more*. Cas was a hundred times the man Jeremy had been. Could Matty really risk getting closer when he'd only have to leave again?

Urgh. He was so bored of his own brain, and he'd had enough. He took another glug of wine. He didn't really have the kind of friends he could talk to about sex and stuff back home. In fact, he was quite a loner. He narrowed his eyes at the sisters, who were watching his internal debate with amusement, as if they knew exactly what he was wrestling with.

"So you're saying you think Cas is really into me, and that I should throw caution to the wind and text him back?"

Shommie blew a raspberry. "I was saying that when we were on the tea. But if it takes vino to make you start seeing sense, I'm gonna go ahead and order another bottle."

"Ohh, and let's get chips," said Esosa eagerly, picking up the menu.

"Oh, um," Matty began, his anxiety spiking, but Shommie arched an eyebrow at him fiercely.

"Now, I know you're not going to stop me and my sister spoiling you, too."

"And we don't even expect to get lucky after," Esosa added wickedly. "We'll let you save that for after your dinner date tomorrow night."

"You have a date, Uncle Matty?"

Shit. Matty hadn't realized that the kids had skipped closer to their table again. They were out of breath and had different colored chalk smudged on their hands and faces where they'd obviously gotten bored of hopscotch and just started rolling on the damn ground. Matt was horrified, thinking of all the germs, and not sure if he should tell Finley off. But without batting an eyelid, both Shommie and Esosa magically produced wet wipes from somewhere and began attacking their squealing kids, in between managing to order another bottle of wine from the passing waitress, as well as some snacks.

Matty blinked, his mouth hanging open in awe as he looked back at Finley. Before he could panic, though, Shommie held out a wet wipe in front of his face, which he gratefully took. It was as if the woman had eight arms like an octopus, she was so on top of everything.

As if the universe was trying to illustrate just how *not* on top of everything Matty was, a voice piped up next to their table. "Excuse me?" a woman asked in a pleasant voice with a Rosavian accent. "But is this someone's phone?"

Matty looked up from his chalk-covered niece to see a slim woman with bright red nails and a severely tight ponytail of long dirty-blonde hair. For the briefest second, Matty wondered if he'd seen her somewhere before, but then he was distracted, because she was indeed holding out a phone.

Matty's phone.

"Oh my god!" he spluttered as he lunged for it. She handed it over without pause. "Where did you-? *Thank you!* Oh god!"

He couldn't afford a new phone, but more to the point, he couldn't be stranded in a foreign country without a way to contact his sister, unless he borrowed Finley's phone. But that would leave *her* without a way to communicate with her mom, and…

He made himself breathe as he clutched the damn thing to his chest. "Where was it?" he managed to ask the woman without passing out.

She smiled kindly, though, and just shrugged, like what she'd done was no big deal. "On the ground by your chair, there," she said, pointing. "I guess it fell out of your pocket or something? I hope it's not cracked?"

Matty inspected the screen and used his fingerprint to unlock the phone's systems. He breathed a big sigh of relief. "No. Everything seems fine. I can't thank you enough."

But the good Samaritan just shook her head and stepped back from the café's outdoor space into the plaza. "It was my pleasure. Have a good day!" She waved at them as she melted into the busy afternoon crowd, and Matty took a long deep breath of relief before placing the phone in front of him on the table where he couldn't possibly lose sight of it.

Because – he realized with startling clarity – if he lost that phone, he'd lose the *only* way he had of contacting Cas. He had no idea what his last name was. He'd saved his contact details as 'Cas Rosavia,' and that wouldn't be nearly enough to find him on any social media platforms.

For all Matty had been avoiding responding to all three of Cas's texts, it hit him like a wrecking ball that he didn't actually want the option to be taken away from him.

Not one bit.

"That was a close call," Shommie commented sagely.

But it seemed not everyone was so easily distracted. "Well?" said Finley impatiently as Matty finally finished cleaning off her hands.

"Well, what?" he asked with a frown.

Finley huffed. "Do you have a date or not? And is it with *Cas?*" she added in a sing-song voice, then proceeded to make loud kissing noises.

Matty huffed. "I feel like I'm being ganged up on."

"That's because you are, sweetie," said Shommie with a wink.

"It's not a date, Finley," Matty said, still unsure if he was even going to say yes despite the scare with his phone. "We don't know each other."

"But that's what dates are *for,*" insisted Finley. "Getting to know each other. Look." She put her little fists on her hips and scowled impressively for an eight-year-old. "When you have a target in your sights, you have to fire! Otherwise you get all wobbly and you might miss."

"This is a little different than shooting an arrow," said Matty weakly.

Finley smirked and crossed her arms. "But *Cupid* used a bow and arrow, didn't he?"

"The kid's got you there," said Shommie as she grinned around the lip of her wine glass.

"Fine," said Matty, all of a sudden giving up. He had too much else to worry about – *real* concerns about his sister's health. Why was he still doubting himself so badly? He picked up his phone and showed it to all the women meddling in his love life. "You win. I'll text him right now."

Finley air punched. "Yes! I *told* you so!"

"Brat," Matty mumbled fondly.

But he was an idiot, truly. He couldn't even *try* and deny the way his heart flipped when he reread Cas's last, simple message. He wanted to bring Matty to his home and *cook* for him. Why was he fighting a good thing so hard?

That sounds wonderful. Send me your address and I'll be there at seven? Thank you.

"And, *send,*" he announced triumphantly as their fresh bottle of wine and snacks arrived.

Finley cheered, so the other kids cheered too without really knowing why, then descended on the bowls of hot, salty fries that Esosa had ordered for them. But Shommie took a second to reach over and squeeze Matty's knee under the cheap plastic table.

"Now, promise me," she said softly and sincerely, "that you'll go and do your very best to have a good time. You're a nice lad. You deserve a holiday romance."

Matty attempted to swallow the small lump that was doing its best to lodge in his throat. "Thank you," he whispered, accepting another top up to his glass.

He was Vacation Matty. And Vacation Matty got a little day drunk and took a chance on gorgeous strangers. He'd only regret it if he didn't.

And, honestly, *really* – what was the worst that could happen?

Chapter Eight

CAS

What the hell had Cas been thinking? He couldn't *cook*.

He pressed the heels of his palms into his eyes and groaned. His rather nice apartment might have been decorated with several bunches of fresh cut flowers thanks to Valentina, but now it smelled like burnt garlic and despair.

He had half an hour until Matty arrived.

A thrill ran through Cas. It was okay. Everything was fine, because Matty had finally texted him back and said he was coming over. So long as he showed up, Cas could gloss over his lack of culinary skills with some dazzling conversation. He'd successfully entertained *far* duller men than Matty during the countless state dinners he'd attended. Cas's witty repartee had healed international relations and secured trade deals in the past. All he had to do tonight was show Matty how much he liked him.

Which, really, couldn't be that difficult.

"Okay, okay, I can *fix* this," Cas muttered to himself as he opened the window and wafted some of the smoke out.

Really, it was an outrage that he and his brothers hadn't been taught to properly prepare any kind of meal. Aside from Jules, but he'd learned in Thedes during university. Sure, he knew how to start a fire with flint and could survive in the wilderness through foraging. He could also speak six languages (including finger spelling sign language) and attempt small talk in at least another three, he was practically a historian with regard to his own country's legacy, and he was a borderline anthropologist in countless other cultures.

But he'd just had to Google *'How do I cook rice?'*

He rubbed his hand over his face and groaned, laughing at himself. At least he was already dressed in his favorite teal cotton shirt and navy dress pants, freshly shaved and doused in just the right amount of cologne. Although, usually, that meant formal events. Not a one-on-one date with a guy he really fucking liked.

He was just playing pretend in this small apartment, acting like he knew what the hell to do with the box of eggs and cubed chicken that were currently mocking him. He was a total fraud, and Matty was going to see right through him. He'd been spoiled his whole life. For heaven's sake – Nanny had buttered his toast until he was ten years old! He should have stuck with the sushi restaurant and ordered take-out. He and Matty only had a short amount of time together, and Cas was wasting his time worrying over how much chili paste to add to this damn sauce. He should have-

There was a knock at the door.

Matty was early, but only fractionally. Cas had been standing there working himself into a state the whole time. He'd wanted everything to be perfect, but when was anything perfect, really? People always said it was the thought that counted. Hopefully Matty would appreciate Cas's good intentions.

He made sure the gas was switched off before dashing from the kitchen. "Uh…just coming!"

He'd just pour Matty a glass of Zasfer, and then continue to muddle through with the recipe that had seemed so simple earlier. This wasn't the end of the world.

Cas hurried through the apartment, stopping briefly to check his hair was okay in one of the mirrors and that he hadn't splashed oil on his shirt or anything. Then he lunged for the door, praying Matty hadn't gotten bored and wandered off in the age it had taken Cas to move his ass across the apartment.

However, when he finally yanked open the door, Matty was standing on the other side, looking uncertainly at his phone. At Cas's sudden appearance, he gasped and looked up. "I-I was just checking I had the right address," he said quickly, waving the phone at Cas.

Fuck. It had only been a couple of days, but Matty was a sight for sore eyes. For the first time Cas had seen, he wasn't wearing jeans. Instead he was sporting a beige pair of chinos with a navy and white horizontally-striped long-sleeved T-shirt. It clung to his body like all manner of sin. He looked up with those blue eyes, so bright against his pale skin.

Cas's insides twisted with want and longing, and his heart fluttered with happiness. "You've got the right address," he murmured, feeling the sappy grin spread over his face.

Who cared if he'd failed at the first hurdle when it came to cooking? Matty was *here*, and they could just damn well order takeout.

"Please, come inside," said Cas, his manners switching on automatically thanks to a lifetime of training. He stood aside and swept his arm toward the living room, which the front door led straight to. "I'm so glad you came."

Matty blushed sweetly as he stepped in and allowed Cas to take the jacket he'd had slung over his arm. It was only in that moment that Cas suddenly realized that Matty must still have the old school hoodie that Cas had lent him for their little picnic. He loved the idea that it was still in Matty's possession, and the strategic part of his brain noted that it gave them an *excellent* excuse to see one another again, should they need it.

The romantic side of him just loved the idea that it might keep Matty warm.

After Cas hung up the jacket, he closed the front door then turned back to face Matty, who was looking a little like a deer in headlights. For an awful second, Cas was frozen with indecision, not sure if they should hug or shake hands or bloody *bow* to each other. But once again, Cas's manners took on a life of their own, and before the moment could become too awkward, he touched Matty's elbow and leaned in to ghost a kiss over his cheek.

"Did I mention it was good to see you?" he murmured as he stood back. After their little hiccup, he figured he might as well make his intentions crystal clear.

Matty took a breath and clasped his hands in front of his stomach. "You, too. Really. Look...I'm *so* sorry I avoided you. I can be a little weird sometimes. My ex-boyfriend liked to play games and mess me up, and my so-called parents have given me a few serious trust issues. And I promise I won't mention any of them again now I'm here." He grimaced and waved his hands. "What I'm trying to say is, thanks for not giving up on me. I'm really excited for dinner."

He offered Cas a hopeful smile, but for a second, Cas wrestled internally.

Should he come clean?

Matty had just been vulnerable and admitted that his ex was a player and his parents had given him trust issues. And here was Cas, hiding a huge part of who he was.

But he wasn't *lying*. Was it so terrible that he didn't want Matty to treat him differently, which he undoubtedly would if he found out that Cas was a damned prince? No, they were just two guys having dinner. Cas would never, *ever* mess Matty around. In fact, he'd do everything he could to keep him safe and having a good time.

So he shook off his doubts and snorted, holding his hand out toward the kitchen. "I wouldn't be too excited. It's all gone horribly wrong. Come on, let's head in so I can ply you with bubbles, and hopefully your meal won't taste so awful."

Matty gave him a curious look as he followed Cas into the next room. Cas was aware out of the corner of his eye that Matty's head was twisting and turning as he took in the high arches between the rooms, the vaulted ceiling, the chandelier, the original artwork, and the view that showed off the river Urden and half of upper Alpina.

Even when he was trying to be simple and modest, Cas wasn't sure he was capable.

Much like his cooking abilities.

"It was supposed to be a Thai curry," he said apologetically as he opened the fridge to retrieve one of the bottles of Zasfer.

He'd had a fondness for Thai food since his school days, when he, Leo and Jules used to sneak into Alpina for dinner, sometimes with Prince Dante of Thedes as well, seeing as he and Jules had always been two peas in a pod in those days. It had been the closest thing to normalcy the four princes had found back then, as the restaurant had never given them the royal treatment. In fact, the family had always gently teased them, making Cas feel like a regular teenager for once. He'd hoped to recreate some of that nostalgic sense of belonging for Matty tonight, but…

"I burned the garlic, and then you arrived. I think I managed to chop up most of the ingredients okay, though," he added brightly as the cork burst free with a loud *pop!* Cas expertly snagged one of the flutes he'd had out already, pouring Matty his glass before any of the bubbly could escape out of the neck.

He handed his date the glass with a shy smile, but Matty's eyes were wide and his brows raised. He accepted the glass almost without appearing to even see it. "I can take a shot at it, if you like?" he asked hopefully.

Cas stared at him. "But…I said I'd cook for *you?*" he replied weakly.

Matty smirked around the lip of his flute and took a long sip, his throat bobbing as he swallowed.

Cas's cock throbbed at just the sight of it.

"Yeah," Matty rasped, a playful tone to his voice. "But you're fucking it up."

Cas barked out a laugh. As much as he adored taking care of Matty, he *loved* it when Matty stopped worrying and started teasing. It was incredibly sexy.

"Oh, and you could do so much better?" Cas asked, equally as playful as he poured his own glass. A full one, this time. He didn't have to drive anywhere.

Matty's expression became quite serious and earnest. "I can already see what I'd do from the ingredients you have out. Were you following a recipe, or can I just improvise?" He blushed again, Cas's new favorite sight. "You've been so kind to me. So generous. I'd really love to reciprocate, if I can?"

Cas's insides squirmed, and his heart ached. Sure, his cock was definitely still awake, but Matty was practically begging to cook for them so he could repay Cas in a way that made sense to him.

Suddenly, that great gulf of a power and wealth imbalance didn't seem so enormous. Suddenly, they were just two guys, fumbling their way through a cute second date.

"Be my guest," Cas said warmly.

Matty took a sip from his glass, then set it down on the counter so he could roll up his sleeves and get to work. He moved with ease around the kitchen, his eyes dancing as he focused on sorting through the ingredients. Cas gave him the recipe that he'd been attempting, telling Matty that he really didn't mind if he followed it or not.

Cas leaned against the counter, sipping his sparkling wine and watching Matty work. He wondered if Matty knew he made little humming noises when he concentrated, or if he felt the smile that was playing on his lips. *Damn*, Cas wanted to step behind him and wrap his arms around his waist and kiss his neck. Matty had smelled of fresh soap and a woodsy after-shave when Cas had leaned in for that chaste kiss by the door. He licked his lips, already craving another hit of the scent that was purely Matty.

But they were still on slightly unstable footing after not seeing each other for almost two days, and Cas didn't want to spook the good mood out of Matty. So they chatted a little about how Finley was getting on with her course, and how thrilled she'd been to get her luggage back, especially her precious bow. Matty chatted about all the requirements for trans-porting what was essentially a *weapon* on a plane as he shifted effortlessly between the pan with the brewing chicken curry and the simmering rice. His fingers glistened with various sticky juices where he'd been handling the ingredients for the sauce, and Cas longed to lick them clean again.

Instead, he made sure their glasses stayed topped up, and put a playlist on his phone of easy-going music to (hopefully) set the mood. As the light faded outside the window, Cas lit a bunch of candles, making his living room far more intimate than any fancy restaurant would have been.

There was so much he longed to tell Matty about his real life. He wanted to moan about all the bullshit his brothers were putting him through, despite him actively trying to step back and stop fussing over them. He wanted to laugh about the circus that was the full-on preparation for the ball, and maybe get a little sympathy for having to dress up in traditional Rosavian formalwear. If he was brutally honest, Cas was convinced he wore it the best of all his brothers. It took a certain style to pull off those rose-patterned pants.

But he couldn't mention any of that, not if he wanted to avoid being caught out in his lie-by-omission. So he kept Matty talking with questions he genuinely wanted to know the answers to, long after Matty had served up their delicious-smelling dinner and they were seated at the dining table. Cas was fascinated by Matty's daily routine in New York, although he kept insisting that Queens wasn't really the city and his life wasn't all that exciting.

He didn't seem to understand that he was *free*. No one knew who he was. No one had tried to map out his destiny since birth. He didn't have a country weighing down his shoulders.

But Matty worried about money. A *lot*. And more importantly, his sister was incredibly sick. Cas felt like he despaired of his brothers nonstop these days, but the thought of any of them becoming ill chilled him to the bone.

He'd walk the world to ease their pain.

It was so tricky, walking this tightrope of truth with Matty. But at least Cas had let slip earlier that he had a little brother in Wren, so he was honestly able to tell Matty how he'd feel if he became sick. It made him feel like the two of them had something *real*.

Cas remembered Matty saying the other day about how he'd love to try living somewhere else for a while, if only he had the money.

Somewhere like Alpina? a voice at the back of his head whispered. But that was crazy. Matty had a whole life in America. There was no way he'd be interested in *really* uprooting everything to come live here. Besides, that was the last thing Cas wanted, anyway. He'd be tormented if he knew Matty was so close to him, and yet still so far away.

"So where would you like to live?" he prompted as they ate their curry – which was *delicious*. It had definitely been the right decision to let Matty take over cooking. Cas gestured to their food, the delicate blend of spices dancing on his tongue. "Somewhere in Asia?"

Matty laughed and shook his head. "Oh, I don't know. Anywhere, I guess. I just feel like I've coasted along my whole life. I need to start taking charge of my destiny more, and for some reason, I feel like that would be easier to do in a new place." He looked out over the city through the window. "Like I could be a different kind of me. I…I like who I'm becoming in Alpina."

Cas knew *exactly* what that felt like.

"Cheers to that," he murmured as they clinked their glasses together.

"How about you?" Matty asked after he took a sip.

Cas blinked. "Me what?"

Matty shrugged. "Did you always want to live in the city? Where did you grow up?"

Danger! Danger! Cas really didn't want to lie to Matty, not once. But he was going to have to be careful to sidestep anything that might give him away without looking suspicious.

He smiled and shrugged. "Yeah, I grew up in the suburbs," he said, which was kind of true. "But I feel like I'm only just getting to know the city properly." Also true.

Matty nodded. "Is that through your job? What was it you said you did again?"

Fuck. Cas knew all he'd said was that he was well off in an attempt to get Matty not to worry about money. "I do public relations for an old family company," he said, relief washing through him. That was pretty much accurate. "Lots of schmoozing," he added with an eye roll. Thinking about how he'd not long ago had to entertain that sleazy Grechzen ambassador Gustav von Jansen for a whole evening when Leo had bailed was a particularly rotten reminder of how true that could be. He smiled and leaned closer to Matty. "You're much better company than the pompous asshats I usually have to deal with."

Matty blushed. "Thanks," he said sweetly. Thankfully, after that the conversation switched again to one of the plays Matty had been working front of house on before coming to Rosavia. "They always let us watch the dress rehearsals for free," he said eagerly. Cas knew he'd promised not to over-whelm Matty with expensive gestures, but he loved the idea of taking him to the theater sometime.

After they'd had their fill of curry, Cas added fresh blueber-ries to their bubbles and revealed the rich chocolate cake he'd ordered to be delivered earlier for their dessert. The ganache shone as Cas cut them each a thick slice, then added a healthy measure of cream to the bowls.

"Oh my god, you're going to kill me!" Matty protested,

clutching his stomach. But he was grinning, so Cas didn't think he was really *that* stuffed.

He quirked an eyebrow as he sat back down, just around the corner from Matty, at his dining room table. "I assure you, this is the specialty of the best bakers in the city," he said, which was true. Even the chefs in the palace couldn't *quite* get the balance of flavors that Pierre's did. "I promise you."

Without stopping to think too much, he reached over to Matty's bowl, which was a comfortable enough distance away for him to pick up Matty's fork, cut off the tip of the cake slice, then held it up and let the excess cream drip off.

Then he met Matty's gaze, asking without words if he could feed him the morsel.

Never mind the cake. It was possible to cut the sexual tension between them with a knife. The candlelight flickered shadows across Matty's face, his blush still clear on his pale skin. He bit his lip and fluttered his eyelashes, but then he looked into Cas's eyes again as he leaned forward, wrapping his lips around the fork prongs, dragging the moist cake into his mouth.

Jesus Christ. There was absolutely no point in Cas pretending he wasn't immediately fantasizing about that being his cock Matty was taking such care over. And that was before Matty let out a ball-tingling moan, his eyelids closing as he covered his mouth and the residual chocolate on his gorgeous pink lips.

"Okay," Matty said hoarsely. He reopened his eyes and licked his lips as he finished chewing and swallowed, dropping his hand to his chest. "I take it back, you were right. That's the most incredible thing I have *ever* tasted. I'm happy to die by chocolate."

Cas carefully looked down at the fork in his hand, then dragged his gaze back up to Matty. He also was not going to pretend he wasn't getting distinctly uncomfortable in his trousers.

"Is that so?" he murmured, hopefully making it crystal clear there was something else he'd quite like Matty to taste. But just in case there was any room for doubt, he cut off another sliver of cake, this time placing it on his own tongue and then sucking the fork clean.

And then sweet, shy, cautious Matty exploded from his chair, knocking it to the floor as he launched himself around the corner of the table, straight into Cas's lap, flinging his arms around his neck, knocking over at least one glass flute, and crashing their mouths together in their first messy, but glorious, kiss.

Chapter Nine

MATTY

Regular Matty had finally given in and let Vacation Matty take the reins. Apparently, this was the result. Finding himself straddling Cas's lap in the blink of an eye, his hot lips pressed eagerly against Matty's, his hands gripping Matty's back, and his hard cock digging into Matty's inner thigh.

Vacation Matty needed to take charge more often.

Cas moaned as their lips moved together, his tongue chasing after Matty's, the rich chocolate lingering on both their mouths. Cas's grip tightened on Matty's back, dragging him closer so they were chest to chest. Matty's hands drifted upward to run his fingers through Cas's hair and clasp the back of his neck. All of Matty's skin was burning with desire and the desperate need to still be closer.

It was as if he'd been holding his breath for this moment since he and Cas had first laid eyes on each other in that sporting goods store. He suddenly felt more alive than he had in *years*.

They broke apart, panting and staring into each other's eyes. "Hi," Matty said weakly with a chuckle. "Uh, sorry for, uh…"

But Cas laughed. "I haven't been so thoroughly tackled since my lacrosse days at school." He rested their foreheads together and grinned. "This was *much* better," he added in a whisper.

Matty sighed and closed his eyes, relishing the feel of Cas's strong hands rubbing up and down his back. His breath held a tang of the sweet wine and chocolate dessert, mingled in with his spicy rich cologne. Matty ran his hand along Cas's neck and shoulder, tracing the solid muscles of his deltoid and biceps. Underneath his thighs, Cas's legs were equally firm, supporting Matty's weight with ease.

He'd pictured being pinned down by this solid body an inordinate number of times over the past few days. Now it might actually be about to happen.

Matty shivered in anticipation, but Cas's expression immediately became concerned. "Are you cold?"

Matty laughed. He dropped his face into the crook of Cas's neck and wrapped his arms around his shoulders, sighing as he watched Cas's pulse thrum. "You're so thoughtful," he said softly. "I'm fine. Perfect, actually."

Cas rested his cheek against Matty's hair, still caressing Matty's back. "I like taking care of you," he said, his voice a low rumble.

"I'd noticed," Matty said, then bit his lip. "No one's ever made me feel like this before, Cas. So…*treasured.*"

Cas kissed the top of his head. "Can I treasure you some more in my bedroom?"

His words were soft and without pressure. Matty had been longing for just this: the two of them, alone and intimate. But still, he felt a very slight spike of fear and hesitation. Regular Matty didn't do one-night stands. But that was because he preferred to sleep with men he knew and liked. And he definitely knew *and* liked Cas. So Vacation Matty took the wheel again, relaxing his body and reminding him this was exactly what he wanted, what he'd been craving.

"Yes, please," Matty said, nodding against Cas's warm neck. Then he raised his head so they could look at each other again, thrilled when Cas leaned in for a chaste kiss on the lips.

"There's something about you, Matty Doyle," Cas said. Matty didn't understand why, but his words seemed so heavy and laden with another meaning. But then Cas shook his head and smiled. "Isn't it funny how many little things happened to bring us together? How we ended up in that spot at the same time?"

"I guess fate works in strange ways," Matty said as he rubbed the back of Cas's neck.

Cas hummed in pleasure, then glanced around the room. "I hate to be a spoil-sport, but would you help me blow out all these candles?"

Matty laughed as he hopped off Cas's lap. "It's okay, I'd rather your gorgeous apartment didn't burn down with us in it," he joked, huffing on the candelabra sitting on the dining table. "Besides, they worked wonders for your seduction efforts. I can't say I've *ever* thrown myself at anyone quite like that before."

He blew out a couple more of the cream pillar candles before he felt a hand running up his spine. He turned to see Cas had stood and was looking at him with a warm smile and something else dancing in his eyes. Something deeper.

"Did I really seduce you?" he asked, sounding amused. But Matty shook his head.

"Not really, sorry," he said softly, a smile tugging at the corner of his lips. "You didn't really need to do all that much in the end. I was kind of a sure thing."

He'd never been good at playing hard to get, and he didn't particularly want to mess around with any games now. Not when he and Cas only had a limited amount of time together, anyway. He wanted them to be honest and open. So his heart leaped with joy at the smile that crept over Cas's face, dazzling in its intensity.

"In case it wasn't obvious," Cas whispered back, "I was a sure thing, too."

Matty felt woozy with happiness and desire as he and Cas did their best to keep their hands off each other for long enough to make sure all the candles were properly extinguished. Matty was almost sad to leave the incredible chocolate gateaux after only one bite, but he knew there was more in the fridge.

Maybe they could have it as a snack…later.

His stomach flipped as he properly acknowledged to himself that he meant post-sex sustenance. This was really happening.

Cas was really leading him toward his bedroom, their hands looped together, with Cas glancing over his shoulder at Matty, just like he did when they'd had their picnic by the log cabin.

He was so stunningly gorgeous, like a work of art. Matty still couldn't believe someone so beautiful would be interested in plain little him, and he thanked his lucky stars. He was done questioning why. Like Finley had said; once you had a target in your sights, you should fire. Otherwise you might miss your chance.

Matty had almost let Cas slip away once. He wasn't going to do it again.

Matty couldn't see much of Cas's room beyond the fact that it was large and had an equally huge king-sized bed. The only illumination was coming from the twinkling city lights through the floor-to-ceiling windows. They were so high up that Matty didn't feel like anyone could peek in on them. It was like being on top of the world, and not just from the view. Matty's heart sang as Cas turned and walked backward, holding Matty's hands as he led him to the bed.

Cas was choosing Matty. And Matty was choosing Cas right back. He thought of their talk of fate or destiny ensuring that they crossed paths at just the right time. The universe had indeed been kind to him for once.

They laughed as they tumbled onto the mattress together. Cas rolled them so they were side-by-side while they kicked off their shoes, kissing messily. Matty trembled as Cas's hands found their way under his Henley, skimming the ticklish skin of his abdomen. He wasn't nearly as buff as Cas, but he was very glad in that moment he wasn't in bad shape. He wanted to feel worthy of all of Cas's ministrations.

He hummed as Cas kissed his neck, their legs tangled together. He could honestly just imagine them making out like this until they fell asleep, like he was a teenager again. But he wasn't so shy anymore, and he was already feeling desperate for release. He did wonder idly if falling asleep was even on the cards. Could he stay the night? He hoped so. He hated the idea of traipsing back to his basic hotel room.

First things first. He needed to focus on the here and now and truly be present, not worrying about later. This was a gift, and he needed to cherish every single moment. He nuzzled his nose against Cas's, loving when Cas then kissed down Matty's jaw and throat. When he pushed Matty's Henley further up, Matty automatically raised his arms to allow Cas to strip his top half naked.

He realized that his skin was prickled with light perspiration as the cool air hit it. His nipples went rock hard, a fact Cas obviously didn't miss. He grinned as he dropped Matty's shirt over the side of the bed, then leaned down to capture one of the raised buds. Matty gasped as Cas's tongue swept over the sensitive skin, then he grazed his teeth over the nub, sending sparks of pleasure straight to his cock.

"Yes," Matty groaned. He carded his fingers through Cas's thick dark hair, drinking in every sensation as he writhed under Cas's touch. When Cas's hand reached between Matty's legs and palmed the bulge there, Matty yelped and jerked, needy for more. He kissed Cas's mouth frantically, nodding as little breaths escaped his lips. "Please, Cas."

Cas's eyes were blown with lust. Matty was doing that, and pride squirmed in his belly. "Can I top you?" Cas asked, his voice low and primal sounding. "I want to take care of every little thing for you."

Usually, Matty took a while to work up the courage to try anal with someone new, but he felt so safe with Cas. He cupped his hands on either side of Cas's freshly shaved face. He nodded as he looked into his eyes. "I trust you," he whispered in the near darkness, then captured Cas's mouth for a searing kiss.

But Cas pulled back, their lips coming apart with a little *'pop.'* Matty's stomach dropped as for a second, Cas just stared at him. He seemed almost panicked.

"A-are you okay?" Matty asked, worried that he'd said something wrong.

Then Cas blinked, like he'd just come out of a trance, and he smiled. "Yes, sorry – *sorry.* I'm great."

He kissed Matty's cheek, nuzzling their noses as he captured his lips and slowly helping Matty to relax again. Matty had no idea what that moment had been about, but he'd meant it: he trusted Cas not to mess him around, even if this was just a vacation fling. So Matty forgot about the strange look and instead tried to get his hands either under Cas's shirt or his fingers to unbuckle his belt. Neither task was going very well.

Cas laughed into his mouth and batted Matty's clumsy hands away. "I'll do that," he said warmly. "You just lie back and think of Rosavia."

Matty snorted, drinking in the sight of his very own Rosavian as Cas peeled off his shirt and flung it to the floor. His washboard abs and sharp obliques were heavenly to behold.

"I certainly will," Matty murmured, reaching up to run his fingertips over the hard bumps. Cas's skin was hot and, like

Matty, he was slightly damp from the exertion so far. He had a delicious dusting of dark hair across his pecs and a happy trail that led down from his belly button, disappearing underneath his pants.

Matty could see how much the material was tented, though. Cas wasn't small, and he was hard for Matty. He wanted to fill him up with that gorgeous cock, and Matty was more than ready to let him. As Cas hovered on all fours above him, Matty reached up and stroked Cas's arousal through his pants.

"Want you," Matty practically whined, placing little fluttery kisses on his lips. "Do you have supplies?" He was too shy to say 'condom and lube,' but of course Cas knew what he meant.

"Hang on a sec," he murmured, pausing to lean over to his nightstand. He opened it with a frown, like he'd forgotten what he'd put in there, then he burst out laughing.

"What?" Matty asked uncertainly.

Cas withdrew a bottle and waggled it for Matty to see. He couldn't read the words even if it hadn't been dark, as they were in Rosavian. But he just about made out the fruit picture on the label. "Blueberry lube," Cas said with a chuckle. "My brother got this for me as a joke a while back. I'd forgotten all about it."

Matty laughed too, but as Cas also retrieved a condom from a box and closed the drawer again, nerves got the better of him. He swallowed his mirth, eyes fixed on the shiny foil wrapping. What if he was no good? What if he disappointed Cas?

Then Cas touched his thumb and finger to Matty's chin, dragging his gaze up to meet Cas's. "We don't have to do anything you're not comfortable with," he said so sincerely, Matty's anxieties melted away.

Of course Cas wouldn't push him too far or hurt him. This was fine. It was *great.* Just what Matty had been craving. He sighed and smiled, caressing the side of Cas's face. "Thank you," he rasped. "But I want everything. I promise."

Cas had a serious look on his face as he nodded. "You can change your mind at any time."

"I won't," said Matty, kissing the tip of his nose, "but thank you."

Mercifully, there were no more hold ups after that. They shimmied out of their pants with relative ease, after which their underwear didn't last long. And then Matty was pinned to the bed, just like he'd dreamed, with Cas's long, gorgeous body pressed against him from head to toe. Their cocks rubbed against each other, pressed between their bellies. Matty could have almost come like that, but who knew if he'd ever get this chance again. He might have had another week and a half in Alpina, but there was no guarantee he and Cas would have sex again. Matty wanted to make the most of it.

"How do you want me?" he asked, feeling daring and a little dirty.

Cas grinned. "Well, I've already managed to get you naked and wet," he growled, reaching between them to squeeze their cocks, slippery with pre-cum. "Anything else now is just a bonus."

Matty whimpered. "Don't tease," he begged.

"Of course," said Cas, immediately dropping the playfulness.

Matty sighed and looked his lover in the eyes. "I don't mean we have to be serious," he said kindly. "But I'm pretty shamelessly desperate for you. That's all I meant."

Cas chuckled and dropped his head. "Fuck, sorry. Even in bed I can't stop fretting. Right. Sexy. I can do this."

Matty dropped his head back and laughed, rolling his hips and rubbing their cocks together. "You can, I swear to you. You're doing great, champ."

Cas snorted, the playfulness back in full force between them. They also seemed more in sync as Cas reached for a pillow and Matty lifted his hips for him to slide it under without them having to say anything. Matty watched as Cas methodically ripped open the condom and rolled it down his hard shaft, then squeezed a great dollop of lube onto his fingers. The bedroom was suddenly filled with the sweet tang of blueberries, making Matty grin.

The unusual scent reminded him that he definitely wasn't in Queens anymore.

Cas stretched him with both care and efficiency, all while kissing Matty and murmuring sweet nothings to him. Matty's heart was hammering as he gasped and quivered, holding on to Cas's strong shoulders like they were his anchor. It seemed a lifetime ago that Matty and Jeremy had been together, let alone with this level of intensity. In fact, Matty had to wonder if they'd ever had this kind of passion. It was like Cas was already inside Matty, under his skin, their hearts beating as one.

"Do you feel ready?" Cas asked, pulsing the two fingers that were stretching Matty's hole, and cupping his palm against Matty's heavy, sensitive balls. Matty's breaths were shallow as he struggled not to lose control. He didn't want to spurt his load the second Cas touched his dick again. He wanted this to last.

He nodded. "I need you, Cas." Matty dug his fingers onto Cas's arms and kissed his mouth, then along his jaw. "I'm good. I want it."

Cas nodded, his breathing equally as ragged as he kissed Matty a few times, spreading more lube on his cock and Matty's hole. Then he was lining up the head with Matty's entrance, and there was no going back.

Matty braced himself, staring into Cas's eyes as he breached him, pushing through that tight ring of muscle. It burned and they both cried out, but Matty could already tell it would ease quickly, and Cas felt so amazing, filling Matty up to the brim. *"Yes, yes, yes,"* he hissed, blinking away the tears leaking from his eyes. It was too much, but not enough. He needed Cas to give him everything.

He took a few deep breaths, relaxing as Cas eased further into him. He changed his angle slightly, and Matty shifted to wrap his legs around Cas's waist. They both grunted and gasped as Cas bottomed out, his tip rubbing Matty's prostate. Cas fumbled with his right hand to entwine it with Matty's left, kissing him sloppily as they both took a moment to relax.

"You feel incredible," Cas murmured.

Matty nodded, already getting used to the intrusion. It was as if he'd been waiting for Cas, and his body knew what to do. "You too," he rasped. "It's okay to move – *please.*"

But Cas took a few seconds to kiss Matty's neck and stroke his cock. It had softened a little while Cas had been penetrating him, but it very quickly sprang back to life in Cas's strong grip. Matty whimpered and bit his own lip, squeezing his eyes shut, and willing himself not to come just yet. He was close, though.

And then Cas began to move his body, undulating slowly back and forth as he drove inside Matty with a confidence and tenderness that took Matty's breath away. Matty felt like he was floating, every inch of him supported by Cas's strong body. Matty had experienced a decent enough amount of sex in his time. But this really felt like what people meant when they talked about *making love.*

Cas kissed him with a fiery desperation, hoisting Matty's hips up to get a better angle. Matty cried out as Cas hit his prostate again and again, making him feel like electricity was dancing between them. He wailed, feeling raw as he and Cas moved together in the dark, discovering the beautiful connection that just seemed so *perfect* between them.

Even as his climax rose in him, Matty kept his gaze fixed on Cas's warm brown eyes, clinging on to his powerful body as their slippery skin pounded together, their speed increasing without either of them needing to say a word. "Cas!" he cried in warning.

Then Cas reached down and circled his hand around Matty's cock, jerking him off and tipping him over the edge. Heat rushed over Matty's body from head to toe as he yelled out and began pulsing hot, thick cum between them. Even though the high was dizzying, he still felt oddly calm and safe in Cas's arms.

Matty realized as he blinked his way back to reality that was probably because Cas had stilled, holding Matty through his orgasm. Matty took a couple of breaths, sleepily pawing at Cas's chest. "You're not done," he mumbled, giving his lips a clumsy kiss. Cas's skin had a sheen of perspiration all over, and his dark hair was dripping wet. He looked like a fantasy, but he was solid and hot against Matty's body. An impossibility made real.

"I wanted to see you come," Cas said, making Matty flush even more than he already was. Cas seemed to like that, grinning and brushing back one of Matty's curls. His hair was probably a complete mess right now, but he didn't care. Contentment thrummed through his veins, making him drowsy and heavy as lead. But he was fretting over Cas's very *hard* situation, still buried deep within Matty's ass.

He mustered enough energy to roll his hips, and was immediately rewarded with Cas flinching, screwing up his eyes and sucking in a sudden breath. His loud moan made it clear it was a completely pleasurable reaction, though.

"Do you want to come in me?" Matty asked, his heart skipping at his own boldness.

He'd never done much dirty talk with Jeremy or his other exes. Sex with them had been warm, safe, and comfortable. Right now, Matty definitely felt all those things with Cas, but with a very important added thrill of confidence and daring. Lying beneath Cas, Matty didn't feel shy or afraid that he might fuck up and say the wrong thing. He felt almost powerful, in command, which was crazy because Cas was clearly in charge here.

Cas moaned and captured his lips for a filthy kiss and he began to slowly rock his hips. "Yes, Matty," he whispered, nipping at Matty's jaw and earlobe. "You feel so good. I want to fill you up."

Matty knew it wouldn't be quite the same with a condom on, but he hoped that was true. He dropped his feet on either side of Cas's legs and stroked his back, urging him toward his climax. "Yes, feels perfect," he murmured, not really caring what nonsense came out of his mouth. "You're so hot, Cas. Fuck me harder. I've got you. *I've got you.*"

Cas gnashed his teeth and jerked forward, scooping Matty into his arms, pressing their sticky chests together. He twitched his hips, shooting his load, breathing heavily and nuzzling his face against Matty's neck. Matty wished he could have come in him without the condom, as if having Cas's seed in him afterward would prove this had really happened. But Matty could feel his cock pulsing deep in his ass, and knew this was no illusion.

This *had* happened. Cas really had just fucked his brains out, and Matty's ass was going to be fully aware of that fact tomorrow. The reality of that made Matty laugh, dropping his head back down on the pillow.

Cas hummed. "Everything okay?" he asked sleepily, pressing his lips against Matty's pulse point.

"Incredible," Matty said, shaking his head. "Amazing. Wonderful. Oh, Cas."

Slowly, Cas withdrew his softening cock and made short work of disposing the condom. He gave Matty a quick kiss before disappearing from his bedroom. Matty frowned. He thought they might at least *cuddle*. But then Cas returned with a damp washcloth and perched naked on the edge of the bed, looking down at Matty.

"May I?" he asked.

If he was honest, Matty wasn't entirely sure what Cas was asking to do, but like Matty had said before, he trusted him. So he nodded, then watched as Cas proceeded to tenderly run the warm cloth over Matty's belly, cock, and between his legs, wiping away most of the mess.

Matty was stunned, not sure if he should say anything or not. He'd always been left to fend for himself when it came to post-coital mess. But Cas hadn't even hesitated, like it was no big deal to perform such an intimate act.

Did he do that with all of his lovers?

Matty bit his tongue, *hard*. He wasn't going to get melancholy thinking about the other men (or women?) that Cas might have been with. He was with *Matty* right here and now, and Matty was going to be extremely grateful for this moment as long as he lived.

So he smiled and sighed as Cas slipped back onto the bed beside him, pulling the covers over them both just enough to cover their modesty, and snuggling up to Matty's side. "Come here," he murmured, and Matty fit perfectly in his arms.

Matty fought the wave of exhaustion that rolled over him. He didn't want this night to end. It had been so perfect he could almost burst with happiness. But it was greedy to expect more. He promised himself that no matter what, when morning came, he would be thankful.

And that was his last thought as sleep finally claimed him. Apparently, he *was* staying the night, which was an incredible bonus on its own.

He wouldn't ask for anything else. No matter how much he wanted to.

Chapter Ten

CAS

Was Cas the biggest fool in Rosavia? Had he made a monumental mistake?

As he watched Matty sleeping in the morning sunlight, so peaceful and perfect all rumpled up in Cas's bedsheets, he honestly couldn't convince himself he'd done anything wrong.

But the reason he'd woken at the crack of dawn was because he'd had some sort of awful nightmare. He'd been back in that intervention with Wren along with his parents, but this time, it had been Cas on trial, his hands in cuffs, a jury sentencing him for crimes against the state. He'd bolted awake, gasping in fear, but then quickly realized it was just a dream.

And he wasn't going to be held hostage to it.

Matty's lips were slightly parted as he slept soundly, his hands tucked under his cheek like a damn angel. His skin seemed extra pale in the fresh dawn light, his hair a glossy, inky black.

His expression when he'd come last night was seared deliciously into Cas's brain.

He knew the risks. He was fully aware of what he was doing. He knew no matter how strong this pull was between them, it couldn't last. And yet he was convinced Valentina was right. He would have deeply regretted it if he'd never found out how Matty tasted, or the way he'd felt under Cas's hands. He was divine, and Cas refused to feel guilty. They hadn't done anything wrong. They were two consenting adults who'd had a wonderful night together.

But Matty didn't know that Cas was a prince. When Matty had said that he trusted Cas last night, in the middle of sex, it had made Cas freeze. People had trusted him to fix their problems his whole life, and this vacation was a chance to stop enabling his family and allow his brothers to fix their own lives. But Matty saying those words had caused a stab of guilt through Cas's chest. He didn't want to deceive Matty, but Cas was holding back a big part of himself so he could have a real chance at normalcy. Was that wrong? Was he hurting Matty?

He desperately hoped not.

Cas sighed and ran his fingers over Matty's hair with a featherlight touch. That couldn't be helped. There was no way Cas could have told Matty that particular truth, not without risking everything. And what he didn't know wouldn't hurt him, Cas was sure. He comforted himself that while he hadn't been able to be totally honest, he'd never *lied* to Matty, either. That was very important to Cas.

They just needed to stay in this perfect bubble while they still had the chance.

Cas was perfectly happy with that. He didn't really want to leave this *room*, but the kitchen was where the food lived, and his stomach was rumbling. After another half an hour of uselessly trying to get back to sleep, he decided to go do something productive.

He knew he was trying to impress Matty without lavishing money on him, but that was okay. If this was only going to last a few more days, Cas wanted treasure Matty, to use their word from yesterday. And not just in the bedroom.

So he got his robe and slippers on, then made his way back into the rest of the apartment. The kitchen was a bit of a disaster zone, but if Cas moved too many dishes around now, whether to wash them or load the dishwasher, he might disturb Matty. That was the opposite of what he was trying to achieve here.

Very carefully, he cleared a few things to the side so he could free up the stove, then looked up another recipe on his phone. This one for pancakes. He chewed his lip, debating whether to go for the very thin French crêpe style or the fatter American type that Matty would be used to. In the end, he decided that the thick American ones would be easier to keep warm, and they'd go perfectly with the blueberry syrup that Cas obviously had in his cupboard as a respectable Rosavian.

He paused briefly, wondering if he had flour and baking powder. But it seemed Valentina had thought of everything. Maybe she'd secretly hoped they'd stay hidden away baking rather than risking getting caught out in public. He grinned, feeling ridiculously domestic.

He might not have been very good at it, but he could see how ordinary cooking was so much better than the survival techniques he'd learned at school. He wished his suite at the palace had a kitchen, but he could just imagine his relatives spinning in their graves at the mere suggestion of renovating the centuries-old architecture, not to mention all the traditionalists still living at the palace who would definitely see it as undignified for a prince to cook for himself. They'd all probably rather he got caught with Matty.

Cas sighed as he mixed some of the ingredients together. He needed to be present in the moment, not worrying about the past or the future. Besides, there was every chance he was going to burn these suckers if he didn't give them his full attention.

He bit his tongue between his teeth as he focused on melting butter in a pan, filling the kitchen with a delicious warm smell, then folded some fresh blueberries into the batter before adding them in four dollops to make sort of disk shapes. They weren't terrible-looking, though, and the way they sizzled made Cas grin.

Leaving them to brown, he started making some rose tea and chopping up bananas to go with the finished pancakes. He frowned. Was there anything Matty might like? Maybe bacon? Would he prefer coffee to tea?

"Wow," a voice rasped sleepily from behind him. Cas spun around to find he'd been discovered by an adorably rumpled Matty. He was back in his boxers, with Cas's sheet draped over his shoulders like a cape. He gave Cas a lopsided grin. "What's this?"

"Breakfast," said Cas proudly. Then he lunged for the pancakes, getting to them *just* before they started to burn, sighing in relief as he flipped them onto the uncooked side. "I didn't mean to disturb you," he said guiltily.

Matty shook his head. "You didn't. I'm still adjusting to the new time zone. When it smelled so good, I had to come investigate."

They smiled at each other, and the energy between them shifted slightly. Before Cas could second-guess himself, he stepped forward and opened his arm out. His heart skipped as Matty moved against his side without hesitation, and they hugged side-by-side. Cas kissed his hair, smelling Matty's unique scent. It was glorious.

"Did you sleep okay?" he asked.

Matty nodded, then smiled up at him. "I'm not used to waking up in these strange beds." He bit his lip shyly at Cas. "Your room was much nicer than the hotel, though."

It was stupid, because this might as *well* have been a hotel room. If Matty searched through the drawers, he'd quickly realize it wasn't a particularly lived-in apartment. But Cas was still pleased Matty liked it.

Cas had promised himself that he wouldn't push Matty, but as they looked into each other's eyes in the kitchen, with the pancakes sizzling and the tea brewing, Cas felt like he never wanted the moment to end. "So, um," he said, uncharacteristically shy, "do you have plans today?"

Can you stay here with me? That was what he was really asking.

"Not particularly," Matty said, biting his lip. Then he huffed and offered Cas a tentative smile. "No. No plans at all. Did you want to do something?"

"Yes," Cas said so fast he made them both laugh. "Shall we have breakfast, then perhaps think of what we'd like to do?"

Matty grinned and leaned up to kiss Cas's lips sweetly. "Perfect," he said. Then he jutted his chin toward the pan. "Don't let them burn."

"Shit!" Cas let go of Matty to yank the pan off the stove and save the pancakes from a crispy fate. "Nice work."

He chuckled weakly as Matty laughed at him, looking around for something to serve them up on. He forgot for a second which cupboard the plates were in. But Matty obviously remembered from the night before, as he produced two small plates in a flash.

Cas sighed in relief. "Right, these may be terrible. So, shall we start with two each? I can always make more."

In the end, he and Matty made their way through a stack of six pancakes each, drenched in blueberry syrup, washed down with buckets of rose tea. They snuggled up on the sofa with blankets, cuddling close once they were too full to eat any more, watching a silly romantic film on the television. Cas was pleased it was in English, so Matty didn't have to read subtitles. However, it wasn't long before they were only half-paying attention to the screen.

In Cas's defense, Matty's mouth was extra sweet after breakfast, and those lips were just so kissable. Sometime before the credits, they slid down the couch, kissing and letting their hands wander, then Cas kicked away the blankets. There was enough heat between him and Matty that they really weren't necessary anymore.

Matty moaned deliciously as Cas pulled off the T-shirt Matty had borrowed from him to put on for breakfast, kissing down his flat stomach and palming his hard cock through his boxers. "Hmm," Cas growled, nipping at Matty's hip, loving how he squirmed. "I'm still hungry. Can I have more breakfast?"

Matty whimpered, rubbing the back of Cas's neck and mussing up his hair. "Oh god, yes, please."

His usually pale skin was flushed over his checks, down his neck, and across his chest. He rutted his groin upward as Cas ran his finger under the waistband of his underwear and nuzzled his cock through his boxers with his nose, mouthing at the tip.

"Smells yummy," he said, meaning it. Cas inhaled Matty's unique musk as he pushed his boxers down, freeing his leaking dick. It bounced as Cas rubbed his cheek against Matty's tight, curly hair and kissed the base of his shaft. "Oh, fuck, Matty," he rasped, stroking his trembling legs, his underwear pinning his thighs together. "I want you to come down my throat."

"God, yes," Matty hissed, screwing up his eyes and fists, his breathing ragged. Then he blinked and looked down at Cas with sincerity in his eyes. "I'd love that." He cupped the side of Cas's cheek, rubbing little circles with his thumb.

Fuck. In that moment, it was as if Matty was seeing Cas right down into his soul. He wanted Cas to touch him and hold him and make him feel good, and Cas wanted that more than anything. Matty was kind and sweet and gorgeous and *his.* Even if only for a few days. Cas was almost overwhelmed with a possessive need to keep Matty safe, and if that meant shutting away the rest of the world, just for a little while, Cas would do it.

The ball, his family drama, the press, the duty that had weighed him down his whole life, didn't seem so important when it was just the two of them, is this small apartment, offering each other their hearts.

And their bodies. Cas took a moment to crawl up the sofa and kiss Matty with everything he had, but he wasn't about to leave his gorgeous lover with blue balls. Matty groaned and shook as Cas wrapped his hand around his cock for the last few kisses. Then he moved back down the couch and wasted no time in slipping his lips over Matty's hot, hard, salty shaft, swallowing him down to the root.

Matty jerked and cried out in surprise, but he soon flopped back down on the cushions, gasping and begging Cas for more, whispering how good he felt in little half-uttered sentences. God, he was gorgeous when he came undone like this. Perfect putty in Cas's hands. Cas watched him as he bobbed his head, sucking and swallowing as he jerked the base of Matty's shaft with his hand, and fondling his balls.

Cas might not have gotten the relationship he'd wanted over the years, but he'd worked *really* hard to perfect his blowjob technique. There was just something that he loved about giving his partner so much pleasure. Sometimes he didn't even bother to come himself afterward, riding the high of knowing that he'd given his lover his all, even just for a few minutes.

Watching a man come was always rewarding, but there was nothing Cas had done previously to compare to how he felt watching Matty on the verge of tears, writhing as Cas built him up to his climax. He edged him a little, slowing down a couple of times. He knew instinctively that Matty could take it, and his orgasm would be that much more spectacular when Cas finally did tip him over the edge.

"Cas, wait!" Matty said frantically, shaking his head and almost trying to shift away from Cas. Cas paused, widening his eyes, asking Matty what he wanted. Had he pushed him too far after all?

Matty bit his lip, his hair completely disheveled and his skin blotchy and shining with perspiration. "I'm close. Are you sure you're okay to swallow?"

What a sweetheart. Cas responded by sucking – *hard* – then giving as much of a nod as he could with Matty's cock down his throat.

Matty squealed and bit his knuckles. "Okay. Okay, then. *Fuck.* You're the hottest thing I've ever seen, Cas. Oh my god."

Cas felt like Matty had probably done enough talking by that point, so he wasted no more time, throwing everything he could into building Matty's climax, sucking and rubbing his engorged cock.

And when Matty came with a loud shout, Cas drank down every droplet of his bitter, musky cum, milking his shaft for everything he had to give. As Matty sank boneless against the couch, gasping for air, Cas took his time to come off his softening cock, licking and kissing the oversensitive skin, and caressing his spent balls tenderly. The sofa was big enough that Cas was able to crawl up it again and lie by Matty's side, wrapping his arm around him and kissing his damp hair as he took several deep breaths and trembled.

"That was incredible," Matty eventually stammered. He clutched onto Cas's bathrobe and buried his face against Cas's neck. "I just – I never – *holy fuck.*"

Cas chuckled and gently stroked up and down his spine. The TV was still playing quietly in the background, and beyond the windows, in the bright, sunny day, traffic rumbled and birds sang. The world was still turning, but for Cas, in that moment, this was it. Nothing else existed but the way Matty's hot body was trembling in his arms, or the way a tired smile was playing on his lips.

"It was my pleasure, sweetheart," Cas said fondly, meaning that to his core. Matty didn't want to be spoiled with riches. Cas had to admit that giving him this intimate kind of gift was far better than a fancy meal and expensive cocktails.

Matty blinked several times, looking like he was coming back to his senses. "Okay," he said, nodding and taking another fortifying breath. "Okay, wow. I could blow you, or did you have something else in mind?"

Cas smiled, meeting Matty's eyes. The earnest tone to his words was incredibly endearing. "I'm fine," Cas said genuinely.

But Matty frowned – no, *scowled* – then looked pointedly down where Cas was half-hard underneath the robe he was wearing and nothing else. Okay, he wasn't *fine.* But he hadn't sucked Matty off just to get something in return.

"Honestly, you don't have to," Cas elaborated, not wanting him to feel obliged. It was wonderful just cuddling on the couch, after all.

However, Matty didn't seem to see it that way. "Oh," he said, in confusion. "Okay. If you don't want me to?"

Oh, hell no. That was a different question entirely. "No, no," Cas spluttered. "I just meant that you don't have to, if you don't want to. You look exhausted."

A light brightened in Matty's eyes. "But if I *did* want to, you'd like that?" he asked hopefully.

Cas's heart twisted. He wasn't sure what he'd done to deserve meeting such a beautiful soul, but Matty was just so perfect.

Cas leaned over and kissed Matty's mouth, running his hand up and down Matty's arm, feeling his goosebumps. "I'd *love* it," Cas told him. "But only if you've got the energy."

Matty beamed and sat up, pulling his underwear back on then grabbing a cushion and sliding to the floor. He knelt on the cushion, batting Cas's knees apart so he could scooch between his legs. Only as he reached for the tie on Cas's bathrobe did he hesitate. "Oh," he said, his confidence visibly fading. "Unless you'd prefer it some other way?"

Cas had to click his jaw shut and clear his throat. Was Matty crazy? Some other way? He looked positively sinful at Cas's feet, eagerly about to suck his brains out of his cock. He was perfect. Well, *almost* perfect.

Cas shook his head and caressed the side of Matty's face. "This is amazing. You look gorgeous. But I'd really love it if you took your boxers off all the way." He rubbed his thumb against Matty's lower lip. "I'd like to see all of you while you give me your mouth."

Matty swallowed, his Adam's apple bobbing. His usually blue eyes were dark, his pupils were blown so wide. His cheeks flushed even darker crimson as he nodded. He kissed Cas's thumb, sucking the tip for just a second. But it was enough to bring Cas to full hardness, immediately making him anticipate when the thumb would be replaced by his cock.

Matty was beyond beautiful, but that was nothing compared to the thrill Cas felt when he smiled and nodded again, agreeing to Cas's request.

"Of course, Cas," he said softly.

Not breaking their connected gaze, he stood and swiftly pushed his boxers down to his ankles, kicking them away, then kneeling back down on the cushion, sitting on his heels with his recently spent cock lying on his thigh. He looked completely open and – more importantly – at ease as he sat naked for Cas.

Cas's breath hitched in his chest. It was rare someone went down on him with the same kind of reverence he displayed for his partners. He hoped he'd made Matty feel this goddamned special a few minutes ago.

Because Cas had spent his whole life as royalty. But in that moment, all the Crown Jewels couldn't compare to the way Matty was staring up at him. Like he was his whole world.

Almost too afraid to breathe, Cas undid his robe and shucked his arms from the sleeves, leaving them both entirely naked in the bright morning light. Matty bit his lip as half a smile crept on his lips. Cas watched his gaze as it raked over Cas's body, drinking it all in. Cas knew he was in great shape, but what did that matter without a gorgeous man appreciating him the way Matty was?

This was different than the night before, where they'd been

shrouded in darkness. There was no hiding from each other now, not that Cas would want to.

Matty hummed, his smile becoming a full one. He ran his hands up Cas's legs, then he shuffled forward and rested his cheek against Cas's thigh, studying Cas's hard cock in awe, like it was a piece of art.

That *certainly* didn't hurt Cas's ego any.

Matty turned his gaze up to Cas's face, apparently unsurprised to find Cas watching him intently.

"Do you want to feed it to me?" he asked in little more than a whisper. He had a small smile dancing on his lips, and his eyes were wide. It was clear to Cas that *Matty* would like him to take charge again. He seemed excited by the prospect, but also strangely calm.

Cas got the overwhelming impression that this kind of confidence – to ask for what he desired – was unusual for Matty.

And Cas was honored.

He sat up and leaned forward, his heart leaping when Matty didn't move an inch. He just kept looking up at Cas's face. "Oh, *Christ.* Yes," Cas growled, running his fingers through Matty's tangled curls. "You're so fucking beautiful. Will you be still, just where you are, and take my cock? I want to slide it all the way down your throat and fuck your mouth slowly."

If Matty was daunted by that in any way, he didn't show it. He just gave a little nod, leaning into Cas's palm. "I will, Cas. I want to make you feel good. You can use my mouth. Tell me if you want anything different."

Cas was so hard and close to the damn edge already he had

to circle the base of his shaft and squeeze it *hard*. At this rate, he was going to blow his load the second Matty's lips touched his cock. To think he'd almost talked his way out of this.

"I will, sweetheart. But I think you'll be just perfect."

Matty's eyes definitely shone brighter at the praise. If he got off on being told he was good and gorgeous and doing everything right, that was the kind of kink Cas would have no trouble with at all. How long had he yearned to care for someone like this? Someone who would let Cas in and blossom under his guiding hand? It was like Cas had been pushing all this energy in the wrong direction his whole life.

He stopped squeezing his cock and instead shifted forward so he could take hold of it and rub the tip against Matty's parted lips, smearing them with pre cum. "You have no idea how glorious you look right now, Matty. I know you're going to make me feel so good."

"Like how you made me feel good," Matty said with a small sigh of happiness.

"Exactly like that," Cas agreed.

Using one hand to guide his pulsing cock, Cas slipped the other through Matty's hair again, bringing them together in a surge of tight, wet heat. Cas groaned loudly, not holding back and clearly letting Matty know how much he was enjoying himself.

Despite his efforts, Cas knew he wasn't going to take long. Not as he slid along Matty's tongue, hitting the back of his throat. Matty was calm as he relaxed, accepting Cas's intrusion, sucking and licking and swallowing eagerly. He brought his hands up to rest on Cas's knees, only bobbing his head a little, but mostly letting Cas fuck him.

Cas would have had to stand up to thrust much more, and he was enjoying the sweet intimacy of being on the sofa with his lover between his legs. So instead he gripped the back of Matty's head, trying not to pull his hair too much, but guiding him all the same to suck Cas off. Matty moaned in pleasure as Cas moved his head and sped him up, sliding him up and down his throbbing dick, bringing him to climax.

"I'm going to come, Matty," he grunted through his teeth. Knowing he was seconds away, he dropped his hand from Matty's head so he could pull off if he wanted to. But Matty didn't falter or even seem to notice that Cas's hand was gone. If anything, he moved faster and sucked harder, chasing Cas's orgasm for him.

And just like that, Cas exploded, shooting cum down Matty's throat, feeling like the orgasm lasted for minutes as he spurted again and again.

Matty swallowed the first load, but then he choked, getting some on his chin as his eyes watered. But before Cas could react, Matty latched back onto Cas's dick, catching the rest of his seed and taking it down greedily. Finally, when Cas was spent, Matty popped off his still hard shaft and wiped his chin with the back of his hand. He looked utterly exhausted as he gazed up at Cas.

"Was that okay?" he rasped, his throat sounding raw from getting fucked.

"Okay?" Cas repeated weakly. He dropped down to his knees and hugged Matty to him, rubbing up and down his spine as

Matty dug his fingers into Cas's back. "Sweetheart, that was spectacular."

He sat on his ass and opened his knees, pulling Matty flush against him, and hugging him with his arms and his legs. Just a big naked ball of deep affection. Matty tucked perfectly under Cas's chin and against his chest. He rested his hand over Cas's heart, and sighed peacefully.

Yes, Cas thought as he looked down at where Matty was resting his palm. *I think that might belong to you now.*

Cas was pretty sure that was a bad idea. He couldn't give Matty his heart, not without causing a hell of a lot of trouble. But as they sat curled up together, Cas realized that he might not have a choice in the matter. He'd just have to deal with the consequences when they came, and hope that they weren't too disastrous.

Chapter Eleven

MATTY - ONE WEEK LATER

"Oh my god! Yay! Hi! I thought I was never going to talk to you again!"

Matty laughed at his sister on the other end of the line, relief flooding him. They'd had the worst luck trying to speak over the past week, only talking through texts. It was wonderful to hear her voice. "I know, right? Time zones are a bitch."

Reghan blew a raspberry. "The clock has lost all meaning," she said, doing her best mystic impression. "Also, I'm napping all the damn time, so I have no clue what the time even is. I honestly didn't know if you'd pick up or not. I just woke up and grabbed my phone." As if to illustrate her point, she yawned loudly.

Matty continued walking down the quiet Alpina street, enjoying the deep shadows from the buildings in the dawn light. He'd always been an early riser, and jet lag was still messing with his body, so he'd embraced it and gone for a walk. It felt like the whole world was his to relish with so few other people around.

"Oh!" Reghan said, sounding surprised and distant. Matty guessed she'd just checked the time on her phone. When she spoke again, she was loud and clear once more. "It's eleven-thirty, apparently."

Matty should have remembered New York was seven hours behind Rosavia, but the last several days had been such a blur, it was as if details he hadn't needed for a while were just leaking out of his ears.

Concern quickly overrode everything else. "Shouldn't you be asleep?" he asked.

Reghan sighed. "It's okay, baby bro," she said. Her voice was kind of hoarse, reminding him of just how ill she was. "I'm doing okay, really. Lola is taking such good care of me while I get used to this hell again. But it is what it is." There was a pause, and Matty battled with the lump in his throat. "I'm going to beat it this time, I *promise* you."

Matty sniffed. "I know," he said, making himself laugh. "You always were a stubborn brat."

Reghan laughed wetly. "Me? *You* were the brat. I always had to bail you out of trouble!"

Matty's heart swelled as he rubbed his face. Teasing was good, after all. It was *normal.* "Is that why you called?" he asked. "Did your sixth sense ping that I'm up to no good?"

There was another very different kind of pause. "Matty, what's wrong?" Reghan demanded. "Is Finley okay?"

"She's fine!" Matty spluttered, cursing himself and his big mouth. He hadn't meant to say anything at all, and he certainly hadn't meant to scare Reghan. "She's had a fantastic week. I've visited her a couple of times, and we talk every night. She said she was calling you guys, too?"

Reghan let out a breath. "Yeah, she has been. And if I was asleep, Lola's spoken to her. I just…it's so tough being on another continent from my baby. I've never even left her *overnight* anywhere before. Thank you so much for getting her there and being her guardian angel."

"Oh, hon, it's fine," Matty said. "I'm glad you trusted me, but Elm Willows is doing most of the work. This is an opportunity of a lifetime for her, and she's doing amazingly, according to the school. Her teachers are so attentive, and I've been speaking to them regularly too. Everything's great here, I promise."

Matty didn't really understand what Finley was doing, other than spending most of her day shooting arrows, but one of her instructors had spoken to him just yesterday and assured him that she was excelling as one of their top students. He told Reghan that.

She sniffed and sighed in relief. "Sorry, I didn't mean to lose it. I wish I could be there so badly."

Matty smiled, wishing he could wrap his big sister up in his arms. "It's perfectly natural to be worried about your daughter," he assured her. "Thank you for having faith in me. I promise to take a hundred thousand videos at the competition tomorrow."

His heart twisted. He and Cas had been lost in a blissful

bubble that had seemed to exist out of time. How was it already Friday morning?

Matty and Finley were flying home on Monday.

Before melancholy could overwhelm him, Matty shook himself. He and Cas had studiously *not* discussed Matty's departure over the past several days, but he'd vowed to himself that he would today. He wasn't sure what future could possibly happen with an ocean between them, but Matty was determined not to let Cas slip through his fingers.

Right from the start, Cas had somehow helped Matty's confidence to grow. After such an intense period together, Matty was already believing in himself more. It almost felt easy with Cas's continuous praise and the way he looked at Matty with such fondness.

Regular Matty was already feeling like the stranger, and Vacation Matty was taking his place. Vacation Matty didn't assume that Cas was going to abandon him like all his ex-boyfriends and, most painfully, his parents had. Cas made Matty feel *enough* in a way that had clearly been lacking his whole life.

Enough that Matty was finally giving serious deliberation to that half-baked plan of his that he could maybe try living somewhere other than Queens for a while.

And perhaps that place could be Alpina.

He'd never even considered anything so crazy in his life, but he'd thrown caution to the wind and trusted Cas, and he hadn't messed Matty around like he'd feared. Everything had turned out fantastic. People moved all the time. Why shouldn't Matty give it a try?

As he talked more with Reghan about Finley's accomplishments over the past week and a half, he knew his family was the only thing tying him to New York. He would never in a million years desert them, like his and Reghan's folks had. But he wasn't slamming the door on them for coming out. He was just thinking about what would make him happy for once, and how he might start truly living his life. Shommie and Esosa had been very clear with him that he wasn't doing Reghan any favors by sitting around and worrying over her. He'd always be there to help, but Matty wanted to see the world and discover more of who he truly was.

He strolled past a bakery that was wafting delicious smells of freshly-prepared pastries through the open doors. He'd gone out with the intention of picking up something tasty on his way back to Cas's place later for them both. As much as he'd made up his mind that he was going to talk to Cas about a tentative future between them later, he still had a hard-wired fear that it was all going to blow up in his face. His stomach knotted immediately as he pictured Cas's beaming smile falling from his face as he rejected Matty's idea.

As if sensing his thoughts, Reghan clicked her tongue. "So, when you said you were up to no good, what did you mean?" she asked. "Something's up. Come on, tell your big sis everything."

She wasn't being pushy, but she was right. Matty bit his lip and paused to admire a fountain in the square he'd wandered into. There were lots of these in Alpina, with cobblestones and centuries-old architecture.

"I..." God, it was going to sound so stupid to say out loud, but he persevered. "I've sort of met someone."

"In Rosavia?"

Matty nodded, even though she couldn't see him. "Uh, yes," he said out loud when he realized. "It was a complete accident. And…oh, *Rey*. He's amazing. Kind and funny and generous and a *terrible* cook, but that just means he thinks I'm great at it." He bit his lip. "We've basically been inseparable for over a week."

"Whoa."

Reghan sighed, sounding like she was blowing out her cheeks. She always did that when she was thinking. That was why Matty had waited to talk with her despite the time difference, and not his new friends Shommie and Esosa. They were fantastic and encouraging, but nobody knew him like Reghan.

"Matty…that sounds kind of serious? I know you don't do casual, but…"

"He lives four thousand miles away in Alpina," Matty finished for her. He blew his own raspberry, meandering around the piazza as more of the businesses came to life around him. "It started out casual, it really did," he said, almost pleading for her to believe him. "I was determined to have a vacation fling, but the longer we're together, the more I'm sure it could be something bigger."

Because as amazing as the past several days had been with Cas – mostly incredible sex and snuggling in his apartment, accompanied by such easy conversation it was almost unnerving – Matty was getting scared. He'd *promised* himself this would just be casual, because he was leaving on Monday. And yet…

"Love isn't logical," Reghan said quietly. They'd always said that, especially in the bad times where they'd been truly broke and in desperate need of their parents. They couldn't help who they were attracted to, just as much as they couldn't stop their parents from switching off their love for their kids because of it. Love was completely illogical.

But that wasn't the point here.

Matty stopped dead in his tracks by a tourist souvenir store. "It – it's not *love*," he spluttered.

"Okay," said Reghan dismissively in that way she had that told him she didn't believe him in the slightest.

"No, that's…" he said, not even sure how to finish the sentence. "He's – I – it *can't* be love, because we just met, and he lives on the other side of the world, and that's insane, and you're a dummy."

"Oh, shit," said Reghan after her longest pause yet. "You really like this guy, don't you?"

"I…I don't know," said Matty sadly.

But he did. He was falling head-over-heels for Cas. And as much as he was trying to convince himself he was seriously thinking about moving *anywhere* in the world, the truth was that as of now he was only considering Rosavia. Because he was hoping that it might give him and Cas the opportunity to let this powerful thing between them blossom, like one of the country's famous roses.

But what if Cas didn't feel the same? What if he was expecting Matty to leave on Monday and that they'd never cross paths again? Was Matty jumping to the wrong conclusions?

He didn't think so. He'd only been back to his hotel room once since their perfect second date that didn't seem to want to end. Matty had grabbed his toiletries, a few pairs of underwear and a few items of clothing, then walked straight back out the door again. Essentially, it had been endless hours of Netflix and chill at Cas's place, and Matty couldn't remember the last time he'd been so unbelievably happy and stress free. Cas had halfheartedly suggested doing a few touristy things, but every time, they'd somehow ended up making love on the sofa again…or the dining room table…or in the shower…

Jesus. Matty was insatiable for Cas. He made him feel so completely whole in a way he hadn't known was possible. Cas worshipped him and took charge totally when they were being intimate, but somehow that made Matty feel like he was king of the universe.

His eyes burned.

"Rey," he whispered. "I think I'm going to get my heart broken."

"Oh, baby boy," Reghan said with such sincerity Matty's throat clamped. "Yeah, maybe? Maybe you'll never see this guy again and remember him forever. Or…" She cleared her throat. "*Or* maybe this is the start of the rest of your life, and you'll get married and adopt a dozen babies and puppies."

"Actually, he has a cat. He's mad about her." Cas had shown Matty about a hundred photos of Bella, who apparently lived back at home with his younger brother Wren. Cas had fondly told Matty how terrible she was with each one. "So it'll be kittens."

"Matty," Reghan said firmly. *"Don't* sabotage this for yourself.

You're a good man with a kind heart and never-ending altruism. You'd give anyone the coat off your back. Just…think of yourself for once, okay? You have my permission to go wild. And *maybe*," she added in that infuriating know-it-all voice she'd always used to correct Matty's homework, "remember how you've talked about leaving Queens and New York and wanting to see the world since – I don't know – *forever?*"

Matty pouted. "Okay, yeah," he mumbled eventually.

He wandered on absently past a clothes store and inside a small grocery store, half-thinking about buying terrible snacks for later after he and Cas inevitably had wild sex again. Their phenomenal bedroom activities were really not helping him think clearly right now.

"But I'm not going to uproot my life because of some *man* I just met. If I move, it'll be for me. Besides, I can't leave you guys!"

Reghan tutted. "Less Frozen and more Little Mermaid for you, my friend," she admonished. "Don't cockblock yourself! I'm not saying that you should be reckless. I'm just saying that sometimes crazy stuff like, I don't know, *love at first sight* really does happen. Embrace the crazy!"

Matty shook his head. Crazy was still way out of his comfort zone. He couldn't believe he was even considering moving. Vacation Matty was wilder, but he wasn't fully ready to accept all-out crazy just yet.

Unfortunately, that was the moment he paused and looked at the newspaper rack, glancing at the front pages with their headlines or, more specifically, the pictures that accompanied those headlines.

Because Matty couldn't read Rosavian. But he sure as hell recognized his own face in less than a heart-stopping second.

It looked like crazy was about to fall in his lap whether he wanted it to or not.

What the ever-loving FUCK! was what he thought. But he forced himself to take a couple of breaths to stop him screaming down the phone, then out loud, he gently interrupted Reghan telling him about how she and Lola had met, and how fate works in mysterious ways.

That was one way of putting it.

"Uh, Rey? I'm really sorry, but I have to go," he managed to grit out.

"Is everything okay?" she asked.

"Yep," he lied, "I just…have to go underground. I'll call you back, okay – bye!"

He couldn't hold it in any longer. He heard his sister's slightly confused goodbye as he closed the call.

Then the floodgates came crashing down.

"Fuck fuck FUCK!" he cried, fear gripping his heart. The logical part of his brain swept over the lone paper, trying to tell himself he just had a doppelgänger out there. But the thing was, it wasn't just photos of him.

They were him *with Cas.*

The store clerk asked something in Rosavian, but the words were all a blur to Matty. They sounded concerned, though.

"I – uh," Matty croaked as he reached for the paper, pulling it out so he could see everything. The foreign words swam in front of his eyes, dark gray letters on light gray pulp paper. But the grainy color photos were unmistakable.

One was of him and Cas at the Alpina rose gardens the other day. Matty had his hand on Cas's arm and was looking at him in concern, clearly an intimate act. And the other was when they'd dashed out from the apartment to grab more food and…oh, Jesus fucking Christ.

More condoms.

What he was looking at simply didn't connect with his brain. Why in the name of all that was holy would *anyone* be taking photos of him and Cas? Let alone be putting them on the front of any newspaper?

He didn't know if he wanted to scream or cry or faint. True, he'd been mildly suspicious that Cas always skirted around details of his job, but honestly? Matty had been with Jeremy for over two years and asked many times about his work, and all he could say to this day was that he'd worked in IT.

It hadn't seemed like a problem, but it obviously was. Who the fuck was Cas? A rock star? A jewel thief?

With a trembling hand, Matty unlocked his phone again and activated the translation app. He held the screen above the headline, waiting for the internet to do its best at explaining what the fuck was going on.

Prince Cassander having regal frolic with aspiring actor American!

Matty blinked. That had to be a translation fail. Aspiring actor? He just checked ticket stubs at a tiny theater when he wasn't bussing tables. And, wait…what? *Prince Cassander?*

Matty felt so faint that he stumbled and knocked into a spinning stand of postcards by the cash register. The old man behind the counter rushed out in concern, rambling in Rosavian as he steered Matty to sit on a round stool that was probably used for restocking the higher shelves. Matty looked guilty at the crumpled newspaper in his hand, and immediately fished out a few Euros from his pocket. The clerk didn't seem to want to take them by the way he threw up his hands, but Matty insisted.

And then he was back with his own panic, staring at the news article through his phone.

Prince Cassander. Cas was short for Cassander? And…he was a prince? That was just so ridiculous, Matty started giggling. There must be some mistake.

So he threw his data allowance to the wind, and started Googling to see if there really was a Prince Cassander of Rosavia.

Oh. Right. It was all okay! Cas was only *second* in line to the throne. Not the actual heir. It was highly unlikely he'd ever be king. No big deal.

No big deal.

"Thank you," Matty managed to whisper as he stumbled from the store, vaguely aware that he was aiming for Cas's apartment.

And then he stopped in front of the souvenir shop which he'd paused by earlier. He hadn't been looking properly at it then.

But now he was.

There were a lot of teddy bears, plates, thimbles, and spoons with the Rosavian flag on them, but also a lot of things with people's faces. Half a dozen handsome young men, to be specific.

One of whom was Cas.

Matty gasped, feeling like Alice falling into Wonderland. It was as if his whole world was being pulled from beneath his feet. Cas – *his* Cas – was on *mugs* and *magnets* and *dishtowels*. They'd made cheap cardboard masks of his face and wobbly-headed dolls. He was *everywhere*.

Matty covered his mouth, the tears prickling at the back of his eyes.

This whole time Matty had been developing feelings for a guy he thought was honest and true and possibly falling for him back. He'd honestly believed that Cas would never mess him around.

Had this been a game the whole time? Matty might have worried Cas just saw their relationship as a vacation fling, but had Matty even known Cas at all? Had he been laughing at Matty this whole time? Did he regularly pick up unsuspecting tourists for a wild week of sex, then never think about them again? *Jesus Christ.* Matty hadn't been impressive enough to keep any of his regular boyfriends. What could he possibly be to a *prince* other than a dalliance, a bit of fun?

Trembling, Matty unlocked his phone once again and Googled 'Prince Cassander new boyfriend.' Sure enough, several online outlets were running stories in English as well now. And there were the same photos of them, with 'Matty Doyle of Queens, New York' written in black and white.

What if his parents saw?

Had Matty been played for a fool, a royal joke, that would reach back to his parents and make them hate him even more? He'd long given up on the idea of a relationship with them, but the idea that they could be even more ashamed of him was almost too much to bear.

He'd been so desperate for affection that he'd allowed himself to be manipulated by someone who might have just been using him this whole time. And now the whole world was about to be in on his humiliation.

Cas wasn't what he said he was at all. Matty desperately resisted the urge to throw up as he stumbled out of the souvenir shop and back into the plaza, sucking down fresh air and squeezing his phone in one hand and clutching the paper in his other.

Had anything Cas said to him been true? Matty desperately wanted to believe he was still the same kind, attentive, dorky, gorgeous guy he'd known for over a week, but all his old insecurities were flooding back to him. In his mind, he saw Jeremy's embarrassment as Matty begged him to stay. His parents' disgust as they threw him and Reghan out of the family home.

Cas was a prince. Matty was a nobody. It had just been a vacation fling. And now the whole world knew it.

Matty was such a fool.

He looked down at the screwed-up newspaper sheets in his hand. According to the online translation, the article was claiming he was some sort of gold digger after the royal coffers. That didn't make sense at all, and Matty felt a tiny bit of relief that he had in fact insisted Cas stop spoiling him so much. He could at least hold his head high and say that wasn't true.

But everything else?

Matty tried to breathe properly as his vision swam. The foundations of everything between him and the man he'd been hopelessly falling for – the man he'd been considering moving to another *country* for – were crumbling under his feet. He'd been so desperate to jump into the fantasy of a hot, successful guy wanting a vacation romance with him, but now Matty had no clue what was real and what wasn't.

And then the fear crept in.

Did people...know who he was? They had his name and knew he was from Queens. Was he being watched right now? He spun around, his heart in his throat as he looked at the people going about their business in the plaza. Who had taken those photos? Was he being watched right now?

Was Finley?

Suddenly, it was like having a bucket of ice water thrown over him. Nothing else mattered. Someone had pried into his personal life, and that was devastating. But would people be willing to chase the story so far that they discovered why he was in the country in the first place?

He was confused and hurt by Cas. But he realized with utter clarity that he'd have to deal with that later as he ignored his whimpering bank balance and called an Uber. Above all else, he had to protect Finley.

He'd been right in what he'd said to Reghan. He was pretty

sure his heart had just been broken. But he'd do what he'd always done, and put his family and everyone else first.

Maybe later he could try and pick up the pieces. But if this had all been no more than a superficial fling to Cas, a joke that the press had then been let in on, Matty wasn't sure he'd ever be able to glue his heart back together again.

Chapter Twelve

CAS

It took a good minute or so for Cas to realize that the pounding on the door was not in fact a dream, but very much happening in reality. He'd been so dead asleep, it took another few moments for him to get his eyes open and blink up at the ceiling in the morning light.

Matty wasn't in his bed.

Cas's stomach lurched and he was immediately awake then, worrying if that was Matty banging on the door. But he'd left a note on his pillow. *'Gone for a walk! I'll bring back breakfast.'* He'd also drawn a little heart which made Cas's actual heart leap with joy.

Okay, so Matty should be okay and back soon. So who the hell was banging on his door at seven o'clock in the morning?

There was only one person who (should) know he was here, and if she was trying to kick the door down, that meant they had a serious problem.

"I'm coming!" he called out, quickly pulling on some sweat-pants and a T-shirt. He didn't want to face any trouble in his bathrobe. He then dashed to the door, already dreading what kind of hijinks his brothers were up to now. Some of the papers were catching wind of Leo and his librarian, Wren and his valet, and whatever was going on between Jules and Dante. It had been a pretty shambolic week leading up to the royal ball for his family. Maybe Ben had accidentally-on-purpose gotten himself photographed naked on a beach again?

But when he unbolted the locks and finally wrenched open the door, Valentina was standing on the other side, her fist raised, mid-pound.

She looked frazzled. Valentina was *never* frazzled.

For the second time in so many minutes, Cas's stomach dropped. "Oh, god," he moaned, stepping aside to let her inside. "Who's done what now?"

But she didn't move. She just stood there with her red hair sticking out at odd angles and her eyes wide and frantic behind her black rimmed glasses. He realized she had a rolled-up newspaper gripped tightly in the hand that hadn't been banging on the door.

"Why didn't you answer your phone?" she shrieked, making Cas flinch. He honestly couldn't remember the last time she'd shouted at him. His apprehension was quickly turning to dread. Whatever was going on was *bad*.

"I-I was asleep, and it's on silent. It's the crack of dawn. Roth – Valentina – *what's wrong?*"

She finally marched into the apartment, and Cas mutely

closed the door behind her. Then she spun around and shook the paper out in front of him. There were tears in her eyes. "I'm *so sorry*, Your Highness," she whispered in distress. "I don't know how this could have happened. This is all my fault. If you want my resignation, I'll understand."

Cas was too distracted by this completely alien display of emotion from his most trusted friend and confidant that he didn't even look at the front page initially. "Your what?" he spluttered. "Outrageous. No, never! Valentina, what would make you think...?"

He trailed off as his gaze dropped to look at the Daily Chronicle. A despicable rag that was less interested in the truth and more concerned with what sensational headlines they could make up to sell papers. Except today...they really did have the truth.

God damn them.

Prince Cassander in royal romp with wannabe American actor!

And there they were. Him and Matty. Holding hands in the gardens and on the street not far from this very apartment.

He'd been such a fool.

"Oh *fuck*," he croaked, taking the paper into his own hands and moving so he could sink into the sofa.

Of course the 'journalist' was Ida von Tarr. Her glee at catching Cas out just oozed from the page. Apparently, they hadn't been as clever as they'd thought when they'd practically walked into her last week. He felt sick as panic rose in him. This was a *disaster*.

"Jesus," he cried as he skimmed the article as quickly as he could. "How does she know so much about Matty? *I* don't know half this stuff!"

She knew where he was from, where he'd gone to school, all about his sister and her wife (whose names she'd shamelessly published as well). There was only a brief mention about Finley, which was odd. Cas would have thought von Tarr wouldn't hesitate to exploit a child, but he chose to be thankful for small mercies.

He covered his mouth as his chest tightened. "No one was ever supposed to know," he choked out, the shame and horror making him dizzy. "Matty, my family, the public…this is terrible. Everyone is going to…"

He couldn't even finish his sentence. He had no idea how anyone was going to react. Naturally, von Tarr was making Matty out to be some kind of common gold digger who had hoodwinked Cas to pay for his sister's medical bills. He had to admit, he'd wrestled with that very idea himself, but obviously Matty had never once mentioned anything like that. He was generous and sweet, and this bloodsucking leech had annihilated him. She clearly wanted people to hate him.

Tears formed in Cas's eyes, but he tried to blink them back. Crying wouldn't do anyone any good now. He had to stay strong and deal with the crushing guilt of letting his family down later. *Damn it!* Couldn't he have one private, precious thing to himself?

Valentina lowered herself to sit beside him, touching his knee in a rare display of affection. It was against protocol, but Cas didn't hesitate to grab her hand and squeeze it tightly, desperate for any reassurance he could get.

She used her free hand to smooth down her blouse and her

hair. "Right," she said, sounding a little more like her usual self. "If you're sure you don't want my head on a silver platter-"

"Absolutely not," Cas interrupted firmly, looking her in the eyes. "This is *my* fault. I'm an adult. I knew what I was doing. And now I need to fix it." He glanced sadly down at the article again. All the major news outlets would have the story now. It would be everywhere. "If only I knew how."

Valentina let go of him and patted his knee. All trace of her previous distress vanished as she sat up straight and placed her hands in her lap. "Right, as I was previously saying, first things first. Where is Matty?"

"He went for a walk," said Cas. "He should be back soon."

Valentina nodded, getting out her phone. "As you weren't with him, your security detail wouldn't have followed. But I'll alert them to keep their eyes open and scoop him up on his return." She threw Cas a sympathetic look. "He'll need to be debriefed now."

Cas nodded miserably. He was aware his security detail was never too far away. He'd been able to forget about them for a few days, but he felt the tiniest bit better that von Tarr had managed to outsmart them too.

"I know we need to tell Matty everything," Cas said dejectedly. "Can I at least be present?"

"Of course," Valentina assured him. "If I may say so, Your Highness, I think this would be much better for him to hear this directly from you."

Cas nodded in total agreement.

It was a small comfort. Cas dreaded seeing the look on Matty's face when he realized Cas had been hiding who he really was this whole time, and that his life had just been cracked open for the whole country to see. *This was never supposed to happen!* Cas thought bitterly. But it had, so there was no point crying over spilled milk. And he was *not* going to let Matty go through this ordeal alone.

So no matter how painful it was, Cas was going to be the one to confess his true identity to Matty and walk him through what would happen now.

Their perfect little bubble of bliss had well and truly been popped.

Cas bit his lip. He couldn't help but have the smallest hope, though, that Matty might be excited when he got over the shock. Cas knew their relationship had started out as a no-strings fling, but…well, Cas knew he was already far beyond that now. And if the cat was out of the bag, why couldn't he keep seeing Matty, somehow?

He cursed von Tarr. If he was going to come clean, this wasn't how he would have wanted it to happen, but he couldn't change that now. He just had to roll with it, and hope his family weren't too angry that he'd caused a front-page scandal two days before the biggest night for their country for a century.

Valentina got on the phone to various people while Cas kept himself busy by tidying the apartment up for the first time since Matty had practically moved in. If there were going to be security agents in here, he'd like the place looking a little more presentable and smelling less like sex.

His heart stuttered as he opened a window. Had he and

Matty made love for the last time? Would Matty want to go anywhere *near* Cas once he found out about his deception? Cas bit his lip and closed his eyes, refusing to let them get damp. He had to keep his shit together and face up to the consequences of his actions. Matty was his priority, that hadn't changed.

It was just that Matty might not trust him now, and Cas wasn't sure his heart could take that.

He sniffed and marched himself into the kitchen. He'd been pretty harsh on his brothers about taking responsibility for their actions, and now it was his turn. He was long overdue for his own fuckup. Knowing he had embarrassed the crown was almost too awful to bear, but he had no choice. So he would keep his head high and deal with the fallout at home later. Now all he cared about was Matty, and he was anxious for him to get back soon.

And really, he thought angrily as he scrubbed the dirty pots and pans and loaded the dishwasher, what had he actually done wrong? Fallen for a man he cared very deeply for? Cas sighed and rubbed his forehead with the back of his wet hand, flicking suds over the sink. He knew exactly what he'd done, and never should have let it go on for so long.

He'd hidden the full truth from Matty, who had deserved the chance to make his own decision about getting involved with a prince or not. Cas had been too busy trying to protect him, but Matty's face had ended up on the front page anyway. Their whole relationship had been based on a lie of omission, and Cas had to acknowledge the wrongs he'd done to the man he cared so deeply for. He'd kept telling himself that it was only for a week or two and nobody ever needed to find out, but that had included Matty himself being kept in the dark, and Cas was a dick for doing that to him.

But Cas sighed as he stopped his pot scrubbing for a second. He also had to be honest that he'd been trying to protect *himself*. He'd never been involved with anyone who didn't know his royal status, and it had been intoxicating to think Matty liked him for being *Cas*. Not Prince Cassander Fabian Ivor van Rosavia.

He dried his hands and came back around to the frustrating thought that he wouldn't have needed to do any of this skulking around if there weren't so many archaic rules about what he and his brothers could and couldn't do. Because it didn't matter what Matty's job was, no matter how von Tarr tried to spin it to make Matty seem more sensational. He didn't need to be an actor or a duke or whatever people might find interesting or appropriate. He just needed to be Matty: kind and sweet and funny and sexy. That was good enough for Cas, and it should *damn* well be good enough for everyone else.

Of course, Cas knew it wasn't like that in the real world. He had responsibilities, and people held him up to certain expectations. He couldn't go gallivanting off and do whatever he wanted. He was born to serve his country.

And that couldn't possibly include being with Matty long term. Could it? Cas chewed on his lip. The press might want to spin falling for a commoner into a scandal because it hadn't happened in the country's history before, but this was the twenty-first century. Why *couldn't* Cas choose a man who made him happy, regardless of his birth status?

He hung up the dishtowel and shook his head. He was getting

ahead of himself. They'd deal with the fallout *after* he'd told Matty everything. But it had been over an hour since Cas had been woken up, and Matty still wasn't back. Worry was starting to crawl into his guts.

"I'll try giving him a call," he told Valentina, who seemed to have done all the logistical work she could for now. By listening to her while he'd been cleaning, Cas gathered the palace's legal team were already on to von Tarr. But what could they do? She might have twisted the facts, but she wasn't exactly wrong about what Cas had done.

The call went to voicemail, which worried Cas. Unlike him, Matty kept his phone on at all times in case Finley or Reghan needed to contact him. Either he hadn't heard it ring, or...

Or he was ghosting Cas.

Could he have seen the paper for himself? The very thought that the news of Cas's deception would be broken to him like that made Cas's stomach curdle. It was unconscionable.

"Go take a shower, then you can call him again," Valentina instructed kindly but firmly. "We're going to need to do a press release at some point, so you might as well be ready."

Cas's stomach dropped at the notion, but of course she was right. So he did as he was told, hurrying through the bathroom, all the while hoping that Matty would call him back by the time he was done.

Nothing.

Cas forced himself to wait until he was dressed to call again, but it was the same result. It just rang several times until it got to voicemail. This time, Cas left one. As much as he wanted to do this all face-to-face, he was becoming seriously concerned.

"Hi, sweetheart," he said, a lump forming in his throat. Was Matty still his sweetheart? "Something's happened. Can you please call me back when you get this, and come back to the apartment as soon as you can? Thanks. I lo…I mean, thanks. See you soon."

He closed the call and stared down at the screen. What had he almost said? It had been without thinking, but his instinct was to close the call with an 'I love you,' which didn't make any sense at all. That was crazy. It was just the pressure of the situation making him want to wrap Matty up in cotton and protect him from everything.

An instinct that only grew as Matty's silence went on for another hour. The apartment was immaculate, as was Cas. He'd opted for the only expensive suit he'd brought with him, instead of the jeans and T-shirts he'd been lounging around in the past several days. The suit had been intended for the fancy date they'd never gone on. Now, though, it would do for facing the press.

But Cas wasn't going to talk to anyone before Matty, and he couldn't do that if he didn't return or pick up any of Cas's many calls. Something was wrong.

"He knows," he said heavily to Valentina, shaking his head. "Either that, or he was in an accident and got rushed to the hospital."

Valentina held up a long finger and gave him a stern look. "He's fine. But…just in case, I will call around the city hospitals while you go to his hotel. It's possible he's hiding from all this there."

Cas puffed out his cheeks and ran his hand through his hair, despite having carefully styled it. Fuck it. He didn't care what he looked like. He cared about Matty. "Okay, yes. Thank you. We'll get an extra security detail sent out?"

Valentina nodded. "I'm on it."

Cas was grateful nobody tried to stop him from driving his own car. He'd always insisted on being allowed to transport himself anywhere and maintain a little freedom and privacy, and appreciated it especially in that moment. His grief at losing the little bubble of make-believe he'd cultivated with Matty was raw, and the last thing he wanted was an audience.

It didn't take Cas long to reach Matty's hotel from his apartment. The look on the receptionist's face when he walked in would have been comical if Cas hadn't been feeling so torn up. She was a neatly-styled woman in her thirties with horn-rimmed glasses and hair in a sleek bun. She glanced up as Cas approached, offering him a polite smile before glancing back at her computer. Then her head snapped back and her jaw dropped as he reached the desk. Thankfully, there wasn't anyone else around at present to overhear them.

"Good morning," said Cas, mustering a smile.

"G-good morning, sir. Uh, I mean, Your Highness." The clerk blushed and visibly tried to compose herself. "How can I be of assistance?"

Ideally, Cas would have liked to have sneaked past her and just gone to knock on Matty's door. Cas knew the number from when they'd nipped back to get Matty some fresh clothes the other day. But now the receptionist had seen him, he needed to do this properly.

No more playing outside the rules.

"I was wondering if you could try calling the gentleman in room three fifteen for me?" he asked. "I'm concerned for his wellbeing."

The receptionist's perfectly drawn eyebrows crawled up to her hairline. "Of course, Your Highness. Do, um, do we need to contact the authorities if you're worried?"

Cas gave her a tight smile. "Not yet, thank you. I'm probably overreacting."

She gave a small, nervous laugh, probably unsure if she was allowed to laugh at a prince or not. "Of course. One moment, Your Highness."

Cas managed to keep his smile on his face, but inside his guts were writhing. He wasn't surprised when there was still no answer after a minute, but Cas had been clinging to the hope that he'd finally find his lover.

The receptionist shook her head and hung up. "I'm sorry, Your Highness. He doesn't appear to be there."

Or if he was, he was avoiding that phone as well. Cas nodded once, keeping his disappointment off his face. "I don't suppose you've seen him?" he asked. It was a small hotel, and there was a chance that the staff would be familiar with their current guests. "He's American, a little shorter and slimmer than me. Dark hair, pale skin, square jaw." *Blue eyes like the ocean and a smile like the break of day.*

The receptionist bit her lip and thought a moment before shaking her head. "I know the gentleman you mean. I checked him in. But I'm afraid I haven't seen him in the past few days."

Dread welled up inside Cas, but he kept his composure. He smiled and nodded politely at her. "Thank you very much for your assistance."

"I hope you find him," she blurted in a rush, her cheeks reddening. "Good luck."

Cas managed to keep his smile going until he turned away from her. Then his crushing disappointment got the better of him. He grimaced as he pushed through the doors back out onto the street.

Where the hell should he go now? A quick call to Valentina assured him that Matty hadn't come back to the apartment. So where else? Cas got back into his car and bit his thumbnail, a bad habit he'd trained himself out of as a teenager. But now he couldn't give a crap.

What if he never saw Matty again?

Cas screwed up his eyes and gritted his teeth. He knew what they'd had could never have lasted, but god damn it, he'd wanted it to end on their own terms. To be torn apart like this was unbearable. He sniffed and finally gave in, rubbing his wet eyes when he couldn't hold back his frustration any longer.

He wished this was another life, and he and Matty could just be together without all this bullshit.

Not knowing what else to do, Cas threw his car into gear and drove to a parking garage he trusted to be secure, then walked back toward the rose gardens. Without anywhere else to look for Matty, it was the only thing he could think of to make himself feel better. Perhaps if he was surrounded by the beauty he'd shared with Matty, he wouldn't be miserable.

Or maybe he'd feel worse. Who knew? At this point, it was something for him to do. He didn't want to sit still and wallow, so he paid the entry fee, ignoring the ticket-seller's startled cry of recognition, and marched onto the grounds.

It was another gloriously sunny day, so the gardens were busy again. In his suit, Cas was far more recognizable as his royal persona, but on the whole people kept their distance. Thank goodness for the Rosavian sense of propriety. Cas kept his head down, walking between the roses and gently touching their petals, thinking of all the family members they repre-sented. It was one of the essential parts of their education in the family's and the country's history, and Cas had a particu-larly good memory for which flower belonged to whom.

So many generations of royals that he had let down with his giddiness at getting some freedom in his life. Princes weren't allowed to have casual flings. They were supposed to match with suitable partners and carefully plan every step of their relationship.

He sighed and shook his head, moving down the path. He was aware that his security detail had to be near, but as usual, he didn't see any of them. He wished that he could be truly alone, but he'd been allowed to indulge in that fantasy for days now, with disastrous consequences. There was no sense in complaining when they were only hovering around for his safety.

He was coming to the realization that he might have to start on damage control before he got the chance to talk to Matty. Because he might never hear from Matty again, and the longer von Tarr's article was out there without a response, the worse it would be for the crown. As much as Cas loathed the idea, he had to face facts. His tryst with Matty was only ever going to be temporary. Crown and country were forever.

Cas knew he should turn back, but he had an inexplicable urge to go look at his own breed of rose, the one Matty had loved. In Cas's head, if he saw those blue flowers and remembered the moment they had shared, he could maybe bring himself to say goodbye to Matty.

There was only one problem with this plan.

Matty was standing in front of Cas's roses.

"Oh, god," Cas choked out in shock. He was there, *he was really there.*

Matty's head snapped up. His skin was blotchy and his eyes red.

He knew.

"I-I've been calling," Cas stammered, taking a step closer. There were people milling around them, but Cas ignored them all. The only person he saw was Matty, whose puffy blue eyes were wide and fixed on Cas. "I was so worried. I…I take it you saw the news?"

Matty swallowed and looked back down at the blue roses, touching the petals of the one closest to him. "This one's yours, isn't it? I saw it when I Googled your name." His lips twitched in a sad smile. "It's still my favorite."

Cas bit his lip, not sure what that meant or where that left them. He took another step towards his lover, wishing like hell he could reach out and hold his hand. But he wasn't sure if that would be welcome right now.

"I'm so sorry," Cas said through the lump in his throat. "I'm so *incredibly* sorry I couldn't be honest with you. I never wanted you to get hurt."

Matty shook his head, sending a knife through Cas's heart. "I'm not sure if I know you at all. Was anything we had real? Am…was I even *allowed* to be with you, Cas?" He sniffed and rubbed his eyes. "Do I have to call you 'Your Highness' now?"

"Please don't," Cas said quickly. "With you, I got to be Cas. I got to be myself. It was bliss."

Matty nodded. He was still looking determinedly at the roses and not Cas. "I'm glad," he said quietly.

"And *yes*, god damn it," Cas said desperately, taking the final step. Any closer, and he'd have Matty in his arms. As much as Cas yearned for that, he didn't feel he'd earned that right again just yet. "It was all real, I promise. You stole my heart. I hoped we could have the time you were in Rosavia to create something amazing." He swallowed and tried not to snarl at the unfairness of the situation. "Even if I couldn't tell you the whole truth. But I should have. You deserved that."

Matty choked back a sob. "I'm just *scared*," he whispered. He balled up his fists and turned toward Cas, his beautiful eyes full of desperation that cracked fissures in Cas's aching heart. "I could only translate so much, but that article said I was a gold digger, and it mentioned my sister and her illness!"

"I know, I know," Cas said desperately. Without meaning to he raised his hands, going to clasp Matty's shoulders and try and offer him some comfort. But he yanked them away again just in time in case Matty wouldn't want Cas touching him now. "I'm so sorry. That's what von Tarr does. She's hateful."

Matty twitched like he wanted to hug Cas, but then he held himself back, crushing Cas's heart. Cas was vaguely aware of people looking at them, but thankfully none of the public were approaching them. He just hoped no one was filming them.

"It feels like you were playing a game with me," Matty rasped, full of hurt. Cas shook his head, but Matty held up his hand and continued speaking. "Were you just playing the part of someone who cared? Do you pick up tourists all the time? Were you going to let me leave on Monday and never think of me again?"

"It was *never* a game," Cas spluttered, shocked that Matty could think that. But then he remembered how Matty's ex had enjoyed laughing when Matty got things wrong, and how his parents had abandoned him for coming out, and Cas felt a whole new level of pain that he'd abused Matty's trust like he had. "I was trying to protect us both," he said. "I've barely dated anyone, and certainly never a tourist before, I promise. I just wanted to have something with someone where they didn't treat me differently for my birth, and that meant keeping a big truth from you, but-"

His voice broke, and he took a second to clear his throat. He looked Matty in the eyes, wanting – *needing* – him to hear him in that moment.

"But my feelings for you were nothing but honest, Matty. You got the real me, just minus one part – the part I never chose for myself. You're incredibly special to me, and the week we've spent together has been the most real time of my life. Please, believe me."

Matty swallowed, visibly trembling. He nodded his head, the

motion sending twin tears cascading down his cheeks, but Cas felt a thrill of hope that maybe all wasn't lost. "Cas," he bit out. "I-"

"There they are!"

Cas snapped his head up at the raised voice, immediately spying the half a dozen people with cameras suddenly rushing toward him and Matty.

Ida von Tarr was leading the charge, naturally.

"Prince Cassander!" she cried, glee in her eyes as she thrust her voice recorder in Cas's face.

Within seconds, he and Matty were surrounded. Bystanders were now turning around and openly gaping at them. Cas didn't think, he just grabbed Matty and hugged him to his side in a vain attempt to protect him. However, it was also just enough time for Cas's security detail to descend in a furious wave of indignation. That didn't stop the press from hurling questions at them, though, as they fought the body-guards to get as close as possible.

"Prince Cassander, how long has this illicit affair been going on?"

"Mr. Doyle! How did you meet the prince?"

"Prince Cassander! What does the royal family think of you dating a commoner?"

"How can this possibly be allowed?"

"People are calling it a disgrace to the nation! Do you have any comment?"

They were all shouting at once in English, so Matty would

have understood it all. He looked terrified, quivering against Cas's side.

Fuck this shit.

"No comment!" Cas shouted firmly, pushing his way through the throng, cameras flashing and people still yelling questions. They knew well enough not to touch a member of the royal family, but they moved like a bubble around them, hindering their escape.

However, there was nothing to stop Cas's security team from manhandling the press, which they did effectively and without remorse.

"Step *back* from His Royal Highness!" they commanded, pushing on chests and covering camera lenses with open palms. They created an opening for Cas and Matty to escape through.

So Cas didn't hesitate. He grabbed Matty's hand, and then *ran*.

Chapter Thirteen

MATTY

Matty was so tired and confused.

He'd wasted no time in checking that Finley was okay by alerting Elm Willows in person that there was a situation. That had been an excruciatingly embarrassing conversation to have, but it needed to be done.

He'd spoken to the school's liaison to the archery program, who had made a goldfish face when she'd realized Matty was the one on the front page of the national paper that morning. She'd informed him that they were used to tight security measures, having been responsible for all five princes during their education. Then she'd pointedly said how much they'd loved Prince Cassander, leaving Matty feeling like he'd just been warned not to break Cas's heart by a concerned parent.

He'd really love to not do that, but he was feeling like reality was spiraling out of control around him. So when he'd returned to the city center, he'd gone back to the rose gardens, hoping maybe if he stared at Cas's flower long enough, he might work out what to do and whether he had the strength to return Cas's calls. It seemed a cruel twist of fate that the rose Matty had loved most had turned out to be Cas's namesake.

Matty was a nobody from Queens. Cas was a prince who'd had an exotic rose bred for him at birth. His face was on mugs and dishcloths. He was insanely rich, and was no doubt destined to marry another prince or a duke or some son of a noble family.

Not anyone so completely ordinary and unaccomplished as Matty.

Why, *why* had he gone to look at the roses? Why had Cas shown up at that precise moment? Was the universe back to being a douchebag, rubbing Matty's nose in his humiliation?

He'd really believed Cas had feelings for him. That they'd made a connection. Matty had even been daring to allow the smallest idea into his heart that they could have attempted some kind of future together.

But now he wasn't sure what to believe or who to trust. It had been so easy for Matty's exes and his own parents to leave him. Why wouldn't Cas just do the same? Matty should have tried to protect himself and stayed away. Yet somehow Cas had *tracked him down*. He could have just abandoned Matty once the scandal had broken, but he'd appeared like magic in the middle of the rose gardens, and Matty couldn't deny there had been a huge part of him that had been over-whelmed with relief.

And now here they were, once again in Cas's car, speeding out of the city.

That press mob had been no joke. Logically, Matty knew it had only been a handful of people, but it had felt like he'd been drowning in those few moments. So when Cas had taken Matty's hand and started to run, Matty had just followed without questioning. And then it was as if Matty had blinked, and they were driving away from Alpina.

Now that he was coming back to his senses, he was starting to feel anxious, which he'd *never* felt with Cas before. Not since the start of their second date. Sadness washed over him. He chewed his lip and was torn between thinking he could trust Cas to take care of him just like he'd done all week, and whether he even knew who Cas was at all.

"Where are we going?" he eventually asked. He glanced at Cas, but then looked away again before their eyes could meet, his gaze on his hands that were twisting in his lap.

"Away from the press," Cas said. He slowed his BMW on the deserted road, pulling off on the side. They were surrounded by trees with the mountains looming in the distance. "But I can turn around and take you to your hotel if you like. I just don't know if they'll find you there." He paused, sounding bitter when he spoke again. "If you're not with me, you won't have any security protecting you."

Matty chewed his lips and warred between confusion and fear. Of course Cas had a security team. They'd probably been around this whole week. Matty hoped they hadn't seen anything embarrassing.

Finley should be safe from the press at Elm Willows. But Matty? There would be nothing to stop the press from banging down his hotel door if they discovered where he was staying. He had no idea how easy that kind of information would be to uncover.

"How did they even track us down in the park?" he asked, his voice wavering. "How did they know so much about me in that article? It's like they hacked me or something." He so desperately wanted Cas to have the answers and make this all okay again. He was only just stopping himself from crawling into his lover's lap. But first, he needed more information.

"Matty," Cas said gravely after a few seconds. "Can you think of anyone strange approaching you over the past couple of weeks? Perhaps that woman who was just asking us questions now? With the ponytail and long red nails?"

Red nails? That jolted an immediate memory in Matty's brain. "Oh fuck," he rasped, jerking his head up to look at Cas. Now that he mentioned it, she *did* seem kind of familiar. "A woman picked my phone up off the floor when I was at a café. Before our second date. She said I dropped it."

"Von Tarr," Cas snarled. Matty thought that might have been the name Cas had mentioned earlier as the journalist who'd written the damning article about them. Cas bit his lip and held out his hand. "May I please see your phone?"

Matty pulled it out of his pocket, handing it over. Their fingers so nearly touched, and Matty felt a thrill that maybe he *hadn't* touched Cas for the last time.

Within seconds, Cas pulled the back off it, revealing its SIM card. And something else. "What?" Matty asked at Cas's grim expression.

"I think your phone's been cloned," Cas said. He pulled the

minuscule disk from where it had been resting inside Matty's phone. "I also think this is a tracking device."

A wave of nausea rolled over Matty. He opened the car door and hurriedly stepped outside and leaned against a tree, taking deep breaths. He wasn't surprised that Cas also got out, but Matty was relieved that he kept his distance. He was too busy panicking to work out if throwing himself into Cas's arms would be a relief or a disaster right about now.

"What's *happening?*" Matty asked. "How is this my life? I thought I was being wild and having a vacation romance, like a normal person. But there's absolutely *nothing* normal about this situation!" He pressed the heels of his hands into his eyes and choked back a sob.

He'd never wanted to be famous, like the actors in the plays he worked front of house for. The last thing he'd ever desired was to be in the spotlight. His life was such a pitiful disappointment, but that hadn't seemed to matter between him and Cas before. But now his personal business was out in the open for all of Rosavia – all the world – to see, thanks to von Tarr. They'd all be asking why a prince would ever be interested in broke Matty Doyle from Queens, who had to work two jobs just to pay rent on the small room he lived in. Someone whose parents didn't even love him enough to stick around.

But the truth was, Matty had truly been starting to believe that no one else's opinion mattered. Reghan, Lola, and Finley all loved him, and that had felt like enough.

Especially if it was possible that Cas might be starting to love him, as well.

"I feel like I've been cracked open for the whole world to see my flaws," he said, his voice cracking as more tears leaked free.

"I can't tell you how sorry I am, Matty," said Cas with such a heaviness Matty had to look. He dropped his hands, spots dancing in front of his eyes. He sniffed and rubbed his face, trying to get a hold of himself as a couple of sobs broke loose from his chest. "It was selfish of me to put you in this position," Cas said, a rueful smile tugging briefly at his lips. "But you're so amazing, I just wanted a normal relationship for the first time in my life. I was afraid you'd see me differently once you knew everything." He shook his head. "But that wasn't fair. I'm so sorry. I don't know how to fix this."

Neither did Matty.

"That woman just splashed my life all over the news," he spluttered, fury and incredulity finally overshadowing his fear and heartbreak. "Like it was entertainment!"

Cas nodded with a sad sign and rueful smile. "Yeah. That's kind of her thing. No one can stop her – believe me. You just…get used to it." He shook his head. "Not that you should have to. I meant me. My family."

Matty blinked, shame mingling sharply in with the anger. For the first time since his awful shock this morning, he began to truly appreciate the situation from Cas's point of view. He'd been born into the public eye. He hadn't chosen to be a prince, and yet he had leeches like von Tarr determined to delve into the depths of his public life.

What Cas *had* chosen was to escape from that invasive life for a few precious days.

With Matty.

He shook his head and hugged himself. "I don't know what to think," he whispered. "I want this to *stop.* I want to turn back the clock."

He wiped his eyes, willing himself to stop crying. He could just see Cas in his peripheral vision, watching him anxiously.

"My plan was to take you back to the cabin," Cas said gently, like he was scared any one of his words might spook Matty and make him flee. There was a strange comfort in that for Matty. Like Cas really cared about keeping Matty around. "It's not an official royal residence, so no one should know about it. But it is mine, and it's protected. My security detail can monitor us from nearby, and there's a panic button should we need it. You'll be safer with me, but..." He sounded so pained, Matty's heart threatened to crack. "But if you'd rather never see me again, I'll make arrangements to protect you to the best of my ability."

"No-" Matty spluttered before he could stop himself.

That was *all* he wanted. For it to just be him and Cas again, with Cas making everything okay. For nothing to have changed. Maybe he was a fool not to be running a mile from the man who had just betrayed his trust and made him vulnerable to the vultures of the press. But...Matty wasn't ready to let go of the perfect fantasy bubble he'd had with Cas just yet.

He cleared his throat. "For how long? Would we have to stay at the cabin, I mean?"

Cas's face lit up with what looked like hope. "Just until the palace PR team can draft a statement for me, and we can work out the best plan to move forward with. Once you go back to America, I'm sure the attention will die down. They'll have a new royal scandal by next week, knowing my brothers." Cas laughed ruefully, but his expression toward Matty was deeply earnest. "So maybe a day or two, if that's okay?"

For a second, Matty thought it *could* go back to how it had been the past week, with just the two of them hiding away. Except this time, they'd be in the picturesque cabin instead of Cas's apartment. But...it couldn't be that easy, could it?

"Okay," he whispered with a tiny smile. Because, realistically, how could things get any worse right now? What did he have to lose by spending some more time with Cas before he got on a plane on Monday? "Are you sure we'll be safe there?"

"Oh, great!" Cas cried breathlessly. "Yes, yes, totally safe. I – thank you, Matty. Thank you for staying a little longer. It'll be okay, I promise."

He seemed unsure what to do with his hands as he flapped them and fidgeted on the spot. And just like that, it was as if Matty was seeing him for the first time that day in the ridiculously hot suit he was wearing. He looked like a supermodel, and Matty's smile got a little brighter even as hot tears pooled in his eyes.

Matty really, *really* liked this stunning, slightly dorky, incredibly caring man. Yes, things had gotten unbelievably strange and complicated between them...but was there a chance that they were still just Cas and Matty? Was Cas still just the gorgeous guy who had rescued Matty from his troubles and shown him endless kindness and devotion? The same guy who couldn't cook worth a damn, but attempted blueberry pancakes anyway and acted like everything Matty made was gourmet?

"Maybe we can talk some more?" Matty suggested shyly, not

sure if he was making a huge mistake. But apparently Vacation Matty was back at the helm, and he was throwing caution to the wind again.

"Yes, absolutely," said Cas with a sniff and a laugh. "Uh, let me just…"

Matty hadn't realized that Cas was still holding the tiny tracking bug until he dropped it on the pavement of the road and ground the heel of his shoe over it. He pressed the back of the phone on again, and held it out. It felt more like an olive branch than it did a cell phone.

"I wouldn't use this yet," said Cas. "Not until we can have someone take a look at it, or get you a brand new one. Von Tarr could still be listening in. But she won't be able to track you anymore."

"Okay," said Matty cautiously. "And those people that saved us from the mob – your security team – they'll be close by?" His heart was beating so fast, and his head was spinning with fragile and tentative hope, so he wasn't careful as he took his phone from Cas's hand. Their fingers brushed, and it was like a lightning strike across all of Matty's skin.

Apparently Matty's body had no hesitations if it still wanted Cas or not.

Cas gasped. Matty was too busy being shocked at his own reaction – specifically *down below* – to guess what he might be thinking. But he cleared his throat and brushed down his suit.

"They will," Cas assured him. "But you won't know they're there, I promise."

God, Matty wanted to believe any promises that Cas made him so badly. "Okay, then. And, um, Finley? The school has gates and good security, but that reporter wouldn't go after her, would she?"

Cas grimaced. "Elm Willows has excellent security, yes. But... I would just remind Finley not to speak to strangers the next time you talk to her. You can use my phone, if you like?"

He offered it out for Matty to use right there and then, which Matty agreed was a good idea. Nothing was more important than his niece's safety. The call went to voicemail, so Matty left a short but upbeat message for her saying that he was okay, but if anyone approached her she didn't know, she should go straight to her teachers. He tried not to worry her, but she was a smart kid and would no doubt have questions, so Matty said she could call back on this number.

Then he also left Reghan a voicemail, as she'd been increasingly suspicious since Matty had closed their call abruptly. No doubt she was sleeping again, as it was still early morning in New York and she was bound to be exhausted from her treatment and the fright Matty had given her. But he wasn't sure what to say. He didn't want to blurt it all out until he knew where he and Cas stood.

"Sorry for cutting the call short earlier," he said into the phone, away from Cas and out of his earshot. "I'll explain more later – it's complicated. But..." He took a deep breath. "I'm working very hard on not getting my heart broken."

He hoped that was the truth.

"What do we do now?" Matty asked after he'd walked back to the car, handing back the cell.

Cas offered him a small smile. "Why don't you sit in the car?" he suggested gently. "I need to call my valet. She'll make sure someone delivers supplies for us. Is there any food you'd like in particular?"

Matty shook his head. The thought of eating right now made his stomach churn. Cas took a breath and nodded in understanding as Matty turned and went back to his side of the car.

He could hear the murmur of Cas's voice as he waited in the car, but none of the specific words. Matty's feelings toward Cas were still complicated, but they were pretty simple about von Tarr. What a despicable person, to use him like that for a scandal just to sell papers.

How far would this news story go?

How much would the press dig into his and his family's lives? They seemed convinced that he was a gold digger seducing Cas for his fortune. They couldn't have been more wrong, but that didn't seem to matter to them. Would Matty lose his jobs over this? How would he get new employment when any internet search would now throw up this scandal? How long was he going to have a black mark against his name? Months? Years?

Forever?

Matty bit his thumbnail and tried not to let his panic spiral. Cas got back in the car, and even just the waft of his familiar scent made Matty's heart clench and his throat clamp.

There was no denying he still felt very deeply for Cas, despite everything.

They were both silent for the rest of the drive back up to the impossibly beautiful log cabin where they'd almost shared their first kiss. That felt like a lifetime ago now. Matty looked around with apprehension at the stunning pond with its waterfall and amazing view of Alpina. What was going to happen now?

When he exited the car in front of the cabin, he turned back toward the woods in the other direction and was surprised to see ominous gray clouds in the distance. Perhaps a summer storm was on its way. That seemed more appropriate to his mood than the glorious sunshine.

He followed Cas as he walked up to the front door and let them inside. It smelled a little musty, but nothing a few minutes with the windows open wouldn't fix. As Matty had suspected before, it was just an open plan, one-room space. There was a sofa and a bed and a few kitchen appliances along one wall, and not much else. With a jolt, he worried he didn't have his phone charger, but he couldn't use it anyway, so it didn't really matter if it ran out.

It seemed like it was just him and Cas in the whole world, which was how it had kind of been in the apartment. Matty was almost scared of recapturing that feeling, unsure if he could trust it again.

He distracted himself by looking around. There was a quaintness to the cabin. A knitted blanket was draped over the bed, and roses were carved into the wall beams. In front of the sofa was a stone fireplace with an ancient-looking clock ticking quietly on the mantelpiece. Rugs stretched across the floor, a stuffed bookcase stood against the wall opposite the kitchen area, and there were well-used pillar candles every-where too. When Matty breathed in deeply, the whole place smelled like warm wood.

He wished he wasn't here under such confusing circumstances. Otherwise, it might be extremely romantic.

As it was, he and Cas looked awkwardly at each other. Matty wasn't sure what to do now they were here, and it seemed like Cas felt the same. Where before they'd had such easy conversation and incredible chemistry between them, now it just felt like they were both holding their breath.

"Um, is it okay if I go for a walk?" Matty blurted out. He had so many turbulent thoughts, some alone time would be really appreciated. "Is that allowed?"

Cas looked appalled. "Of *course* that's allowed, sweethe-" He grimaced, cutting off the endearment midway. They were back to awkwardly holding their breath. "Of course, Matty. You're not a prisoner here. Just, maybe stay close to the cabin. I'll be here when you get back."

There was a loaded pause between them, the weight of what that might mean. Cas would be here when Matty returned... and then what? They knew each other so intimately now. Their bodies might need one thing, but their hearts and minds another. Matty didn't know what the hell he wanted.

Best to go clear his head and put some space between them, before he did something he'd regret. Like run across the small cabin, leap into Cas's arms, and kiss him like the world was ending.

Because it wasn't. He'd get through this. Yes, it was horrifying to think his privacy was being invaded and the man he'd been developing feelings for hadn't been who he thought he was. But all that really mattered was Matty's sister's health and his niece's safety. Right? His heart would mend.

That was what he kept telling himself as he stepped outside, thunder rumbling ominously overhead as he walked toward the forest. If he kept insisting to himself that he'd survive this heartbreak, then perhaps his heart might finally start listening.

Because as far as it was concerned, losing Cas really *was* the end of the world.

Chapter Fourteen

CAS

Cas awoke with a start to the sound of pouring rain. He blinked for a second, completely confused as to where he was. Then his memories came flooding back and dread filled his heart.

Matty.

Cas had obviously fallen asleep on the sofa. He sat up, cracking his neck and rolling his shoulders. The cabin was dark, and outside, a thunderstorm was raging. Checking the clock on the mantel, Cas saw it was late afternoon. The last thing he remembered was meeting Valentina outside in the driveway with the bags of supplies she'd procured for them. Then he'd sat on the couch, anxiously waiting for Matty's return and going over and over what he was going to say once he eventually came back.

"Matty?" he called out as he stood up, but he already knew the answer to his question.

Matty wasn't there.

Fear lanced through him as he lurched for the front door. He'd fallen asleep in his fancy suit with his shoes still on, so he didn't hesitate as he wrenched open the door and stepped out onto the covered porch. "Matty!" he bellowed over the torrential rain. It might have been a summer storm, but there was a nasty chill in the wind that blew water against Cas's face. Was Matty out in this?

Cas's car was still standing in the drive, so at least Matty hadn't taken it and driven off somewhere. But where was he?

Cas gritted his teeth, trepidation flooding him. He'd spent all morning frantically searching for Matty. He wasn't sure he could go through that again.

He should try calling him before jumping to conclusions, so that was what he did. But just like that morning, the call rang out. Cas realized with a thrill of hope, though, that he had a very important advantage now.

He called Valentina.

"Hey," he said without preamble once she picked up. "Does the security detail have eyes on Matty?"

Valentina hummed in displeasure. "Yes, they have eyes on him. We were getting concerned, and I was debating contacting you soon. Did he wander off to go find himself for a bit?"

"I don't know," said Cas truthfully.

Valentina sighed. "Do you want his coordinates, or would you like the team to pick him up?"

"No," Cas said immediately. "I'll go get him. Just tell me where he is."

Cas had been using this little cabin as his hideaway for even longer than his apartment in the city. He knew the woods like the back of his hand, and had never lost the orienteering skills he'd learned as a child. When Valentina told him where they'd last seen Matty, Cas knew exactly the spot she meant.

He thanked her, then hung up. He didn't bother getting changed into the more appropriate clothing that she'd sent over. That would waste precious minutes. Instead he just grabbed an umbrella from the stand and closed the front door. The cabin only had a basic lock, but Cas used it anyway, just in case. Then he plowed into the rain.

Knowing it would take about twenty minutes to reach Matty, Cas tried calling him again a couple of times, but to no avail. Cas prayed Matty hadn't moved from where the team reckoned he was. Was he hurt? Was he stranded in the middle of the forest with a twisted ankle or something?

He sped up, his dress shoes slipping on the muddy ground. Rain streamed off his umbrella in rivulets, the wind trying to tug it from his hands, and thunder rumbled overhead. Once or twice lightning forked across the sky, but thankfully, the storm looked to be moving away as evening drew in.

After feeling like he'd been walking forever, Cas finally came across the clearing where, thank fucking god, Matty was huddled on a tree stump, his arms wrapped around himself as he shivered. He was soaked through, but he was there, and for the second time that day, that was enough for Cas.

"Matty?" he called out as he walked down a small hill, careful not to slip. It would really suck if he got all the way out here only to twist his own damn ankle.

Matty's head snapped up, and in a blur he launched himself off the tree stump and flung himself at Cas, hugging him desperately and sobbing against his neck. "Thank fuck!" he cried as Cas squeezed him tightly, his heart aching at Matty's obvious distress. "I'm such an idiot! I got lost, and you said not to use my phone, so I couldn't get maps up or answer your calls. I'm sorry, Cas, I'm so sorry!"

Before Cas knew what was happening, they looked at each other, and then their lips crashed together in a passionate embrace. Matty whimpered into Cas's mouth as their tongues met and they gripped each other's backs for dear life. Cas kept the umbrella over them as he hugged Matty's trembling body to him.

"It's okay," he said as they broke apart. Cas rested his temple against Matty's and rubbed his back as the rain pounded down around them. The wind had done a good job spraying water onto Cas despite the umbrella, but now Matty's clothes were soaking Cas's fast. "It's okay, sweetheart."

"No, it's not!" Matty cried, banging his fist half-heartedly against Cas's chest. "It's all fucked up and I want to be mad at you for putting me in this situation, but I don't think I can! Why didn't you trust me, Cas? I wanted this to be real so badly. You didn't give me a choice! I've been so scared, going over and over in my mind what's going to happen to me and my family – they pried into my *whole life*. Why didn't you tell me you were a damn *prince?*"

Cas closed his eyes and just held Matty as he cried against

Cas's neck, his fist balled around Cas's damp shirt material. There was nothing he could say to make this better or change what he'd done, but he tried anyway.

"I'm *so* sorry," he said, mustering all the sincerity he possessed. "This got completely out of hand. You have every right to be angry with me. I just wanted a bit of normalcy instead of the puppet show I've grown up in. But then I met you and you weren't normal – you were *extraordinary*. I never should have let it go this far, though. It was selfish and completely unfair, and the very, *very* last thing I ever wanted to do was hurt you. But, Matty…"

I love you. That was what he wanted to say. He knew it to be true. He'd never felt this way about anyone, not even close. It was like a physical ache in his chest, a feeling of completion like the slotting of two jigsaw pieces together. It wasn't an excuse for his behavior, but it was a fact.

He loved Matty Doyle. An American who would be leaving the country in a matter of days, who had no social standing, whom no one would approve of him being with. And even so, how could Cas ask Matty to take on the kind of media scrutiny he'd experienced today, just to be with Cas? It was unreasonable.

Matty leaned back, blinking at Cas with raindrops glistening on his dark eyelashes. He was so beautiful it hurt.

"What?" Matty whispered, hope dancing in his eyes. "What were you going to say?"

Cas shook his head. He couldn't give Matty any hope, because it would be shaky at best. As much as Cas wanted it, there was no guarantee they would be able to be together.

That would be cruel to Matty, and Cas had done enough damage. "Come on," he said, moving to take Matty's hand. "Let's get you warm and dry, okay?"

Matty allowed Cas to take it, and his skin was indeed like ice. Matty bit his lip, his blue eyes searching Cas's face. Then he surged up on his tiptoes, pressing another firm kiss to Cas's lips. Before Cas could wrap him up and kiss him some more, Matty pulled back. "You've said 'sorry' a hundred times today. But *I'm* sorry, too, okay? I handled this badly."

Cas spluttered. "What, sweetheart? No, I-"

"Wanted some real life," Matty interrupted, shaking his head. "I understand that, I do. And I'm so happy you found that with me. Yeah, I hate that von Tarr did this to us, and I wish you'd been able to tell me the truth. But I shouldn't have run off on you. Twice." He smiled sheepishly.

Cas sighed and hugged his lover tightly. "There are things we maybe both could have done differently, but life doesn't come with a script. I'm just glad we're here, now. Let's head back to the cabin. Maybe a hot shower first? You must be frozen."

Matty hummed and leaned into Cas's side as they began to walk. "A little bit," Matty admitted. "I'm so glad you came looking for me."

Cas wanted to promise that he'd always be there to look after Matty, but he knew he couldn't guarantee that, no matter how much he wanted to. So instead he lifted their joined hands and kissed Matty's knuckles.

They spent the rest of the walk back in comfortable quiet. But unlike in the car earlier, it had real warmth to it, despite the awful weather. Cas rubbed the back of Matty's hand with his thumb, and every now and again, Matty would glance over at Cas and then squeeze his hand as he gave him a small smile.

By the time they got back to the cabin, Cas was cold and wet, so Matty must have been really suffering.

He looked over at Cas and frowned as they approached the driveway. "I didn't see a bathroom before?"

Cas shook his head. "The original property had a dreadful outhouse when the family acquired it. After it became my favorite haunt, I had that torn down and replaced. This way."

Anticipation tingling in his belly, Cas led Matty around the back of the cabin to the new building he'd installed. Opening the door and turning on the lights, he got a little thrill of pride as Matty gasped and stepped inside out of the rain. It looked like another small log cabin on the outside, but inside was a wet room that Cas had often used as a sauna because it got so hot and steamy. He couldn't think of a better place for Matty to warm up.

"There are towels in the waterproof locker there," Cas said from the doorstep. "And you can use any of the products you like."

Matty turned and looked at Cas, biting his lip. "Do you want to join me?" he asked eventually.

His words were so vulnerable, they broke Cas's heart all over again. He'd been trying to be strong and give Matty space, but he could only be so pious. "Do you want me to look after you, sweetheart?"

Matty hugged himself and looked down at the wooden slats on the floor. Then he nodded.

That was all the encouragement Cas needed. He came inside and closed the door, kicking off his shoes and socks as he propped the umbrella up in the corner before wrapping his arms around Matty in a firm hug. After he'd kissed the top of his head, he moved quickly to crank the heat up and get the water going in the shower in the corner. They might have been out of the storm, but this room hadn't been used in a long time, and it was still pretty chilly.

That done, he turned back to Matty, who was still hugging himself and looking unsure. When Cas placed his hands on Matty's shoulders and began rubbing them, Matty leaned into the touch and groaned.

There wasn't anything sexual in the way that Cas undressed them both. He peeled off their sodden clothing and guided Matty toward the hot water. But Cas couldn't help but be moved by seeing Matty this way, regardless. He was vulnerable and small and trusting Cas again, and Cas wanted to do everything in his power to earn that confidence back.

After making certain that the temperature was just right, Cas gently encouraged Matty under the water, relishing in the way he groaned and shuddered. Yes, it was sexy. Matty was *always* sexy. But above all else, Cas was just happy that Matty was safe and content.

He sent a silent prayer of thanks to Valentina once again, because there were brand-new products waiting for them to use. So Cas reached for the rich and creamy Thedian olive-infused shampoo and conditioner to clean their hair, then lathered Matty up in a delicious wild blueberry and mango body wash. Matty allowed Cas to warm him, swaying into his every touch with little hums, his eyes closed in complete trust.

Cas wanted to be able to do this any time Matty was upset. He wanted to be the one who caught this kind, beautiful man whenever he fell. But he forced himself to stop thinking about tomorrow and focus on tonight. He'd thought he'd never get to see Matty again, let alone care for him like this. Their time together was a gift, and he refused to squander it.

When he turned off the water and wrapped them both up in big fluffy towels, he realized he'd made an error. He chuckled, the sound startling him after their somber day.

"What?" Matty asked with wide eyes, huddled in his massive white towel. His skin was flushed from the hot water, his wet curls even darker than usual.

Cas grinned and rubbed Matty's arms, enjoying the moment of silliness. "I forgot to get us any clothes."

"Oh!" Matty managed a small laugh too, lifting Cas's spirits even further. "Whoops."

Cas leaned over and pressed a kiss to Matty's forehead. "Stay here," he said as he stepped back. "Keep drying. I'll be back in a flash."

"But-" Matty said. Then he relaxed and nodded. "Okay, thank you," he said.

Cas smiled at him, his hands still on Matty's shoulders. "Were you going to suggest we both run back through the cold rain?" he asked, knowing the answer.

"Maybe," Matty mumbled. Then he closed the space between them and leaned against Cas's chest. Cas happily wrapped his arms around him as he smiled against Cas's neck. "But I'm still cold, and you said you wanted to look after me. So it's okay to let you."

"I really do want to look after you," Cas said, his heart full and warm. Things were so much simpler when it was just the two of them. He allowed their little fantasy bubble to creep back around them again. "Thank you for letting me."

Matty licked his lips and frowned, looking up at Cas. "It's not…" He huffed and shook his head. "Is it selfish that I love you making all the decisions and taking charge like that? Do you think I'm lazy?"

Cas couldn't help but smile and shake his head. "Not in the slightest. What we have is precious and unique." *I was terrified we might have lost it forever,* he almost added. Instead, he said, "It makes me happy and at peace in ways I can't really express. I want to look after you, and when you let me, it's like you give me a gift."

Matty bit his lip. "Wow," he said sadly. "We really do fit well together, don't we?"

That damned lump threatened to rise in Cas's throat again. "I think so," he said softly.

Before he could dwell too long on the doomed nature of their relationship, he kissed Matty's dark curls, then turned to shove his damp feet back into his already-ruined dress shoes. He made sure his towel was wrapped securely around his hips before throwing another one over his shoulders, grabbing the umbrella, then fishing the keys out of his trousers on the tiled floor.

It only took maybe thirty seconds to get around to the front of the cabin and let himself back in. He flicked on some of the lamps so he had enough illumination to see by, then used the lighter to get the fire going. Matty hadn't been wrong. Despite a hot shower, Cas was still shivering from being wet, and the dash back through the cold evening air and rain wasn't going to help either of them. At least the cabin had been warmed by the summer sunshine earlier.

He hurriedly pulled on his own sweatpants and hoodie from the bag Valentina had pulled together for him from the apartment. But when he came to picking an outfit for Matty, he stalled.

Among the various clothes, Valentina had packed Cas's worn out Elm Willows hoodie. Did she realize Matty had been wearing it all week? Did she have any idea that it smelled like him – his sweet musk and woodsy aftershave? Cas bunched the soft material up in his hand, inhaling deeply as he hugged it to his chest, his throat tightening. There was still a faint whiff of the palace detergent as well, mingled in with pure *Matty*. Cas still wasn't really sure where they stood, but he wanted that feeling they'd shared in the apartment back so badly. Their perfect, private bubble, where they were both safe from the outside world.

Cas debated for a second, then grabbed a pair of sweats and T-shirt that actually did belong to Matty to go with the hoodie. If Cas was going to wear his heart on his sleeve, he might as well go big or go home.

Matty had been wearing his only sneakers out in the woods, so he'd have to suffer them for the short run back from the wet room, but Cas laid out some thick woolly socks for him to change into once they were back in the cabin.

While he worked, Matty's words rolled around in his head. *'We really do fit well together, don't we?'* Cas sighed. How long could he fight his feelings? This wasn't some fling. He wasn't playing commoner by jumping into bed with the first ordinary guy he'd met, no matter what that vile woman printed in her newspaper. Cas's affection for Matty was as deep as it was startling.

He wasn't sure he'd ever feel whole again once Matty left, not now Cas knew what it felt like to have him complete his life.

He shook his head and stuffed his feet back into the dress shoes. He was thinking too much again. He'd spent his whole adult life problem-solving for his family and being the perfect son who steered them all to safety. Enough. All that mattered right then and there was getting Matty warm and dry again. That was about all Cas could control at present, so he needed to concentrate on that.

When Cas returned to the steamy wet room, Matty's face lit up in the first real smile Cas had seen on him all day. It made his heart sing. Matty had asked if he was selfish in allowing himself to be fussed over by Cas, but the truth was Cas felt the same way. He felt too lucky to have met this man who blossomed under Cas's ministrations. Maybe Cas didn't deserve such a perfect guy after everything that had happened, yet here they were, and he was done fighting his moral compass. At least for one more night.

Matty was sitting on one of the ledges around the wet room, his soaked clothes folded up next to him. He watched Cas with a smile as he came over to him, waiting for Cas to dress him rather than reaching for the clothes himself. Cas loved that with every fiber of his being.

Matty was perfect as he stepped into his sweatpants and lifted his arms so Cas could slip the T-shirt on him. "That's it, well done, sweetie," Cas said fondly, tucking Matty's hair behind his ears. "We'll deal with those in the morning," he said, gesturing to the damp towels and wet clothes. "I got this for you to wear as well, if you want?"

His heart in his mouth, he offered up his favorite hoodie that he'd loved seeing Matty in over the past week. Sure enough, Matty's blue eyes went wide. He didn't miss the significance of Cas picking that particular garment.

He licked his lips.

"Thank you, Cas," he whispered. A small smile tugged at one corner of his mouth as he held his arms out again, inviting Cas to slip it over Matty's head. Cas swallowed, not wanting to let his emotions get the better of him in this moment. He was looking after Matty, so he needed to keep it together. But inside, he was bellowing in relief and happiness.

Once it was over his head, Matty wriggled into the too-big sweater, looking utterly perfect as he gazed up at Cas.

Cas sighed and cupped the side of Matty's jaw. "Let's get you back to the cabin, okay?" He took Matty's hands and rubbed them between his own, giving them a little extra warmth before they made a run for it.

They dashed from one building to the other under the umbrella, then Cas was finally able to lock the door on the world, making it just the two of them again. "Oh, that feels so good," Matty said with a sigh, immediately going over to warm his hands over the fire. "Thank you, Cas."

Cas came and wrapped his arms around him from behind.

His skin was still too chilled for his liking. He'd hate it if Matty got sick for the precious few days he still had in the country. Cas had no idea what was going to happen between them after tonight, or even during the next few hours, but it was his privilege to do everything he could to look after Matty right then.

"Can I warm you up?" he murmured against Matty's neck. "No funny business, I promise. But we need to get your core temperature up."

Matty looked over his shoulder at Cas for a second, then nodded. After they both kicked their shoes off, Matty let Cas lead him by the hand over to the bed. Cas yanked back the covers.

"I mean, with body heat," Cas clarified.

What he was really asking was if it was okay for them to get into bed together after everything that had happened. But Matty just nodded and crawled under the sheets. That was enough to warm Cas from the inside out.

"And you need to put these on," Cas fussed, fetching the thick woolly socks he'd put aside for Matty earlier.

Matty laughed. He really threw back his head and laughed, and the sight made Cas want to cry with relief and happiness. "Those are the dorkiest things I've ever seen!" Matty gasped. "What are you, a hundred years old? There's like a whole sheep in those socks!"

"Frostbite is dorkier," Cas insisted with a raised eyebrow that just seemed to make Matty laugh harder. Good. Cas loved carefree Matty a lot more than stressed Matty, especially when Cas knew he was the source of the stress. But he'd managed to find a way to fix that, even just a little, so he allowed himself to enjoy Matty's smiles and laughs. *Live in the moment*, he reminded himself.

When Cas got into the bed and pulled the covers over them, Matty snuggled up to him immediately, tangling their legs and hugging onto Cas's chest like a life raft. The sense of rightness was as overwhelming as it was painful. Matty had been yelling at Cas that he wanted to hate him not two hours ago, and yet now here he was, pressed up against Cas head to toe, sighing contentedly like the foundation of their whole relationship hadn't been shattered today.

That was the problem. When it was just Cas and Matty, it was perfect. It was everything else that fucked it up.

Cas carded his fingers through Matty's curls until they were dry and Matty's breathing was heavy and even. Cas wanted to stay so badly, but he'd done his job. Matty was warm and safe, and Cas couldn't ask any more of him than that. So he began to carefully untangle himself, trying to extract himself from the bed.

But Matty's eyes flew open and he grabbed the front of Cas's hoodie. "Stay," he rasped sleepily. But there was also a hint of panic in that one word.

Cas immediately moved back under the covers and allowed Matty to cling to him. "I was going to sleep on the couch," he said, unable to keep the sorrow from his words. "I figured it was for the best. I don't want to hurt you any more."

Matty shook his head and yawned, blinking as he roused from his almost-sleep. "No, stay," he repeated. "You didn't hurt me, not really. It's just…the way things are." He rubbed his eyes and met Cas's gaze. "It'll hurt more when I leave for good on Monday, so stay here while we can. Please? Oh, unless you *want* to sleep on the couch-"

"I don't," Cas said emphatically. "I was trying to do right by you and be respectful. But I want you in my arms all night, Matty. I don't ever want to let you go."

God, how he meant that from the bottom of his heart.

Matty sighed and held on to Cas tightly. "We can just cuddle if you want?" Matty said.

Cas stroked back a wayward curl and cupped the side of Matty's jaw, feeling the prickly stubble against his palm. "What do you want, sweetheart?"

Matty licked his lips, then gently pressed them to Cas's mouth. The kiss itself was chaste, but Cas still felt like it was potent by Matty initiating any kind of intimacy. "I want to make love," Matty whispered. "I want to be close to you again, like before. Without the secrets."

Shame and guilt threatened to rush through Cas, but Matty's words weren't an accusation, they were just honest. And Cas realized that he wanted that, too.

Matty knew the truth now. He knew that Cas was actually Prince Cassander of Rosavia, second in line to the throne. There was no more deception.

Being with Matty made Cas feel whole, but now Matty knew everything, Cas was truly himself. The man that Matty had grown to know over the past week, as well as the state figure with a past tied to the entire country. Cas wanted to be vulnerable and naked in every sense of the word for this wonderful man who'd stolen his heart, even if it was for just one last time. They would at least have one night that was completely honest, not an illusion of make-believe.

"Without the secrets," Cas repeated, kissing Matty's mouth again with a little more heat. "I'll give you everything, I promise." And he meant it. Everything that was in his power to give was Matty's.

He didn't think he could give him his future, but Cas could give Matty his heart, and that would have to do.

Chapter Fifteen

MATTY

Cas's lips were warm and comforting against Matty's skin as they made out in bed. He clung to Cas's solid body, already feeling the awful stress of the day melting away. He'd had a lot of time to think when he'd gotten lost out in the rain.

He'd felt so stupid, so small. On top of everything that had happened, it had taken him an embarrassingly short amount of time to get completely turned around. He hadn't even been able to guess the direction of the cabin, and the panic had set in as the sun began to dip beyond the mountains.

He'd really thought he was going to have to sleep out in the cold and rain.

And as he'd sat there shivering, feeling frightened and alone, it was as if all the drama and hurt had suddenly cleared from his mind, leaving Matty with what really mattered.

Cas.

Yes, Matty's family was incredibly important to him, and he'd do anything for them. But he'd never been all that good at doing what was right for *himself.* And whether he'd known it or not, he'd jumped at the first chance he'd gotten to 'prove' to himself that what he had with Cas wasn't real. That – yet again – he was being used by a guy who would dump him at the drop of a hat. Matty suspected he had been so upset because if he expected to be treated badly and got ahead of it, he could maybe somehow control it.

But there was no controlling his heart. He was in love with Cas. It didn't matter if that scared the shit out of him. Lost and feeling utterly hopeless out in the forest, he'd been forced to acknowledge to himself that he could be as furious with the situation as he liked. It wouldn't change the way they felt about each other.

And Matty could be afraid and run away from that again. Or he could remember the overwhelming relief that had cascaded over him when Cas had stepped into the clearing and come to his rescue.

It was like Matty was suddenly home.

Yes, he'd been hurt that Cas had omitted to tell Matty a big part of who he was, but after some time to reflect, Matty could get where Cas was coming from with that. And the harsh truth was, Matty was even more hurt because he wanted Cas to trust him with *everything.* He didn't want Cas to feel like Matty would judge him or betray him. Because Matty wanted to do anything for Cas. Like he'd said in the shower, they fit together perfectly and balanced each other out.

They couldn't control the outside factors that loomed over Cas's public life. But it was more than within their power to fix this communication failure between them and mold the kind of relationship they wanted, regardless of the outside world. It didn't matter if it had no future. Matty wanted his time left with Cas to be authentic, even if it was short-lived.

And that started right now, here, in this bed.

"I understand," he mumbled against Cas's lips, rubbing his back. They blinked their eyes back open to look at each other.

"Understand what?" Cas asked with a frown.

"Why you weren't totally honest about who you were," Matty told him bluntly. Cas winced and looked away, but Matty cupped his hand to his cheek and encouraged him to look back at Matty. "I understand why you wanted a vacation from your real life, and why you couldn't say no to this. To us." He smiled. "I did the same thing, after all. This isn't real life. It's a temporary fantasy. But I wanted it so badly that I pretended it would be okay."

Cas's frown deepened. "You didn't do anything wrong, though."

Matty bit his lip. He'd been so raw with hurt for most of the day, but now that was fading, he found he was better able to see both sides of the coin.

"Neither did you, not really," Matty said. "You just didn't tell the whole truth, and I can see how that would seem okay, especially if no one found out." Cas opened his mouth, but Matty held up a finger to signal he didn't need to apologize again. "Sometimes we get movie stars at the theater," he began to explain, "when they do a play off-Broadway for a while. I mean *big* celebs. And the way people treat them…"

Matty shook his head. "You grow up thinking it would be amazing to be rich and famous. But fans get crazy, invading these people's privacy, like they actually think they know the actors they've seen on screen. Like they have a right, and the actor doesn't get a choice. And then there are the trashy magazines, the online blogs, whole TV channels dedicated to gossip. They twist every tiny thing these celebrities do for entertainment, forgetting they're real people. I imagine being a prince is a bit like that, but from birth?"

Cas bit his lip and glanced away. "Kind of, yeah," he admitted.

Matty sighed and rested their foreheads together. They both closed their eyes as their embrace got tighter. "I'm sorry," Matty said truthfully. "At least people choose to become actors or singers or football players. You were just born into this, and…" He took a deep breath. He'd decided when he was lost out in the rain that if he was going to be honest, he was going to go all the way. "I'm honored you chose me to try and find something real with."

Cas laughed and kissed Matty on the lips, his hands clasped around Matty's face. When their cheeks brushed, Matty felt Cas's were slightly damp. "Oh, Matty," he said heavily. "I don't know which life is 'real' anymore. It's supposed to be the one back at the palace. But here, with you, *that's* what feels real." Then he laughed again, nuzzling their noses together. "And I didn't really *choose* you. From the moment I saw you, it was like I was done for. There wasn't a choice at all. My heart just knew. 'Sure thing' – remember?"

Matty opened his eyes, glad to see Cas looking at him as well. "Of course I remember," he said warmly, caressing Cas's jaw.

He was getting too hot, so he kicked back the covers, glad there were a few lamps on so they could see each other. He recalled their first night together. They'd been in the dark in more ways than one. But now they'd stepped into the light, Matty never wanted to go back.

"I know you can't be with someone like me," he said, laying his heart on the line. "But I want you to know that if the rules were different, I'd want to be with you. I'd want to *try*. Despite all our differences and the ocean between us. I...I think I love you, Cas. That's why it hurt so badly when I thought it was all a game for you. I think I've fallen in love with you."

Cas gave a shaky laugh. "Oh, sweetheart. I've definitely fallen in love with you. And it scares me to death, because I don't know what – if *anything* – we can do about it. But I want to say again that this was never, ever a game. I don't think I really deserve your forgiveness, but I'm extremely glad to have it."

"You do have it, and deserve it," Matty promised, his heart full of relief and happiness and maybe even the tiniest bit of hope. "I mean it. I understand."

And that was it. The air was cleared between them. Matty had made his peace out on that tree stump, but to hear Cas's sincere apologies and that he returned Matty's love...well, that was all that mattered for tonight.

They couldn't control what tomorrow would bring. But Matty could at least hold on to the smallest dream that this wouldn't be goodbye forever. It was a million times better to think that Cas would be somewhere in the world thinking of Matty with love and affection, rather than the idea that he might have used Matty for kicks.

Matty had said all along that he trusted Cas, so he trusted him now.

This was what was real.

It was almost like their first time all over again. Even though they'd had sex in every room of Cas's apartment (and it had been *spectacular)*, there was something different sparking between them tonight. Their lips came together again and again, hands desperately holding on to whatever they could as their bodies moved in sync. Without needing to say anything, Cas's energy was already shifting as he took charge, pulling off the T-shirt and hoodie he had so tenderly dressed Matty in to warm him up.

They had a much better way of keeping warm now.

Matty gasped and writhed as Cas sucked and rubbed his nipples. They were both obviously hard in their loose-fitting sweatpants, and Cas crawled on top of Matty, bumping their cocks together as they rutted groins and pawed at each other with grabby hands.

It was messy and tangled, and Matty was loving every second of it.

Cas had tried to be so smooth and polished when they'd met. He'd confessed that their first date had originally been meant to be a fancy dinner at a restaurant and a night at the theater. Matty was so grateful that Cas had changed his mind. On reflection, he'd been as authentic as he could all along. And now they'd been freed from his biggest secret, there was nothing at all between them.

Literally. Cas made short work of their sweatpants, but he

waggled his eyebrows at Matty's fluffy socks as they pinged off.

"I should make you keep those on, after the fuss you made," he growled playfully. Matty's cock liked that *a lot.*

"You could make me do anything, I'm sure," Matty teased back, grinning as he bit Cas's earlobe. "We've already established I'm kind of a slut for doing what you tell me."

Cas laughed. "You're just a slut for me in general, aren't you, sweetheart?"

Matty hummed and nodded. "Guilty, I'm afraid. It's your fault for being so insanely hot."

Cas ran his hand up Matty's side, making him shiver at both the touch and the hungry look Cas had as he trailed his gaze over Matty's naked body. "I don't think you know how hot *you* are, do you?" Cas murmured, caressing along Matty's sensitive thighs. He was so close to Matty's straining cock, but he didn't touch it yet.

Matty whimpered. "Please," he whispered.

But Cas just tilted his head, turning his lust-blown eyes on Matty's. "I will. I promise, sweetheart," he said, rubbing Matty's stomach in a way that managed to be both sexy and soothing at the same time. "But we said we'd be honest. And you need to hear the truth. I've *never* been with anyone while I've been out in the city. I haven't even been tempted to break the palace's rules. The risk seemed too great. Until you. Do you understand how special that makes you? How unique?"

Matty squirmed, feeling his cheeks flushing in embarrassment. "I'm just me," he mumbled, looking away from Cas's piercing gaze. "Some broke guy from Queens who doesn't even know what he's doing with his life."

Cas cupped the side of Matty's face and made him look back at him. "No," he said firmly. "You're a man who dropped everything to care for his family. You're kind and generous and fun and sexy. I couldn't care less what your job is or what's in your bank account. To me, you are precious. I said I'd treasure you, because you're priceless." He bit his lip and didn't blink as he looked so deep into Matty's eyes it was as if he was searching his soul. "Can you say something for me? It'll make me happy, because I think you need to say it to believe it."

Matty swallowed. He'd been so relieved they were having fun, loving sex after the awful day they'd experienced. He'd thought he couldn't feel any more raw. But this was a whole new level of vulnerable, stretched out naked, with Cas saying all these unbelievable things to him.

But Matty wanted to do whatever Cas asked. He wanted Cas to take care of him, because right from the start Matty had just known that Cas's instincts were good. Even if sometimes, they were misdirected. So he continued to trust him now. Matty could surely manage a few words for him, couldn't he? Especially if Cas said they were good for him.

"O-okay," he stammered.

Cas's beaming smile made Matty feel more relaxed immediately. "I know you could, Matty. You're so good to me." Those words were like butter melting over freshly baked bread for Matty. He brushed the backs of his fingers against Cas's dark stubble, shivering a little at the prickly sensation.

Matty breathed deeply and smiled, confidence swimming

through his veins. *Cas will take care of me. Cas loves me. I love Cas.* He thought the words clearly, like a mantra.

Cas kissed him softly on the lips. "I want you to say, 'I'm worthy.' Can you do that?"

Suddenly, Matty wasn't so sure that he could. For just two words, it was almost impressive at the fear they caused him. "Uh," he croaked. Cas still had his hand resting against Matty's cheek, effectively trapping him, so he was locked in with Cas's gaze.

So Matty closed his eyes.

"I-I'm worthy," he mumbled.

There was a pause. "No, Matty," Cas said. Matty's disappointment was so swift his eyes flew open as his stomach dropped. But then Cas smiled again. "That's it. Keep your eyes open. I know you can do it. Look at me and say what I asked you to, please."

Fear was still curled around Matty's heart. He never would have guessed something so simple would be such a problem, but Cas obviously knew. So Matty swallowed and gripped firmly onto Cas's wrist. In turn, Cas caressed Matty's cheek with strong, soothing rubs of his thumb. Matty blinked, but then he held Cas's gaze.

"I'm worthy," he said in a rush. He exhaled, and Cas beamed, looking proud. Matty gave a nervous laugh, a little surprised he'd managed to do it. "I'm worthy," he repeated, feeling a calmness easing the fear out of his chest.

"Perfect," Cas said, placing a sweet kiss on Matty's lips. "Can you try a couple more?"

Matty nodded. He was still clinging to Cas's wrist, but he flopped the other hand by his head and continued concentrating on his breathing, the calmness spreading from his chest through the rest of his body, like tendrils of smoke, curling all the way out to his fingers and toes.

"I can do it, Cas," he said. And he wasn't just doing it for his lover. He was doing it for both of them. It was as if he hadn't had permission to say something like that before about himself, but now he could.

"I am worthy of love," said Cas. Their locked gazes were hypnotic.

"I am…worthy of love," Matty repeated, only tripping up slightly. But he kept his eyes open.

"I am beautiful."

"I am beautiful," Matty said without pause.

Cas grinned. "I am treasured by the man who loves me, no matter what."

Matty bit his lip. Cas sounded so confident when he said that. "No matter what," Matty whispered.

That was the really important part to Matty. Cas meant that. They probably couldn't be together. It was just too impossible. But that didn't mean what they'd shared wasn't real or of immeasurable value.

"I am Matty Doyle," he said quietly but clearly. "I am worthy, beautiful, and treasured by the man who loves me. And I love him, too," he added, feeling light headed.

Was this the kind of euphoric rush people felt when they

jumped out of airplanes? Or when they spoke in front of crowds? Matty felt like he was ten feet tall and flying, perfectly content in his own skin. Like he was exactly where he was meant to be.

"Now you," he said softly, like his tongue had a mind of his own, and his brain wasn't even sure what he meant.

Neither did Cas, apparently. He quirked a smile and tilted his head. "Now me what?" he asked gently.

"Now you say…" Matty was floating, so it took him a second to think of what he wanted – what he needed. But it wasn't so much about what *Matty* needed… "I am Cas, and I am my own man."

Cas's eyes widened in what was maybe shock. "I am Cas, and I am my own man," he said. Then he frowned before a smile played on his lips. "I *am* my own man. Not my brothers' keeper. I don't belong to the state. I'm just…Cas."

Matty grinned. He probably looked crazy or punch drunk, but he didn't care. Those words filled him with joy, turning the calmness in his bones to love and happiness. "We're just Matty and Cas, and we're amazing," he said with a giggle.

Cas kissed him passionately, rolling him on his back so he was pressing Matty into the mattress. Their cocks rubbed against one another as Cas held Matty's jaw and Matty dug his fingers into Cas's back. "We are," Cas mumbled against Matty's lips.

Then he moved, kissing Matty's neck, hard enough it was probably going to mark.

Matty wanted Cas to claim him with a hickey so badly. "Yes," he hissed. "I'm yours, Cas."

Cas hummed and he sucked and nipped at the tender skin. "You are," he assured him.

When he was apparently satisfied with his work, Cas took one of his hands and slipped it between their hot, damp bodies. Matty moaned as Cas wrapped his strong hand around both their members, helping them to glide together as they thrust. They kissed until they were gasping too much, and then Cas held his face just above Matty's as their breaths mingled, their lips grazing against each other as they stared into each other's eyes.

Matty could feel himself coming undone as sweat poured from his burning skin. All his nerve endings were on fire in the best possible way as his orgasm built in him.

"Cas," he uttered in warning.

Cas nodded. "Come for me, sweetheart. Make a mess of us both."

Matty nodded and clawed Cas's back, trying to keep himself anchored as his orgasm rushed up to greet him. He was dimly aware that his fingernails were probably marking Cas just as much as the hickey on Matty's neck.

The next thing he knew, his back was arching as thick, hot cum spurted between their bodies. He quivered and panted for air, clinging to Cas like a life raft. Cas milked him for every last drop as Matty flopped boneless against the bed.

"Fuck, you're gorgeous," Cas growled, kissing Matty's lips and jaw. "You look incredible."

Matty managed to keep his eyes open just a crack, and looked at Cas sleepily through his lashes. "Now you," he mumbled happily.

"Oh, yeah?" said Cas. He braced one hand beside Matty's head, then loomed over him as he stroked his hard, leaking cock luxuriously. "You're bossy tonight. I love it. You like watching that? You like me touching myself?"

Matty nodded, still grinning. "So hot," he whispered. He traced his fingertips along Cas's abs. "Want you to come on me."

Cas bit his lip and nodded. "Whatever you want, gorgeous." He gasped and leaned his head back, exposing his neck and the ridge of his Adam's apple. Matty touched it and the lines of Cas's collarbones.

In his sleepy, sated state, he was able to muster up one thought. The whole world could think they knew Prince Cassander of Rosavia. But not one other person alive had seen him like this. Of that, Matty was certain.

With a shout, Cas came explosively, shooting all over Matty's chest, even hitting his chin and hair. Matty giggled, enjoying the mess they'd made. Cas grunted and rested both elbows on either side of Matty's head, kissing him leisurely as he slowly came down from his high.

"We're going to need another shower," he said eventually, making Matty laugh.

"Later," Matty whispered when he recovered himself. He caressed the side of Cas's face and gave him another sweet kiss. "I want to just stay like this for a while."

Cas nodded. "Me, too."

He did find some tissues by the bed, though, and carefully mopped up most of the cum. As much as Matty wanted to stay covered in it as proof of their special moment, he knew it would be uncomfortable once it dried. "Did I look good?" he asked, fishing for the compliments he knew Cas would want to give him.

Sure enough, Cas grinned, and he gently ran a tissue over Matty's hair. "You looked better than good," he said. "You looked delectable."

Matty bit his lip. He was exhausted after a long, emotional day, and he couldn't seem to stop the words spilling out. "Did I look like I was yours?"

Cas paused, looking back down at Matty with a more serious expression. "Very much so."

Matty nodded. Thankfully, Cas was done with his cleanup, and he pulled Matty in for a cuddle. No matter what happened, Cas would always be able to remember Matty blissed out and covered in both their cum. Matty hoped he'd remember their walk in the rose gardens, and eating donuts, and making meals together in his apartment – all the good stuff.

No matter what, no one could take those memories from them. That was the thought Matty clung on to as he fell asleep in Cas's arms, safe and protected for just one more night.

Chapter Sixteen

CAS

Something wasn't right. Something *aside* from the fact that Ida von Tarr had apparently decided to ramp up her hate campaign against not just Cas, but the entire royal family in the run up to the five-hundred-year celebration ball on Sunday. That was bad enough.

But the palace's response to Cas's shocking scandal was causing him just as much worry.

Because there hadn't been one yet.

From a quick internet search, almost every news publication in Rosavia was reporting on the story by Saturday morning. Even neighboring nations like Grechzen were putting it on their front pages. It seemed everybody had something to say about Cas's illicit affair with a supposed gold digging commoner. But when he had woken up in the cabin expecting to have heard from Valentina regarding an official palace statement, there was still silence.

It made Cas nervous. Not as nervous as he had been yesterday, when he'd cared more what other people had to say, but still. This was a public humiliation for the crown.

Wasn't it?

Cas texted Valentina for an update before he urged Matty to wake up. Matty grumbled adorably as Cas cajoled him back into the shower to freshen up, then they dressed and Matty started making them breakfast from the supplies they'd received the day before. In all that time, Valentina just replied saying 'things are still in motion' and to 'hang tight.'

Cas would have expected to have been raked across the coals by yesterday afternoon. Why wasn't the palace's PR department already tearing him a new one? What was Cas missing here?

Initially, his gut reaction was to hide his worries from Matty. But then he realized with a jolt that they'd promised not to do that anymore. Their future was uncertain, but after last night their present was clear.

It was built on a solid foundation of honesty and truth.

Cas had *never* felt like that with anyone before. Not even when he and Matty had been having sex for several days in his apartment. Cas had known Matty needed to say those personal truths out loud, as if declaring them to the whole universe, not just himself and Cas. The fact that Matty had done as Cas had asked, and that Matty clearly felt better for doing so, was heady. Even though they'd just frotted, it had felt like the best sex of Cas's life.

And he'd woken up expecting to have to get in front of the cameras and publicly denounce Matty, and then possibly stay away from him forever.

But there was still nothing. Was it wrong of Cas to hope?

So Cas told Matty all of this as Matty cooked for them. Cas divulged all the worries bouncing around his head, but also how good he felt after their night together. And Matty smiled and smiled until he abandoned their bacon and eggs for a minute to come sit in Cas's lap on the sofa.

Cas had worried Matty would look at him differently if he found out that Cas was a prince. And he *did* look at him differently today. But Cas suspected it wasn't because he thought of Cas as having tons of money and power.

It was because he saw Cas's heart. And that was far more valuable than anything Cas got from being a prince.

"I agree," Matty said, playing with Cas's T-shirt. "What we did last night felt right in a way I can't even explain. Thank you."

Cas kissed the tip of his nose, his cheek, and then his lips. "You're welcome," he replied, flushed with pride and a sense of accomplishment. It seemed crazy that he'd initially thought he'd make Matty happy by paying for fancy stuff. *This* was the gift Cas had to give in taking care of his lover. His words and actions were far more valuable than any trinkets he could bestow on him.

But as confident as he was with their relationship just between the two of them, there was still the palace and the country to consider. He'd never be allowed to be with Matty in peace, he was sure.

"You're worried that you haven't heard from your family," Matty prompted.

Cas shook his head. "I've heard from my brothers. Some of

them, anyway." Leo, Jules, and Wren had been strangely sympathetic. Ben hadn't said a thing, but there was a good chance he hadn't seen the news in the past twenty-four hours, depending on where Aunt Geraldine had sent him off to. "But not my parents. And certainly not from the palace's legal or PR departments. If I didn't know better, I'd say my valet was stalling."

Matty frowned. "Is that something she usually does?"

"Nope," Cas shook his head. "Never. She's blunt to a fault. It's one of her best qualities. She never bullshits me."

"Maybe she's protecting you?" Matty suggested.

Cas raised his eyebrows. "By keeping me in the dark? Not a good plan."

"As we've discovered," Matty agreed, poking Cas lightly on the chest. Damn, Cas felt lucky they were already able to tentatively joke about his fuckup. That went a long way to convincing Cas that Matty really had forgiven him. "Okay, well, there's nothing we can do about it right now," Matty said. "Come and eat your breakfast before it gets cold."

Matty hopped up to start dishing their food onto plates, but Cas followed and threw his arms around his waist and kissed his neck, making Matty squeal.

"I wanted to do that the first time you cooked for me," Cas growled, his cock stirring in his pants. "You're so cute when you're concentrating."

Matty hummed and turned slightly so they could kiss. "We have more eggs if you want something *else* for breakfast," he said, waggling his eyebrows.

Cas thought that was a great idea. So of course his phone went off at that precise moment.

"Ah, damn," he said with a sigh. He would love to ignore it, but it was almost certainly an update on the situation, so he needed to grab it. "Sorry, babe."

Matty kissed his cheek. "I'll keep your food warm."

Cas snatched up the cell before the call rang out. It was Valentina. "Hey. What's the news?" he asked as he jogged outside. The summer sunshine was back, and everything smelled incredibly fresh from the night of rain.

"Good morning, Your Highness," Valentina said. "I hope you slept well."

There was a teasing note to her voice, which confused Cas. Ordinarily, he wouldn't mind a little ribbing at all from her, but under the circumstances, he expected her to be more serious. Wasn't he still fucked?

"As well as to be expected," he said neutrally. In fact, after he and Matty had reconciled, he'd gone out like a light. No doubt the great sex had helped him sleep, too. But that was more information than Valentina needed. "Is there a statement ready for me yet? Or is a representative going to speak on behalf of the family?"

"Neither," she replied.

Cas wandered down the short jetty and looked out over the small lake with its usually soothing waterfall splashing away. Cas was a little too on edge to appreciate it now, though. He frowned. "Neither?"

"Your father wants to speak to you," Valentina said briskly. "I need you to take Matty back to your apartment, where we're making arrangements for him to stay somewhere the press can't reach him. I've gotten him a new phone and we can collect all his things from the hotel and the apartment."

Cas shook his head. "It's Finley's graduation tournament today. Matty will need to get to Elm Willows – if he's allowed?" God, that would be awful if he had to miss her competition. But before a fresh wave of guilt could engulf him, Valentina responded.

"Oh, of course. Right. Well, still bring him to the apartment, and I'll work it out from there. Whether or not you'll still be attending will most likely depend on what His Majesty has to say."

"Right," Cas said faintly, still feeling like he was missing something.

This wasn't how he'd expected this to unfold at all. But he and Matty had already established that they couldn't control what was happening in the outside world. They could only control their relationship, which was now in much better shape after last night. So perhaps he needed to stop worrying about what he'd expected to happen, and just roll with it.

"Okay," he said, exhaling. "We'll pack up here and see you shortly at the apartment. If anything changes, let me know."

"Certainly, Your Highness. Say 'hi' to Matty for me," she added playfully.

Before he could respond, she hung up, leaving Cas staring at the now blank phone screen. He was less surprised that she'd guessed the two of them had made up, and more confused as to why she sounded so happy about it.

What did she know that Cas didn't?

Matty had taken this development much better than Cas. He was eager to get back to some kind of normalcy, and he was thrilled that he'd be able to attend Finley's graduation after all. Cas was supposed to be adjudicating that tournament, ironically, but that had been two weeks ago, when his whole vacation in the city had needed covering up. He wasn't sure now what counted as official duty and what didn't.

He'd worry about that later, though. First, he and Matty quickly had breakfast, packed up all their things, made sure their phones were charged, and locked up the cabin once more. Cas wondered if they'd ever be back there. He had no way to know, but at least now he clung to a glimmer of hope.

During the ride back into the city, Cas had the radio on and chatted about whatever popped into his head, extremely pleased when Matty joined in. They could almost pretend that everything was fine and the sword of Damocles wasn't hanging above their heads, waiting to drop at any second. Because it might never fall.

So when Cas parked outside of the apartment, he gave Matty a searing kiss goodbye, running his fingers through Matty's black curls and touching the hickey mark just below Matty's T-shirt collar. Cas looked into Matty's wide, slightly dazed blue eyes as he cupped the side of his face.

"I'll see you later," Cas promised, knowing he would do everything in his power to make sure that happened. He wasn't going to let Matty just disappear back to New York. Cas would go and find out what the hell was going on, then he'd come back to the man he loved and make some sort of plan with him.

This *wasn't* the end.

"O-okay," Matty stammered, then he smiled. "Later. At the tournament?"

Cas smiled and gave him one last kiss. "I'll do my best."

He watched as Matty exited the car and retrieved his bags from the trunk. Then he was greeted by Cas's security detail as he approached the apartment building. Cas couldn't see any reporters lurking around, but it was difficult to tell with the long-range lenses they worked with. Either way, Matty nodded at something the guy in charge said, then turned and gave Cas a wave before disappearing inside.

There was nothing left for Cas to do but turn his car around and head back to the palace.

To face his father.

Cas appreciated that he didn't have the sort of relationship with his parents that most people would consider normal. But what was normal, anyway? Yes, the king and queen had been distant and painfully formal during most of his life – especially his childhood and teenage years – but they were loving in their own ways. Definitely not like Matty's asshole folks ,who had turned their backs on their kids just for their sexuality. That was impossible to even consider doing to a child, in Cas's opinion.

But even so, Cas tended to think of his own parents as the king and queen first, and mother and father second. So for King Alphonse to request an audience with Cas before releasing an official statement meant he wanted to discuss the matter in an official capacity, rather than a father-son chat.

And Cas had no clue as to what he might have to say.

Valentina was waiting for him in his suite and, after Cas taking a moment to pet Bella, his valet helped him quickly dress from his casual wear into a suit. He'd used the back entrance, but there were press camped outside the palace with their damn cameras, and it would be best if he were properly clothed if they caught a glimpse of him.

"Is he angry?" Cas finally asked when it became clear from Valentina's silence that she wasn't going to offer any information willingly.

Sure enough, she arched an eyebrow as she ran a clothes brush over Cas's limbs, catching any stray hairs from Bella. "I couldn't possibly say," was her reply.

Cas sighed impatiently. "I mean-"

"Look," she interrupted, dropping the brush back in the drawer and closing it with a bang. She placed her hands on her hips and fixed him with a stern glare that she usually reserved for discussing Cas's troublesome brothers. "You know how you feel about Matty, correct?"

Cas blinked. "Yeah?" he said slowly.

She nodded. "Then that's all that matters. Not crown or country. You two and your hearts. Does he hate you?"

Cas exhaled. "No. I'm pretty sure it's the very opposite of hate, actually," he said in relief.

Valentina nodded again and pointed to his door. "Then you

get out there and say what you need to say, okay? Stop living for everyone else and do what's right for *you*, Your Highness."

Cas raised his eyebrows. "It's just that easy, is it?"

Valentina shrugged. "I don't know. Why don't you go find out?"

Cas narrowed his eyes at her, but she just swept her arm toward the door again.

So Cas had little choice but to straighten his tie, then go and face his father, trying his best not to feel like a schoolboy who'd been caught making out with the captain of the lacrosse team when he should have been in chemistry class.

Not that Cas had ever done that.

As he walked down the palace corridor, he realized he had a shadow. "Offering moral support, or just want a front-row seat for my execution?" Cas joked down at Bella. But she simply swished her tail and carried on trotting alongside his feet. It was silly, but he didn't feel quite so alone as he neared his father's study.

Cas sighed, pausing just before he knocked. He'd been here not long ago to give Wren a stern talking to. Cas should have known it would only be a matter of time before it was his turn. Wren hadn't left that meeting very happy.

How was Cas going to feel?

There was only one way to find out. He knocked firmly twice, then took a step back to wait to be called in. It only took a second for his father's booming voice to call "Enter!" through the thick wooden door, and Cas didn't let himself hesitate. He just turned the handle and swiftly walked inside.

Bella slipped through the door before he could close it, but the palace was so full of cats it wasn't all that unusual. Besides, her presence wouldn't stop the king from saying what he wanted. And there he was, sitting behind his large desk, surrounded by bookcases and portraits of Cas's grandfather and great-grandfather. King Alphonse had silvery hair, but he was still a robust man, even if his face showed a few more lines these days. He was writing something with a fountain pen, but as Cas approached, he finished with a flourish and screwed the cap back on, looking up at Cas with a smile.

"Sander," he said fondly, indicating one of the chairs on this side of the desk for him to sit at. The queen wasn't present, possibly too busy with preparations for the ball. Cas pushed down a fresh wave of guilt at having caused a scandal when all eyes were already on Rosavia and the palace.

He had the same usual reaction to hearing the name that had felt so alien and uncomfortable to him for so long. But for the first time, it felt within his power to do something about it. Matty had given him that confidence. He was his own man.

"Um – Cas," he said.

The king raised his eyebrows. "What was that?" he asked pleasantly.

Cas cleared his throat and sat down. "Actually, I prefer to be called Cas," he said, folding his hands into his lap and holding his dad's gaze. "Obviously, officially, I'll always be Prince Cassander, of course. But at home, I'd like to be called Cas."

The king blinked and nodded once. "I see. Well...I don't see how that should be an issue, particularly. Cas it is."

A wave of something unidentifiable washed over Cas. It was kind of a relief, but also a sort of euphoria. 'What's in a name?' Shakespeare had asked. It turned out, for Cas, a lot. If he could let go of Sander, he could let go of all those burdens he'd placed on himself to be responsible for every damn thing in this family.

Sander had thought he had to be Rosavia itself, the palace personified.

Cas was a flesh and blood man who was finally allowing himself to pursue his own happiness.

So he smiled at his father, feeling a hell of a lot less like he was facing a firing squad. There was no sense in beating about the bush, therefore Cas just took a breath and jumped right in.

"I take it you've seen the news?" he asked, stating the obvious. Why else was he here?

King Alphonse raised his eyebrows, looking down at some of the documents on his desk, of which there were many. No doubt the system made sense to him and would be tidied by the end of the day, but now, to Cas, it just looked like a sea of paper. "I have indeed," said the king. "You've caused quite a stir."

"I apologize profusely," Cas said, completely sincere. "That was never my intention. I should have behaved with more discretion."

The king hummed. "How about you tell me what's happened in your own words?" He frowned and rolled his pen between his index finger and thumb. "That von Tarr has never been a friend to the crown, so I wouldn't trust her in any case. But it seems like there's been a new scandal every day this past week. And *now* there's a new issue with the Thedes press as well this morning. I swear she wants this ball to be a disaster."

Cas's interest piqued, along with concern for Jules and Dante. But he'd have to look into that later. He completely agreed that von Tarr seemed to have made it her personal vendetta to drag the royal family into the mud this week. Cas wasn't sure what they'd done to deserve that, but the result was still the same. They were walking a dangerous line for Rosavia's reputation right now, and Cas was here with his father because of the role he'd personally played in that.

It was time to be honest, like he and Matty had promised.

"I've met someone wonderful, Father," Cas said before he could chicken out. "The man in the photos with me isn't some dalliance. I think I might be in love, in fact. But I'm fully aware that he won't be considered appropriate for me to date."

Or marry, a voice whispered at the back of Cas's head. That was skipping ahead enormously, but the thought lingered, regardless.

The king placed the pen down, folded his hands on the desk, and fixed Cas with a steady look, his expression neutral. "Perhaps you could tell me what he is, rather than what he *isn't?*" A smile twitched ever so slightly at the corners of his mouth, giving Cas the encouragement he needed to open up. He hadn't been expecting this kind of warmth at all. Maybe he had underestimated his father?

"He's kind," said Cas in a rush. "Thoughtful, dedicated. He dotes on his niece and worries about his sister. She's sick with cancer, but there's every hope she can still make a full recovery." Cas tried to stop the grin that was no doubt sappy from creeping onto his lips, but he couldn't. "He's a great cook, a music and movie lover, and I think he'd enjoy the theater immensely if he could afford to go more. He doesn't have a career path yet, but I think he just needs to find the right calling."

The king hummed again. "Sounds like someone suited to sit on a board of directors of a charity or two, wouldn't you say?"

Cas raised his eyebrows. Charity work? That was a classic occupation for anyone who married into the royal family.

"Uh, yes," he said, trying to process this new information as fast as possible. Was his father giving him his *blessing?* That couldn't be right. There was no precedent for a prince to be with a commoner. However, Cas was done omitting facts. "I feel you should also know that he's American. He and his sister are estranged from their parents, as they didn't approve of their children being gay and lesbian. He comes from absolutely no money or social standing." *And yet he's utterly perfect and makes me feel complete in ways I can't describe.*

After a second or two, the king rose from his chair and placed his hands behind his back. Taking his time, he walked across the room and looked out of the large window, over the palace and the city beyond. "It's a blessing and a curse that Rosavia is such a small country," he said. Cas suddenly felt like he was in an impromptu history or politics lesson. Unsure what his father was getting at, he stayed quiet. "We've never had much sway in Europe, other than simple trade agreements and, in the last few decades, tourism. The rest of the world is never very interested in listening to what we have to say." He turned and looked back at Cas. "But that means that they never really pay attention to what we're up to, either."

"Father?" Cas finally prompted. He didn't want to jump to any conclusions, but it was difficult to keep his hope at bay.

"I disagreed with my father on a lot of things, but it's easy to judge from afar. When you're the one on the throne, though, it's very easy to just maintain the status quo for ease and simplicity." He shook his head, a fond smile tugging at his features. "My sons have turned out to be anything but simple or easy."

Cas shifted on his seat, throwing a guilty look down at Bella, who gave him a tiny meow of encouragement. "Sorry," he said, looking back up at his dad.

The king gave a small short laugh and looked back at Cas. "I wouldn't have it any other way, I assure you. Although it has made me take a serious look at some of the protocols we have in place, and whether we should still be blindly following them." He sighed. "Nothing is more important to me than my children. I know it should be crown and country, but I'm only human in the end."

Cas swallowed around the lump in his throat. He'd never heard the king – his *dad* – talk like this before. Maybe all the drama Cas and his brothers had been going through these past months had opened his eyes to something?

"We all are," Cas said softly.

His dad nodded. "If we only marry royalty and nobility, how are we possibly going to be expected to keep in touch with our people?" said King Alphonse. He raised his eyebrows and shook his head, looking once again out over Alpina. "We are *for* the people. We *protect* the people. But by saying we cannot befriend them, cannot love or marry them, aren't we also saying 'we're better than you, common folk'? Why follow arcane rules put in place in a completely different time, when *we* are the rule makers? What is the point of power, if we cannot wield it for what we feel is good and right?"

Cas's throat had gone dry. His heart was pounding, and he realized his mouth was hanging open. He managed to snap it closed with a *'click'* just as his father turned back around again. The king looked cautiously amused.

"Father," Cas said slowly, rising to his feet. Bella immediately rubbed herself in a figure eight around his legs, like she was giving him her support. "Is that...can I take that as your blessing?"

The king's smile grew. "Your mother and I want to meet this young man. Matty, is it?" Cas nodded, hardly daring to breathe. "Why don't you invite him to the ball tomorrow night? If that's not throwing him in too much at the deep end?"

All the blood rushed from Cas's head, and only years of training in decorum kept his knees locked and stopped him from dropping in shock back into the chair he'd been occupying.

King Alphonse van Rosavia had just invited Matty Doyle to the most important social and political night in the country's past hundred years. As Cas's official date.

"I think," Cas said, finally collecting his wits enough to speak, "that would be wonderful. We'd be honored, Your Highness."

King Alphonse snorted and sat himself back down. "None of

that when you introduce us. You always were a stickler for protocol and tradition, Cas." He winked. "I hope this young American continues to loosen you up. Now, off you go. I believe you have an archery tournament to oversee?"

Cas beamed, feeling a little dizzy he was so overwhelmingly happy. "Yes, Father. I do. Thank you, from the bottom of my heart."

The king hummed and shooed him off, his attention already back on his documents. Cas didn't mind the quick shift. His father was a busy man.

But he was also a kind and compassionate one, too.

Cas walked back out into the hallway with Bella at his feet. His thoughts were whirling around his mind as he walked down the corridor, hardly paying attention to the people who passed him. That was until a few turns later, when his baby brother, Wren, materialized from one of the rooms, a mixture of anxiety and hope on his face.

"Hi," he said breathlessly. "How'd it go?"

Cas didn't need to ask how Wren knew what was going on, or if he sympathized. He'd been through something very similar in the past few days with his own love life. So Cas just smiled, trying not to get his hopes up too much. He still had to talk to Matty, and they still had so many obstacles to consider.

But Cas had his father's blessing. That meant he had the blessing of the crown, and everything else paled in comparison.

He and Matty had a chance.

"I think it went well," Cas said, nodding. An emotional lump rose in his throat, but thankfully this was a happy reaction for once. "Good. I...I have a date for the ball. His name is Matty. I can't wait for you to meet him."

Without warning, Wren threw his arms around Cas's neck and hugged him fiercely. Cas stumbled as he blinked, then patted Wren's back.

"I'm so happy for you!" Wren cried into Cas's shoulder. When he pulled back, he laughed, wiping his glistening eyes. "And I'm *so* sorry I was such a dick to you the other day. You've always looked out for me, even when I've been an absolute terror, and I want you to know that I love you, Sander. You deserve happiness. And no one should get to tell you what that happiness looks like."

Cas rested his hand on Wren's shoulder. "The same to you. I'm glad things worked out well for you, too."

Wren beamed. "They really have. Sander...I'm *so* happy."

"Good." Cas licked his lips and dropped his hand. "And...is it okay if you call me Cas? Sander doesn't feel like who I am anymore. I'm not sure that person ever really existed." He laughed. "I'm pretty sure he was just a lot of pomp and nonsense in a trench coat, pretending to be a prince."

Wren snorted. "He was a bit of a stick in the mud," he said devilishly. From that glint in his eye, Cas was sure there was still some brat left in his baby brother. But the maturity of the past few months that now accompanied it was a welcome relief. Cas hoped that now Wren was settling into adulthood, they'd finally have a chance to be the friends that the years between them had always made difficult.

Cas was about to give Wren a hard time, and act like he

wouldn't have *had* to be a stick in the mud if Wren hadn't caused so much trouble, but the clattering of feet announced that a couple of people were coming around the corner.

Sure enough, two men emerged in the corridor. It was Ben and his valet Paul, and they were walking silently side by side at quite a pace.

"Ben!" cried Wren in delight. The other two men slowed as they approached Cas and Wren, their looks almost apprehensive. "I thought you were stuck on active duty! Did the Army let you off for the ball?" That was what Cas had thought, too, although he knew what Wren didn't: that it hadn't been the Army who had been keeping him away.

Ben looked very surprised to see his brothers in the palace where they lived, which struck Cas as odd. His eyebrows were practically lost in his hair, and he hesitated before speaking. When he did make to answer, Bella beat him to it from where she'd been winding around Cas's feet. She hissed and arched her back, which wasn't like her at all.

"Bella," Cas admonished, reaching down to pick up his cat. But she darted away from him and vanished from sight. How odd. "You made it, then?" Cas asked Ben as he stood back up, prying for more information. What he was really asking was if everything was okay with Ben's mission.

"Oh, you know me," said Ben with a grin. "I never miss an opportunity for a party. But I wanted my entrance to be a big surprise, so mum's the word, okay?" He held his finger to his lips and made a *'shh'* noise. Then he winked and strode off.

For just a second, Cas caught Paul the valet's eye, and he had the strangest look on his face. It was almost like panic. But then he too was gone.

"Did anything about that strike you as odd?" asked Cas. He couldn't put his finger on it, but…something was giving him pause for thought.

Wren, however, shrugged. "Nah. It's Ben. He's probably already been on the blueberry vodka." He cackled. "Anyway, I was looking into American species of roses, and they have this big fat red one called a Knock Out, which I think you guys might love, and-"

"Whoa, whoa, whoa!" Cas cried, throwing up his hands and laughing. "Slow down there, Wren. I'm not Leo. I'm not announcing any *engagement* tomorrow night. Matty doesn't need his own rose, okay?"

Wren's grin was sly, and made all of Cas's usual fears around his brother's mischievous ways come flooding back. "Yet," he said, walking backward with a dangerous sparkle in his eyes. "Not engaged *yet*. But these things take time to breed. You'll thank me later."

"Wren," Cas pleaded. "We haven't even tried *dating* yet."

But Wren just turned, walking forward and waving a hand over his head. "Trust me, big bro. I know what I'm doing."

Cas chewed his lip and watched him disappear around the corner, leaving Cas all alone. For a second, his thoughts competed to overwhelm him.

And then he let them all go.

He took a deep, slow breath, and smiled as he exhaled. It wasn't his job to try and juggle everything anymore. His brothers were always going to be trouble in one way or another, he suspected, but that wasn't Cas's responsibility to fix. In fact, without his fussing, he hoped they might actually be starting to flourish. And with the permission of his father, that meant Cas had the blessing from the palace to go and do the same.

All that was left was to go and find out what Matty felt about the whole situation now they had all the facts.

Cas didn't walk back down to his car.

He ran.

Chapter Seventeen

MATTY

"Uncle Matty!" Finley cried as she ran across the grass, throwing herself into Matty's arms. "You made it!"

Matty sighed and hugged her tightly. "Of course, Nibblet! I wouldn't miss it for the world! Are you all ready? You look ready to kick butt! And this is so cool!"

He indicated the stadium that was apparently normally used for the school's lacrosse games. Although, with its wooden stalls and flags flying everywhere, Matty would have been more prepared for a game of Quidditch to start than anything else. Finley gestured eagerly at the row of targets that had been set up, reminding Matty of what they were really here for. It was early enough that lots of parents and other spectators were still milling around on the grounds, safe from any of the arrows that would be flying around later.

"It's *amazing!*" Finley hissed, jumping up and down in excitement. Someone had braided her black hair, so with the bow she'd be holding shortly, she really would look like a mini

Katniss Everdeen. "Everyone here is *so* good." She chewed her lip, suddenly anxious. "I might not even *win*," she whispered.

Matty kneeled down and smiled as he looked her in the eye. "And that's okay, Nibblet. Have you had fun this last couple of weeks?"

Finely blinked her eyes, looking like she was really giving his question some thought. "Yes," she finally decided.

"And do you think you've learned a couple of things?"

Finley gasped. "Oh, yes, *so* much!"

Matty grinned and squeezed her shoulders. "Then all you have to do is your best. You know your moms and I love you, no matter what. You're our shining star, so full of talent! I need to shake some out so I can have a little bit!" She squealed in delight as he tickled her sides. "Wow, yeah, I feel more talented already!"

"No, Uncle Matty!" she cried between her giggles. "I need it! I want to win!"

He grinned and pulled her into a hug. "Now you go out there and give them hell, all right, Nibblet? You show 'em how we do it in Queens."

She struck a pose like a ninja, still giggling. But then suddenly she gasped and looked up at Matty seriously. "But...what about *you*?"

Matty arched an eyebrow. "I don't think they'll let me compete," he joked. "I'm too old."

"*No*," said Finley emphatically. She grabbed his hand with

both of hers and swung on it. "With you and *Cas!* I got your voicemail from his phone saying you'd lost yours, and my teacher told me not to talk to anyone who asked about you guys! Why would anyone ask about you and Cas?"

Matty bit his lip. He'd really hoped they could have waited until afterward to discuss this, because he wasn't sure what the hell to say. He felt a hundred times better now everything was out in the open between him and Cas, and they knew where they stood. But he still didn't know if they were *allowed* to have a relationship. There was still a strong chance that Matty might never see Cas again. His stomach plummeted at the mere thought.

But then he remembered that last red-hot kiss in the car, and how Cas had looked him in the eye and promised faithfully that they'd see each other later, so Matty clung to that hope. Depending on how his meeting went with the king, Cas was supposed to be here to judge the graduation tournament today. But after the rollercoaster they'd been on over the past couple of days, he didn't want to bank on anything.

"It's complicated, Nibblet," he said eventually. "But Cas and I are still friends, and we're hoping to make things less complicated real soon."

Finley narrowed her eyes at him. "Yeah, but are you *boyfriends?*" she asked shrewdly.

Matty spluttered out a laugh. "There's no fooling you, is there," he mumbled, rubbing his eyes. "Uh, that's the complicated part, hon. But we like each other very much."

"Then why's it complicated?" Finley demanded.

"That's a fair question," a new voice chimed in.

Matty snatched his hand away from his eyes, blinking against the sunshine at the woman who had materialized out of nowhere.

This time, he recognized her.

"Ida von Tarr?" Matty said warily to the blonde reporter smiling at him.

She had her hands clasped in front of her thighs, her phone clutched in one of them. He wondered if she was recording what they were saying on that voice recorder she'd waved in his and Cas's faces before. Just because he couldn't see it, didn't mean it wasn't stashed somewhere on her person. From what Cas had said about her, he wouldn't be surprised. Her red nails shone in the summer sun, and she squinted at him without any sunglasses on. Her smile seemed quite fixed.

"Hi, sweetie," she said, ignoring Matty's inquiry over her name. She bent down and offered out her hand. "You must be Matty's niece, Finley. I've heard so much about you."

Finley frowned and stepped behind Matty. "From who?"

Von Tarr laughed like tinkling bells, standing up as if her handshake hadn't just been snubbed by an eight-year-old. "Aren't you adorable? I'm sure your mother wishes she could be here."

Anger flared in Matty. How dare this poisonous woman have the audacity to mention Reghan. "No comment, von Tarr," he said firmly.

The reporter batted her blonde eyelashes at him. "I haven't even asked any questions yet, Mr. Doyle."

"Finley! Finley!"

Matty turned as several other children called out his niece's name. He'd expected them to be other archery students. But with a lurch he recognized the familiar faces of their moms first, as Shommie and Esosa weaved through the crowd with their gaggle of kids.

Finley squealed and rushed to meet her friends. Matty's heart leapt. If ever he needed backup, it was now. "Shommie, Esosa," he said weakly.

"Matty Doyle!" Shommie cried and wagged a finger. "Why haven't you been answering your texts?"

Esosa reached him first and yanked him into a momma bear hug. "You've been in the *papers! The internet!*"

"Why didn't you tell us Cas was *Prince Cassander?*" Shommie demanded as her sister let Matty go. "What the hell?"

Esosa nodded. "You can bet I'm *really* jealous of you now."

Matty was almost excited to tell them everything for a second, but then he remembered who he'd just been talking to. He scowled and glared at von Tarr, who was taking everything in with a *very* interested expression on her face. "Excuse us," Matty said, trying to move his friends away.

But von Tarr leapt into action, literally jumping in front of him and holding her phone up, abandoning all pretense that she hadn't been recording him. He should have realized she could use that in place of the voice recorder. *Damn.* From out of nowhere, a large man appeared with a huge professional camera, the lens pointed in Matty's face. Matty had no doubt he'd been snapping shots from a distance, the realization making him feel sick.

"I absolutely did not give you permission to record my niece,"

Matty snapped. He stepped in front of Shommie and Esosa, who suddenly looked very confused. "I have nothing to say to you. You've violated my rights, and I will be suing both you and the Daily Chronicle."

Von Tarr hummed in amusement, her smile still big and false. "Oh, Americans," she said with a chuckle. "Perhaps your British friends here would like to give a comment on your affair with our beloved Prince Cassander?" She tutted and shook her head. "It really was wicked, the way you seduced him like that."

Matty's guts dropped. That wasn't true, but if that was what everyone thought, what was the use in trying to deny it? He was just one small voice against the tide of bullshit they'd inferred or made up about him.

"Uh," said Shommie, holding up a single finger with its long, colorfully painted nail. "Who is this?"

"Do you remember when someone found my phone when we were at the café?" Matty asked grimly. "It was Ida von Tarr who pickpocketed it off me in the first place. She bugged it to spy on me and Cas."

Von Tarr gasped and placed her free hand on her chest. "I would *never* do such a thing, Mr. Doyle," she said, scandalized. "That's illegal."

Matty gritted his teeth. He wanted to yell at her that he'd had no idea that Cas had been a prince until she'd broken her hateful story, but he didn't want to admit that fault between them. She didn't need any more information to attack their relationship with.

Before he could open his mouth and say something dumb,

Shommie and Esosa stepped around either side of him. "Oh," said Esosa, tilting her head. "You're a pap, are you?"

"We don't care much for paparazzi in the UK," Shommie added cheerfully, but her smile didn't reach her eyes. "Vultures, the lot of you. In fact, here's a quote for you. How about you take that camera and shove it up your-"

"Shommie!" Matty cried, before his new friend could also get herself embroiled in an international incident.

"Why don't you run along now," said Esosa more diplomatically, shooing at von Tarr with her hand, "and leave our friend alone."

Von Tarr didn't move an inch, though. She was still smiling like a deranged mannequin. "Ladies. Mr. Doyle. May I remind you that this is a free country. *My* country. I have every right to report the news to Rosavia." She put on a look of deep sadness and clutched her hand to her chest in a fist. "You are merely guests in Alpina. Whereas the good people of Rosavia are counting on me to let them know what kind of person is hoodwinking their beloved prince. They deserve the truth!"

"Yes, they do."

Matty's heart almost stopped as relief flooded through him. He'd recognize that voice in a *heartbeat.*

As he turned, the crowd was parting like the Red Sea. Through the gap walked Cas, dressed to the nines in a gorgeous suit, his gaze laser-focused on von Tarr. People were gaping as he approached. Shommie and Esosa's mouths dropped open. And suddenly their kids reappeared, chasing after Finley.

Who threw her arms around Cas's waist and shrieked as she hugged him. "Cas!"

He stopped immediately and looked down at her before smiling and resting his hand on top of her head. "Hey, Finley," he said warmly. "I told you I'd be back."

"Your Highness," said von Tarr breathlessly, her massive fake smile back on her face. "Care to make a comment? I was just discussing your relationship with Mr. Doyle here. What do you have to say to the people of Rosavia? Why hasn't the palace released a statement yet? Surely they can't endorse" - she waved her hand back and forth between them- "this completely inappropriate scam?"

Cas straightened his spine and offered Finley his hand. She released him from her hug and took it, and the two of them walked over to von Tarr. The sun flashed on the camera lens as it swung to follow Cas as he stopped in front of the journalist. Esosa and Shommie's heads turned, their kids clustered around them. The growing throng gathered around them seemed to be collectively holding its breath.

Then Cas smiled, and extended his other hand out.

Toward Matty.

"I would like to introduce the people of Rosavia to my dear friend, Matty, and his lovely niece, who is here competing at the archery tournament today. She's a very talented young lady." He gave von Tarr a look that one might reserve for a naughty child. "However, your report yesterday was full of quite a few inconsistencies, Ms. von Tarr." He tutted. "Your readers expect better of you, I'm sure."

She blinked, clearly thrown by Cas's response to her questions. "So...Mr. Doyle isn't your secret lover?" she challenged, the gleam back in her eye as she sensed blood in the water.

Matty's heart was racing in anticipation of Cas's response. Surely he'd have to lie. Or denounce Matty there and then.

Except he did neither. He took Matty's hand in his own, and rubbed the knuckles with his thumb as he smiled at Matty with such warmth. "You can be my everything, if that's what you want?" he murmured, so quiet Matty wondered if anyone else could hear. "Because that's what I want. More than anything. We're allowed."

Suddenly, as if by magic, it was as if they were back in their little bubble, just the two of them in the whole world. Except...this was no longer a fantasy.

Cas had just asked Matty if he wanted this to be their reality. He wanted to stop playing a part and be his own man.

With Matty.

"Y-yes," he whispered back, squeezing Cas's hand as tears sprung into his eyes. "Yes, Cas. That's what I want."

He could weather any storm, take any lies the media wanted to accuse him of. If he was with Cas, he could rise above it all, come rain or shine. He'd protect his family, and they would be stronger as one. Nothing could stop them if he and Cas were together.

Cas's smile was like a rainbow after the rain. "Yes?" he repeated in a whisper.

Matty giggled with relief. *"Yes,"* he confirmed emphatically. They held each other's gazes and hands for a second. It was as if in that moment, Matty could see his whole, glorious future unfolding like the petals of a beautiful blue rose.

"Secret?" Cas announced loudly, looking back at von Tarr with such happiness Matty almost felt faint. "No. In fact, King Alphonse and Queen Aubrey have just given me permission to invite Matty to our celebrations tomorrow night for the country's anniversary ball." He raised Matty's hand, then placed a gentle kiss on the back of it. "As my official plus one and partner."

Matty's vision threatened to black out as the crowd gasped and burst into a wild buzz of chatter, tightening around them even closer. Von Tarr gaped like a goldfish, and Finley squealed.

"Are you boyfriends *now?*" she demanded above all the commotion. She was still holding Cas's hand, so when she grabbed Matty's, it made a little circle between them.

Matty looked down at her, then back up at Cas. Shock was stopping his brain connecting with his mouth. But then he registered the naked hope in Cas's eyes.

"If that's what your Uncle Matty wants," Cas said softly. His gaze on Matty was unwavering. "The palace has given its blessing. We can take it slowly, but-"

He might have had more to say after that. More reasons why Matty should think really carefully about whether or not dating a prince was what he truly wanted. Except Matty didn't want to hear them, and had already let go of Finley to yank on Cas's hand, jerking him forward to crash into Matty's mouth as he lunged forward for what felt like the kiss of his life.

The crowd roared. Shommie and Esosa whooped and clapped. Finley squealed again. And Cas cupped his hands on either side of Matty's face, kissing him back with the force of a hurricane.

By the time they resurfaced, von Tarr had a face on her like she'd been sucking lemons. But Matty hardly noticed. He was just looking at Cas, who was grinning down at him.

"That's a yes to all this lot, then?" Cas asked, not so subtly jerking his head toward von Tarr.

Matty laughed as the ruckus continued around him. He got the impression that the Rosavian people were very much in support of their prince, and couldn't care less what the nasty journalist had to say.

"Yes, it's a yes," Matty said. "Yes to the ball, yes to boyfriends, yes to *you*, Cas. I don't care how scary that is." He also indicated von Tarr. "So long as what we have is *real*. If that's what comes with it, so be it."

Cas hugged him tightly. When Finley huffed loudly, they both laughed and stepped apart enough so that Cas could pick her up and sit her on his hip. "I'm sorry, Nibblet," said Matty. "We hijacked your tournament."

She sighed and patted his shoulder. "It's okay, I forgive you. But only because I like Cas."

Matty smiled at his *boyfriend*. "I like Cas, too," he told her.

After that, things calmed down. The event staff managed to disperse the crowd and get things rolling on the tournament again. Von Tarr was told she could stay if she was actually reporting on the kids, but surprise, surprise, she didn't have the proper clearance, and security looked positively gleeful about escorting her and her cameraman off the Elm Willows premises.

Finley was whisked off to go get ready, but a frazzled-looking woman approached Cas wringing her hands. "Your Highness," she began apprehensively. "I know you were supposed to be part of the adjudication team today. But, uh, unfortunately, the rules state, um…"

Cas didn't seem the least bit bothered by her hesitation. In fact, Matty watched in confusion as he grinned. "But now I'm considered biased," he suggested, hugging Matty to his side and smiling at him. "Because one of the contestants is family?"

Family? Matty's eyes threatened to fill with happy tears. Did Cas really consider Matty's family his own already? Now there was nothing standing in between them, was he really jumping into their relationship that quickly?

Apparently so. And Matty loved it.

The woman let out a big sigh of relief. "Thank you so much for understanding, Your Highness. We want to make sure everything is fair for the children. They've worked so hard. Can we offer you and your partner a VIP box to watch from instead?"

A VIP box? Damn, this school really was fancy.

Cas didn't seem fazed, though, presumably because he'd spent several years here. Perhaps the king and queen had come to watch him play lacrosse from such a box?

Cas smiled politely and effortlessly. He really did look like a statesman, used to dealing with public relations. "That sounds wonderful, thank you. But only if my boyfriend's friends can join us. Is that all right?"

Shommie and Esosa had been gossiping fervently nearby, but they were rendered mute, if only for a second or two, at being acknowledged by one of Rosavia's princes. "Us?" Shommie squeaked.

Esosa elbowed her. "We'd be *honored*, wouldn't we, kids?" Their brood clapped and whooped in delight, making Matty laugh.

"Are you sure?" he murmured into Cas's ear. "They're very rowdy."

Cas just grinned at him, though. "I love kids, sweetheart," he said, kissing his cheek. "I want some myself, one day. That's probably something you should know, maybe?"

Holy crap. Matty figured that answered his question about how committed Cas was to him already. He'd just announced that someday, he wanted to be a father.

Matty wondered how long he should wait before slipping into the conversation that he *also* wanted to have kids down the line. When he met the right guy.

Had he?

He watched Cas's smiling face as they were all shown to a room at the top of the stalls for them all to fit comfortably in. How long would Matty get now to study every expression?

A lifetime?

Now who was rushing in with both feet? Matty shook his head at himself and helped himself to the refreshments that appeared out of nowhere. The kids were given juice and ice cream, while the adults were lavished with sparkling wine and canapés.

"Wow, mate," said Esosa to Matty, leaning in so she wouldn't be overheard. "I can't even be jealous anymore. I'm just so happy for you. You did *good.*"

"Thanks," said Matty gratefully. "I'm so glad you guys are here to share this with."

She winked. "Of course. That's what mates are for."

He was still a little shaky with adrenaline, but mostly that was wearing off and had been replaced with excitement. He and Cas were going to have a real shot at being a couple. Matty still wasn't sure what that would entail, but he wasn't too worried.

He and Cas would figure it out.

With thunderous applause from the crowd, the tournament began. Matty pressed up to the glass, filming every second of Finley as she competed, so Reghan and Lola could watch at home in New York. Cas came and stood beside him, resting his hand on the small of Matty's back.

That simple gesture said *'He's mine.'* And Matty loved it.

When it came to the results, Matty video-called his sister so they could all watch together, and they all screamed when Finley got the silver in her age category. *Silver!* Matty cried, he was so incredibly proud of her. And he had Cas rubbing his back and grinning along with him, sharing in the triumph with Matty's family and new friends.

It was perfect.

But it was also noisy and nonstop. So when the tournament was over and Matty went to go find Finley to congratulate her, he was glad that the school stadium was starting to empty out. The kids had a full day of fun and games tomorrow to wind down from all their hard work, and then Matty was supposed to pick Finley up on Monday morning, ready for their flight home.

Not leaving him and Cas much time to work out what they were going to do moving forward.

Matty felt like an awkward teenager after a school dance, not sure if he should hold hands or kiss his date. Or if they were even going to go home together.

There was a lot he didn't know.

"Hey," Cas's voice murmured in his ear after they'd first waved goodbye to Finley, then Shommie, Esosa, and their kids. They were still surrounded by people who kept looking their way as they went past, and no doubt Cas's security detail wasn't that far away. But for the first time since the kiss in Cas's car in front of the apartment, Matty felt like he could breathe, and all he really had to worry about was him and Cas.

"Hey," he said back, trying to calm his nerves. This was Cas. He didn't have anything to fear, not really. Or did he?

"Everything okay?" Cas asked, probably picking up on Matty's slight apprehension.

Matty laughed and nodded. "Yes. There's just a lot of things to think about." He puffed out his cheeks. "What happens now?"

Cas sighed and brushed back one of Matty's always wild-curls. The fingers of his other hand were threaded with Matty's, and he rubbed his knuckles soothingly. "Some alone time, to talk?" he suggested. "I thought we could head back home. Have some dinner and start thinking about the future."

Matty relaxed, relief coursing through his body. "Going back to the apartment sounds like a dream," he admitted. "I, um, I wondered if I'd ever see it again."

Cas bit his lip, a look of concern flashing briefly across his face.

"Um…no," he said carefully. Then he took Matty's other hand so he was holding them both. "Not the apartment."

"Then where…?" Matty began to ask.

Then the penny dropped. He gulped.

"Oh," he managed to whisper.

He couldn't help but gape through the window of Cas's car as they approached the palace. This was on every *Top Ten Things To Do In Alpina!'* list, for crying out loud. Most people came here to watch the changing of the guards.

And now Matty was about to walk through the front door.

"Are you really sure about this?" he asked for the tenth time. He was trying to be confident, but he was wearing jeans, a T-shirt, and sneakers. Hardly formal attire.

Cas pulled his car up the drive. "Absolutely, sweetheart," he said, smiling over at Matty. "No more hiding, remember?"

Matty nodded, trusting that Cas knew what he was doing. People in matching uniforms approached the vehicle even before they'd fully stopped. Once Cas killed the engine, they opened the doors for both Cas and Matty, bowing as they stepped out of the car. Matty tried his best not to look too bewildered.

Once Cas took his hand, it became much easier to breathe and relax. *I'm not an imposter. I belong here.* If he kept repeating it, perhaps he'd really believe it.

For the first time since this whole messy business had turned his life upside down, Matty actually felt a thrill of excitement. His boyfriend was a *prince!* They were walking into a *palace!* Matty was living in a *dream!* Except Matty knew Cas was as real and true as they came.

As they stepped into the cool marble foyer of the palace, they were greeted by a woman in her late thirties with red curls tumbling past her shoulders, a crisp suit, and shiny pumps with pencil-thin three-inch heels. She looked at Cas with a strange mixture of fondness, pride, and a glint in her eye that suggested she wanted to also give him hell.

"Your Highness," she said, dipping her head slightly. When her eyes flicked back up, they went straight to Matty, giving him the warmest smile. "Mr. Doyle. It's an honor to make your acquaintance."

"You know you want to add a 'finally' to that," Cas grumbled as he placed his hand on Matty's back and indicated the red-headed woman. "Matty, this is Valentina, my dear friend and valet. Basically, my life wouldn't happen without her. And

Valentina, this is Matty Doyle." He beamed down at Matty. "I realized my life wouldn't happen without him, either."

Matty was tempted to feel overwhelmed with emotion, but he was done being surprised with Cas's love. From now on, he was going to treasure it. He trusted Cas and believed his words. He didn't want to live without Matty.

And Matty felt exactly the same way about Cas.

Matty reached over and shook hands with Valentina. As he expected, she had a firm, no-nonsense grip. "I could have told him that days ago," she told him in a conspiratorial tone. "Can I count on you to keep knocking some sense into him from now on?"

Matty laughed. "Absolutely," he promised.

"Good." She nodded once and dropped his hand. She'd been holding a leather portfolio in the other, and now she clasped it with both hands in front of her. "I have some official business to discuss with His Highness regarding the Royal Ball, but that can wait until tomorrow. In the meantime, Your Highness, your suite has been prepared for you." She waggled her eyebrows. "It's *fully* stocked."

With that, she spun on her heels, click-clacking away and out of sight.

"What does that mean?" Matty asked.

Cas snorted. "I'm pretty sure that means there will be *several* bottles of blueberry lube waiting for us."

Matty choked in shock. That wasn't what he'd been expecting him to say at all. But then shock was quickly replaced by lust.

They'd had a ton of spectacular sex in Cas's city apartment. They'd made love the night before in the cabin after baring their souls. But now they were an official couple. Boyfriends for all the world to see. And Matty was in Cas's damned palace, about to go to the room he actually lived in, not the apartment he used for an escape. This was his *home*.

Like he'd thought on the palace steps: this was as real as it got.

How many first times was Matty going to get with Cas? It was like their relationship was never going to stop being full of wonder and surprise. And he loved it.

"Well," he said flirtatiously, slipping his hand back into Cas's. "Don't you think we should go find out just how much blueberry lube there is? Maybe do a quality-control test?"

Cas hummed, his eyes suddenly darkening with want and desire. He leaned down, capturing Matty's lips in a kiss that felt far too filthy to be shared out in the open. And yet, Matty didn't care. They were done hiding. "Excellent point, Mr. Doyle," Cas growled. "Let me give you a tour of the palace."

"Starting with your bedroom?" Matty asked hopefully.

"Starting with my bedroom," Cas agreed.

Chapter Eighteen

CAS

Matty was in the royal palace. It should have felt so wrong, but it was the rightest thing Cas had seen in a long time. Matty had come into his heart and made him feel whole, and now he'd stepped into his home and brought it to life.

Cas watched, overflowing with love, as Matty's head swiveled back and forth, drinking in the opulence of the palace, not with fear or self-doubt, but with excitement and joy. Sure, he almost certainly still had some apprehension around Cas's royal status. He'd definitely given off a slightly panicked vibe when they'd talked more in the car about the ball and meeting the rest of Cas's family. But whenever Matty looked like he might be about to spiral, Cas just took his hand or kissed him, and he would calm again.

Cas didn't want him to feel out of place. He belonged here. What was the point of dating a prince if he didn't get to enjoy all the unbelievable perks that came with it? In time, hopefully Matty would come to see these walls and the centuries of history within them as an everyday occurrence.

But it was understandable that the first time might be a little overwhelming.

"Do you like it?" Cas asked, squeezing Matty's hand as they walked closer to Cas's suite.

Matty blinked, as if coming out of a reverie. "Like it?" he said in confusion. "Cas, it's incredible! All these works of art and chandeliers and carpets so thick I want to sleep on them. The history is awe-inspiring, and it's just so beautiful! Who in their right mind wouldn't love it?"

Cas bumped their shoulders and smiled warmly at him. "I don't care about anyone else's opinion, I care what *you* think, sweetheart."

Matty blushed. "I think it's stunning. I still can't quite believe I'm here."

Neither could Cas. But he couldn't be happier. He'd gone from thinking he and Matty could only have a couple of weeks in their little bubble, to thinking he'd lost him forever... to daring to dream that they might have a real future together.

Cas was getting ahead of himself. They had time to dwell on that and talk it all through. But right now, they had other more pressing matters at hand. Matty might have gotten swept up in his wonder of the palace, and Cas in his wonder of Matty, but now they were at Cas's door, and more primal urges were taking over.

Cas hummed as he pulled Matty in for a kiss. They tumbled through the door together, laughing like giddy, horny teenagers, and then Cas very firmly locked the door behind him. They didn't have to hide away anymore...but there were still things that he wanted to be *completely* private between them.

Matty grinned from ear to ear as he turned on the spot, absorbing the view of Cas's rooms. True, Cas had worked with the palace's interior designer to keep them traditional, but there were also a lot of personal touches from his life, especially his travels. The city apartment might have been his secret space, but he'd kept it purposefully neutral to try and trick himself into forgetting who he really was.

But now, he didn't have to forget. Cas got to be the man who fell in love and no longer had to hide. He didn't have to pretend to be a watered-down version of himself. And that was all because of beautiful Matty, who was currently looking at Cas's fan collection from Japan and mosaic art from Thedes. "You've done so much," he said in wonder.

But Cas shook his head. "There's a difference between traveling and living." He made a come-hither motion for Matty to hold his hand. Matty skipped over willingly, smiling excitedly. "You brought me to life, sweetheart," Cas murmured. "Maybe someday we can travel together?"

"I'd love that." Matty ghosted his lips over Cas's lips, looking through his long black eyelashes. "I love you," he whispered, like it was a secret. But they had no more secrets, and Cas had never felt freer.

"I love *you*," Cas repeated, tugging Matty toward his bedroom. The four-poster bed was a couple of centuries-old, and the blue velvet drapes at least several decades. But the mattress was pretty new, thank goodness. Cas hoped it was going to get a *lot* of use in the near future.

He and Matty had made love in the dark and the light, they'd fucked wildly and they'd gently tended to one another. But Cas was starting to appreciate that his favorite intimate moments with his lover were when they just let the hell go and had fun. As they stumbled toward the bed, kissing messily, they fumbled to pull the other's clothes off. Matty had already made quick work of Cas's suit jacket and tie, which were strewn on the floor like a trail of breadcrumbs, along with both their shoes and three-quarters of their socks. But as Matty divested Cas of his shirt and slung it on the bed, there was a loud, indignant 'meow!' and a silver ball of fluff shot out from under the garment in indignation.

Matty suddenly lost interest in Cas's lips and gasped. "Bella!" he cried, reaching for her.

Cas had forgotten how many photos he'd shown Matty of his beloved cat. He showed no fear as he stroked her fur and cooed over her. As usual, sensing she was about to be adored, Bella flopped on her back and immediately began purring like a car engine as Matty petted her belly.

"Who's a beautiful kitty, hmm?" Matty asked in delight.

As Matty fussed over Bella, Cas caressed Matty's neck and ran his fingers through his hair, delighted when he visibly shivered. "You're so sweet," he murmured. "Can you be my beautiful kitty?"

Matty threw his head back and laughed, then batted his eyelashes at Cas, making his cock thicken in his pants. "I'll be your anything, lover," he rasped.

Cas hummed, his skin electric as he traced his thumb along Matty's square jaw then over his lower lip. Matty's mouth opened, showing his wet, inviting tongue just behind his teeth.

"Sorry, Bella," Cas said, moving swiftly to remove his cat from the room. "We'll pet you later, I promise." He kissed the top of her head before placing her on the floor of his living room. Then he closed the door on her and marched right back to Matty.

Matty, who in those few seconds had stripped his T-shirt, jeans, and remaining sock off, and was now leaning back on his elbows with his feet dangling over the edge of the bed, just off the floor. His dick was hard and bulging against his briefs as he followed Cas's approach with lust-blown eyes.

Cas crowded over him, palming Matty's cock as he kissed him hungrily. Matty moaned and gasped as Cas squeezed and rubbed his erection. Their eyes were open just a sliver, watching each other as they kissed sloppily. "What do you want, lover?" Cas asked.

"You," Matty replied immediately with a grin, running his hands up Cas's torso. "I want to be your fantasy."

Cas hastily undid his trousers and kicked them off. Within seconds, he was lying on top of Matty, their underwear the only thing between their hot bodies.

He kissed Matty and carded his fingers through his hair, slowing the pace for a second. "You might have started off as my daydream, Matty," he said sincerely. "But now *you're* real life. You know that, don't you?"

"Yes," Matty replied happily, his fingers skimming up and down Cas's back. Their eyes met. "I really do, Cas. Thank you for letting me into your life. I know you like taking care of me – and you're *very* good at it." He grinned and prodded Cas's chest. "But I want to take care of you, too, okay?"

Cas laughed and nuzzled their noses together. "I feel so calm with you," he mused, kissing Matty's neck. His skin tasted of sunshine and salt and Matty's own tangy musk. "Of course you take care of me. And I don't just mean in the kitchen."

"Oh my god!" Matty said with a cackle. "It makes so much sense now! I couldn't work out how you could be so hopeless, but you've had people cooking for you your whole damn life!"

Cas tickled his ribs and bit his earlobe. "Shut up," he said playfully as Matty giggled and squirmed.

But then he grabbed either side of Cas's face and kissed him hard. "Will they let me cook for you here, though? You don't have a kitchen in the suite, do you?"

Cas caressed the side of his face, deeply touched. "We'll work something out. The future is an open road."

Matty sighed contentedly, flopping under Cas with his hands above his head, totally open and wanton and *Cas's*. "It is, isn't it?"

Cas nodded, then kissed his lips, feeling the smile playing on Matty's mouth. He fully realized in that moment that their ticking clock had been taken away. Yes, Matty would probably have to fly back to New York after the ball, but then they had options. Cas was no longer in a mild panic about how long they had together before it was all over.

Potentially, they now had forever to discover each other's bodies.

All Cas wanted now was to look at Matty and memorize him. He didn't want to spend hours teasing him or switching between several positions or anything like that. He just wanted to see him, and for them to exist in delicious simplicity.

"Is there anything in particular you want now, sweetheart?" Cas asked.

Matty smiled, slightly dazed, and shook his head. Cas was sure that some time soon he wanted to push Matty a little and get him to ask Cas for his deepest desires, but Cas knew a big part of what Matty loved was being at Cas's whim. So, for now, they would just play out Cas's wishes in glorious, real-life Technicolor. Later, Cas would see what he could help Matty ask for, just like he'd helped him to say all those wonderful truths about himself.

"You're so perfect, Matty," Cas whispered, licking and kissing at one of his nipples, their gazes still joined. "What are you?"

Matty giggled fondly. "Perfect, Cas."

Cas grinned. "Thank you, sweetheart. You're so good for me."

Matty hummed and let his eyes flutter shut as Cas moved further down, kissing Matty's belly and slipping off his briefs. He nuzzled his nose through his dark curls, then kissed and licked at the base of Matty's hard, red hot shaft. Matty whimpered and arched his back as Cas fondled his heavy balls. "More," he begged.

Cas obliged, wrapping his lips over the tip and swallowing him whole, gliding his tongue over Matty's gorgeous cock, the pre cum mixing with Cas's saliva. He pulled off again, despite Matty's pout and groan of disappointment. But Cas just laughed and leisurely jerked his slippery length as he moved to kiss Matty's lips. "Can you stay hard for me, sweetheart? While you ride me? I want you to climb on top of me and fuck my cock with your pretty little ass." He bit Matty's lip and squeezed his shaft hard. "Then, I want to watch you come all over me."

Matty panted and grappled to get a purchase on Cas's back which, like the rest of his skin, was slick with perspiration. "Yes, please. Do we have to use a condom?"

Cas blinked. "Don't you want to?"

Matty bit his lip, swollen from Cas's kisses and nips. "I got tested right after I was…when I became single. You?"

Cas took a moment to brush back one of Matty's curls. "We have regular check-ups. I should be totally fine, but-"

Matty surged up and kissed Cas, hard. "I trust you," he rasped, flopping back against the bed covers. "I want you to feel me. I want your cum inside me, for real. If you think it's safe."

Cas took a slow breath, then nodded. They were consenting adults, and he knew his own status for sure. He trusted Matty, and he wanted there to be *nothing* between them. This time, it felt important.

"Okay," he said, feeling a little lightheaded and excited. "I want that, too."

Matty grinned, kissing Cas's mouth a few times. "What else do you want, Cas?"

"Well…" Cas waggled his eyebrows and reached for his bedside drawer. He'd almost forgotten Valentina's promise until he opened it. He burst out laughing.

"What?" Matty asked, grinning just as much he raised up on his elbows to see as Cas indicated the drawer. It was packed with half a dozen bottles of the same blueberry lube as before – along with fluffy handcuffs, dildos, cock rings, butt plugs, the works. "Oh my god!" Matty cried. He dropped back on the bed, covering his face in apparent mortification. "Your *valet* bought you all of that?"

Cas chuckled, grabbing the top bottle of lube and ignoring the rest of the toys. They had plenty of time to play, and he still wanted this time – their first time as boyfriends – to be relatively simple. "It's her way of saying 'go for it.' It means she likes you and wants me not to fuck it up."

Matty dropped his hands as Cas hovered over him again, leaning up to kiss him sweetly. "You're allowed to fuck up a little," he whispered. "We both are. We don't have to be perfect. Perfect isn't real."

Cas sighed and just rested their foreheads together for a second. "Bullshit," he said with a laugh. *"You're* perfect, remember?"

They laughed and kissed for a few minutes, but Cas didn't want either of them flagging too much. So he soon had his underwear off, and spent a while playing with both their cocks, lubing them up and generally making Matty squirm. Then he guided Matty's hand, getting him to hold it flat by his hip before he squirted lube all over his fingers. Cas sat up, aware that Matty's eyes were wide as Cas took his hand again, moving it between his legs.

"I want to watch you stretch yourself out," he said. "You're so beautiful, can you do that for me?"

He half expected Matty to balk, but he'd come a long way

since they'd met. Instead, he draped his other hand over his head, his favorite position for Cas, apparently, and kept eye contact as he pushed his middle finger into his hole. His knees were up, and his glistening, rock-hard cock bounced above his belly as he thrust against his hand.

"Like that?"

For a second, Cas couldn't speak. "Y-yes," he rasped, rubbing Matty's belly the way he'd enjoyed before. "Just like that. Jesus Christ, Matty. You look gorgeous."

Matty flushed even more pink than he already was. "You help me," he said. "You found me."

Cas knew he didn't mean in that sporting goods store.

He meant his heart.

Cas bent down to kiss Matty's lips. But he was soon back up, moving further down the bed so he could watch the two fingers Matty now had gliding in and out of himself. Cas caressed the inside of Matty's closest thigh to him, kissing by his knee.

"I think," he said, glancing back up at Matty, "one day soon, I'd like you to use one of those dildos. I'll watch you fuck your ass and touch your cock. I think I'd like to just look on while you take your time to make yourself come for me."

Matty whimpered, utterly disheveled with wild curls every-where and sweat pouring off him. "Cas," he begged.

Cas kissed his thigh again. "Would you like that?" Matty nodded eagerly. "Do you want that now?" Cas had to ask. It wasn't what he'd planned, but Matty seemed to *really* like that idea.

However, Matty shook his head just as vehemently. "Want to ride you, like you promised," he said desperately.

Cas sighed happily. "Of course," he said. "Do you need more time, or-"

"Now!" Matty barked. He whipped his hand from his hole and pushed at Cas's chest with a laugh, rolling them over so Matty was now straddling Cas's hips. "I need your naked cock in my ass now, okay?"

Cas laughed, too, as they hurriedly rearranged. Cas might have gone a little soft, but Matty squirted on a whole load more lube over his cock and jerked him off until he was like steel in Matty's grasp once more. Then he climbed back over Cas, dripping half the damn lube bottle down his ass crack, then lining up his entrance with Cas's throbbing length. The air was potent with blueberries and their mingled musk. Cas could taste the unique flavor on his lips.

Matty gasped and moaned as he sank down. He was hot and tight and – as always – perfect. Cas gritted his teeth and grabbed Matty's hips, feeling every flinch as he slowly bottomed out. "Oh my god," Matty mumbled between gasps. "Jesus Christ, yes, so good. Oh, Cas. *Yes!*"

Cas watched him hungrily as he started to rock and writhe on Cas's dick, grinding it deep inside him. Cas forced himself to stay as still as he could, letting Matty pleasure them both and look after Cas like he'd asked. He also restrained himself from touching Matty's cock just yet, sticking to their original plan. Instead, he ran his palms up Matty's sides, over his shoulders, then down his arms. Matty had his hands braced on Cas's chest, so Cas encircled his wrists and held them tight, pinning him down. He could only be so passive, it seemed.

"You feel incredible," he grunted, his gaze locked with Matty's. "God, sweetheart. So beautiful."

Matty bit his lip and rocked with slow purpose on Cas's cock, making Cas gasp. "Are you going to come in me, Cas?" he asked with a lustful glint in his eyes. "Are you close?"

Cas nodded and squeezed Matty's wrists. "Fuck yourself on me, gorgeous," he rasped.

Matty dropped his head back as he thrust faster and faster, moaning deliciously. Cas should have probably told him to keep it down. Sound traveled like a devil along these stone hallways. But he didn't care. He'd been the good son who'd never caused any trouble his whole life. He was allowed to have sex with his stunning boyfriend in his own damn bedroom.

"Close," he managed to utter, gritting his teeth. He chased his orgasm, moving his hips as Matty slammed down on him. Then Matty lifted his head back up and looked Cas in the eyes, and that was all it took to send Cas crashing over the edge.

He bellowed as he pulsed deep inside Matty's ass, filling him up and truly claiming him as his own. Matty moaned and gasped, slowing down but still rocking on top of Cas and milking his throbbing cock for every last drop of cum. Cas breathed heavily, slowly coming down from his high, but still hard within Matty. He managed a smile and let go of Matty's wrists to cup either side of his face.

Matty grinned, glistening with sweat and panting as he

leaned down to kiss Cas sweetly on the lips. "Do you want to watch me come on you now?" he asked, waggling his eyebrows.

Cas hummed. "Desperately." He rubbed his thumb over Matty's lower lip, but Matty captured it to suck on while he wrapped his hand around his leaking member and started jerking himself off with fervor.

If he'd been able, Cas would have come again at such an erotic sight. Instead, he drank in every inch of Matty touching himself with Cas still buried inside him. Cas wanted to have a rich and full back catalogue of memories like this to rely on when he and Matty were apart.

"Beautiful," he murmured, rubbing Matty's thigh and pulsing the thumb Matty was still sucking on. "Gorgeous. Perfect. I love you, Matty."

Matty's fist was a blur, and it wasn't long until he arched his back and let go of Cas's thumb with a yell. Thick, creamy ropes spurted over Cas's chest and streaked over the bedsheets, making a glorious mess. After several moments, Matty collapsed on top of Cas, shivering and clinging to Cas's shoulders. Cas rubbed his back and kissed his neck, sated so deeply there was contentment in his bones.

"I've got you, sweetheart," he murmured. They were breathing slowly in tandem. He suspected Matty was matching Cas, so Cas took even bigger breaths, helping them both come down from their highs. "I've got you."

And he meant it in every way possible.

Chapter Nineteen

MATTY

Matty wasn't sure who the guy standing in the mirror was, but he was pretty sure it wasn't Matty Doyle of Queens, New York. It couldn't be. This guy looked like…*somebody*.

He turned left and right, slowly cataloguing all the changes. It had been quite the day. While Cas had been off working on ball preparations, Valentina had invaded Cas's suite and declared that she and Matty were having a spa day.

Matty had thought she'd been joking, but the palace actually had a fully-equipped spa on the premises. He'd wondered what else was hidden in these walls.

He'd gotten a thrill as it sank in that he'd get a chance to find out for himself one day.

For now, though, Valentina had restricted his palace tour to just the spa. He'd had a facial, a massage, his nails had been manicured, and his hair cut and styled. When they'd arrived back at Cas's suite, Valentina had arranged for a portable rack of various suit pieces to be there waiting for him, as well as a tailor ready to jump in and make any necessary adjustments.

And now here Matty was, practically sparkling as he carefully touched one of his curls. The haircut hadn't been drastic – just a trim, really. Now that he'd been looking at the finished result of his whole look for a while, Matty was starting to realize that was true of everything. He wasn't somebody else. He was still Matty. Just a nicely polished version of himself.

His outfit wasn't a showstopper, in that it was just a black suit with a teal and sky-blue patterned tie. But the tie brought out his eyes, making them look like sapphires. The crisp white shirt showed off the color he'd gotten from the sunshine the past two weeks. And the immaculate fit of the suit was anything other than 'just.' He'd owned a couple off-the-rack suits for prom and his sister's wedding, but they'd always felt baggy in the wrong places and too tight in others. This simple two-piece fit him like a glove.

He bit his lip, enjoying the quiet for a moment after all the staff had left him alone to gather his thoughts. Everyone had spoken English around him and made him feel perfectly at ease. Valentina had even arranged for lunch to be brought up for them, so Matty didn't have to worry about nerves on an empty stomach. He swallowed and smoothed down his lapels.

He could do this. He looked like he belonged here, in a palace, going to a fancy ball. Because he *did* belong here. He belonged anywhere Cas was.

But...no. It was more than that. He licked his lips and took a long, slow breath. He had every right to be here today just because of who *he* was.

Cas had chosen him to be in his life because he loved Matty

for who he was deep down. And that was exactly why Matty had chosen Cas. The omission of the full truth might not have been ideal in the beginning for them, but now that the shock had completely worn off, Matty was able to see that it had allowed him to fall head over heels in love with Cas. Not Prince Cassander. As much as he'd like to think he wouldn't have treated Cas any differently, if he was honest, he was sure that he never would have had the confidence to be open with Cas like he had if there had been the added pressure of knowing he was a prince.

For so long, Matty had raged against the universe for being a douchebag to him. But now he was starting to suspect that it had just been biding its time, waiting for the right moment to bring Matty to his destiny at just the right time in just the right way.

He and Cas were fate. A love story written in the stars. And who was Matty to argue with that kind of destiny?

"You look stunning."

Matty had been so lost in his thoughts that he hadn't even sensed Cas reentering the suite, let alone seen him leaning against the doorframe, watching Matty with such warmth and fondness on his face.

Matty grinned, feeling himself blush a little. "Thank you. So do you."

Cas rolled his eyes and laughed as he gave Matty a twirl. "The Rosavian formalwear, everybody!"

Matty knew Cas liked to moan about the black pants with the red rose pattern, but honestly, with the way they clung to his firm ass, Matty was *not* complaining. Besides, coupled with the black jacket embroidered with a subtle black-stitch floral design, black shirt, and black and red rose tie, the whole thing looked sort of Gothic. Like a '00s emo band, in the best kind of way.

Finishing the look was a gem-encrusted crown sitting perfectly on Cas's dark hair. Cas pointed at it with a grin. "Sorry I wasn't here sooner. For some reason, they only just sent me my coronet." He smiled warmly at Matty. "I got changed in one of the guest rooms. I wanted to show you the full effect."

Crown or no crown, Cas looked every inch a prince as far as Matty was concerned. He stepped over to Cas, running his hands down his arms, feeling the exquisite silk under his palms. "I was reading online that the rose pattern is like your version of Scottish kilts and tartan. That each family in Rosavia has their own, unique colors and designs that you wear to all fancy occasions. It's not just for the royal family."

Cas was watching Matty touching his suit with the lightest of brushes. When Matty glanced at him, he was sporting an amused but loving smile. "That's correct," he said.

"So," Matty said casually, hardly believing his own daring, but surprisingly not feeling nervous. He was with Cas, after all. There was nothing to be afraid of. "If we got married, would I get my own rose pattern?"

For a second, Cas's eyes just went wide. Then he broke into a beaming smile. "Yes, you would. You'd get your own royal rose, too."

"Something to complement your pretty blue one?" suggested Matty.

He laid his hand over Cas's breast pocket, just below where one of his gorgeous blue roses had been made into a boutonniere. That also meant his hand was over Cas's heart, and Matty could just feel it thumping, even through his clothes. It was going a little fast, actually.

"Are you okay?" he asked. Oh no. Was Cas having second thoughts?

Of course he wasn't. He chuckled and brought Matty's hand up to kiss his knuckles. "I can't believe I'm going to be able to introduce you to my family in just a few minutes. I feel so lucky that this is really happening."

Matty kissed his lips lightly. "Me, too," he agreed.

Cas tugged on his hand. "Come on. You already look completely scrumptious, but I have a couple of little somethings to add."

Intrigued, Matty allowed himself to be led from Cas's bedroom back out into the living room. There on the tabletop were two black boxes, one about the size of Matty's hand, the other smaller. His own heart rate picked up a little as he wondered what Cas had in store.

Smiling bashfully, Cas picked the bigger box up first. "You would get a rose to complement mine, yes. But until then…" He drummed his fingers on the box. "I know this is an American tradition for prom dances," he said, looking sweetly shy. Cas didn't get flustered. Matty thought it was adorable how much this obviously meant to him. "So, um, this is for you."

He opened the box to reveal a second blue boutonniere exactly like his own. It was Matty's turn for his eyes to widen as tears threatened to pool in them. He blinked them back.

There was no reason to be unsure or overwhelmed. Instead, he allowed himself a huge smile.

"You'd like me to wear your rose?" he asked, double-checking that he wasn't jumping to conclusions.

But Cas also grinned and nodded. "We'll be announced as a couple. But this way, even if we aren't together side-by-side, people will know that we're *together.*"

Matty practically vibrated with pride. "I'd be honored. Thank you." As Cas removed the very nice but now vastly inferior pocket handkerchief from Matty's suit and replaced it with his beautiful boutonniere, Matty was reminded of the hickey still lurking on his collarbone and the scratches on Cas's back from their night at the cabin. Except this was a way to show the whole world that they'd marked each other as their own.

Despite being determined not to get overly emotional, a lump did rise in Matty's throat. He was stepping into a whole new world, and he felt like a Disney princess, living the dream. If he wasn't careful, he was going to burst into song.

"And these," Cas said, picking up the second smaller box, cracking it open. "Are traditional for Rosavian royalty. They've been made by the same jewelers for hundreds of years, and it's a design unique to our family."

Matty stared in awe at the beautifully intricate rose cufflinks that he guessed were made from platinum. The design was so complex for something so small. The petals that folded around one another looked so lifelike, and the stems that wrapped around the bottom had perfect, absolutely tiny thorns.

"You're really letting me borrow these?" he asked.

Cas laughed softly, making Matty look up from the box. "No, sweetheart. These are yours to keep."

Matty's mouth dropped open. "But how did they make them so fast?" It was safer to ask the practical question, rather than nervously questioning if Cas really meant that big a commitment so soon.

Although…they'd already talked about marriage and children. Matty could accept some damn jewelry without fainting.

Cas winked, then carefully removed the first cufflink from where it was nestled. "People around here aren't blind. I think they realized love is well and truly in the air for me and my brothers. So there were some more pairs made recently."

He stepped closer to Matty, lovingly turning his arm and gently removing the other – again, very nice but now completely outdone – cufflink so he could fix his gift to Matty's wrist. After both were secure, Cas put the old ones in the box and closed it, then held Matty's hands in his own. They both admired the way the silver roses glinted in the evening sunshine.

Matty was trembling, ever so slightly. Not from nerves, but purely from happiness. These weren't just cufflinks. They were a promise of the future he and his love had before them.

Cas leaned in and softly kissed Matty's forehead, then released his hands and offered Matty his arm. "Do you, um, want to take a selfie?" he asked, blushing a little. "Seeing as we're about to be announced as a real couple. One last moment in our little bubble?"

Matty's heart swooped with pride and happiness and no small amount of butterflies. He loved it when Cas got a bit nervous, but he loved his suggestion even more. They *were* boyfriends now, and boyfriends took photos as a couple.

"I'd love to," Matty replied bashfully.

Cas jutted his chin back at Matty. "Why don't you take it? Then you could, um, send it to your family?"

Matty had to laugh. Prince Cassander of Rosavia was anxious about making a good impression with Matty's family? He didn't have to worry there. After he'd spoken to his sister and explained everything as best he could, he knew that Finley had gushed to her moms about Matty's new man. They were all thrilled with the way destiny had treated Matty.

But he absolutely wanted to capture this moment, for many reasons. He and Cas were stepping out from the bubble into the world, after thinking they could never last as a couple. And, more to the point, they were looking *hot.*

Cas hugged Matty close as they positioned Matty's phone and took several shots to choose from. But when they looked through them again, they both cried "That one!" at the same time in unanimous agreement. It was the photo where Cas had tickled Matty's side, making them both laugh and look at each other instead of the camera. It was natural and relaxed and utterly perfect.

Matty sent it to his family group chat with the comment *Cinderella is off to the ball!* He bit his lip, still not quite believing that was really true.

But then they straightened themselves out and Cas took Matty's arm again. "Are you ready?" he asked.

This was it. Never mind what von Tarr had been printing in her terrible newspaper. *This* was Cas and Matty's official coming out as a couple.

And Matty was more than ready.

"I am, Your Highness," he said a little breathlessly. It was the first time he'd tried using Cas's official title, and for a second, he questioned if he'd made a mistake.

But Cas's smile didn't falter. In fact, his eyes crinkled and he leaned in to kiss Matty on the lips. This time, though, it was with real heat. "You can call me that," he murmured against Matty's ear, giving the lobe a quick nip, "only if you truly believe that one day I'll be calling you that as well. And so will the rest of Rosavia."

Matty gulped, but he met Cas's gaze as he leaned back again. With a shaky breath, he jutted his head toward the door and squeezed Cas's arm. "Come on. We don't want to be late...*Your Highness.*"

Cas sighed happily before kissing Matty's temple. "No, we don't," he agreed.

The palace thrummed with life as they stepped out into the hallway. Matty could feel the low rumble of hundreds of voices through the floor more than he could hear them. Apparently, it was customary to allow most people to arrive before announcing the royal family, which they did from youngest to oldest. So almost everyone would have arrived by the time he and Cas made their carefully-timed entrance.

Despite his best efforts, the thought of so many dignitaries and international heads of state all looking at him at once was leaving Matty a little lightheaded. He clutched onto Cas's arm, hardly noticing the corridors they were walking down or the footmen leading the way.

At Matty's change in grip, Cas lifted his other hand and rubbed the back of Matty's, kissing his head as he did. "It's going to be absolutely fine," he promised in a low, soothing tone. "I've got you, sweetheart. Remember?"

Matty exhaled shakily and nodded. Cas was there to protect him, not that he should need protecting. But Matty wasn't on his own. "I remember, Cas," he said, feeling a little better.

Cas kissed the top of his head again. "So perfect," he murmured.

The voices were getting considerably louder as they descended a staircase and approached an open set of double doors. Light was spilling out into the hallway, and Matty could feel the air had gotten warmer, so he suspected this had to be the ballroom, filled with people. The sound of crystalware clinking and a melody from a harp mingled in with the constant flow of countless conversations. He and Cas paused as one of the footmen held up a hand, making them wait a few feet from the door, out of sight from the rest of the guests that were already present.

"This is it," Cas said softly. Matty looked up and met his gaze. "Are you ready?"

Matty breathed deeply, then nodded with a smile. "Yes, I am," he said honestly.

Who on earth would have thought that when Matty had stepped off that plane just two weeks ago, this was where he'd end up? If someone were to have told him that losing his luggage would lead to the best thing that had ever happened to him, Matty would have assumed they'd lost their mind.

The footman nodded at Cas. Cas gave Matty a quick kiss on the cheek, his spicy aftershave wafting over Matty and enveloping him. "Just follow my lead," he told Matty.

And then they were standing in the bright light from a dozen chandeliers, each dripping with dazzling crystals that reminded Matty of the waterfall at his and Cas's magical cabin. The room seemed to turn as one, an impossible number of eyes looking to Cas and Matty.

Matty held on to Cas with his head high. He belonged here. Hopefully, in time, he'd get used to the attention. He *might* have even enjoyed it in that moment, just a little.

"Prince Cassander Fabian Ivor van Rosavia and Matty Doyle."

Surprise hit Matty like a truck, but he absolutely refused to show it on his face as he and Cas waited a moment, then began walking down the steps into the ballroom. He'd fully expected the palace to announce him as his full name – Matthew – which he hated. However, they'd gone with his informal, hardly impressive, but much-preferred moniker.

"Matty?" he whispered to Cas as Cas plucked two glasses of Zasfer from a passing tray. Blueberries bobbed in the tall glasses as Cas passed one to Matty.

"Of course," said Cas with a grin. "That's your name. You don't need to pretend to be anyone else for anyone here. You're good enough, just as you are."

Matty bit his lip, bursting at the seams from the praise, then used that pride to fuel his confidence and kiss Cas on the cheek in front of all these important people. "Thank you."

"You're welcome, sweetheart," Cas said warmly.

He placed his free hand on the small of Matty's back, making it abundantly clear to anyone looking their way that they were there as a couple. Matty might have been tempted to look around and see the reactions of the people nearby. After Ida von Tarr's scathing attack on his low birth and accusations of gold digging, there might be those who disapproved.

But Matty realized he didn't care. The only thing that mattered was Cas, and he was looking at Matty like he'd hung the moon.

"Well, look at this disgustingly happy sight," someone cried playfully. Matty turned, only feeling slightly apprehensive as a young-looking man with chestnut brown hair skipped up to them. Judging by his matching formalwear, Matty realized this had to be one of Cas's brothers, and that his family introductions were about to begin.

As much as Matty really did only care about Cas's opinions, he couldn't help the flash of nerves that rushed through him. But they vanished just as quickly as the young guy thrust his hand forward and grinned at Matty.

"I'm Wren, Cas's favorite brother," he announced, waggling his eyebrows as Matty accepted the handshake. "So *you're* the man who finally got the stick out of his ass?"

"Wren," Cas growled, rolling his eyes.

But Wren just batted his eyelashes as he released Matty's hand, then punched Cas lightly on the shoulder. "What? It's a good look on you! Matty, keep doing what you're doing." He winked, and Matty only blushed a little.

"I intend to," he said, looking fondly over at Cas.

"Okay, bleurgh," Wren said with a laugh, waving his hands at them. "That really is disgusting, stop it."

Another man with close-cropped hair who was a little broader and taller than Wren appeared behind him. He touched Wren's lower back, murmuring something into his ear.

It was such an intimate moment, Matty looked away for a second, not wanting to intrude. But the man appeared to have a real calming effect on the young, bouncy prince, diffusing any awkwardness before it even really began.

"Yes, Thom," Wren said softly. Then he turned back to Matty and Cas, and Matty recognized the same manners switching on in Wren as he'd witnessed with Cas. "Cas, you already know my valet, Pierce, but he's here tonight as my date, Thom. And Thom, I'd like you to meet Cas's friend, Matty."

"My boyfriend," Cas corrected swiftly and easily, squeezing Matty's shoulder.

Wren didn't seem to mind being corrected. In fact, he preened. "Oh, yes, *boyfriend*. I knew it."

Thom shook both their hands, then looked curiously at Cas. "So it's officially 'Cas' now, Your Highness?"

Cas nodded. "It suits me much better than 'Sander.'"

A strange mix of pride and awe flushed through Matty. Cas

had been going by 'Sander' before? Had he changed it since meeting Matty? Had Matty been one of the first people to call him by his preferred name – or maybe the very first? He loved that idea.

He didn't get the chance to ask Cas just then, however, as another man approached their little gaggle who was also wearing the royal rose formalwear. His hand was linked with another man's who was dressed in regal, flowing white cotton and a bright blue vest with gold buttons. Judging by his own crown and formalwear, Matty guessed he was also some kind of royalty.

"Matty," said Cas, indicating the new arrivals with his hand. "I'd like you to meet my brother, Jules, and a dear friend of the family, Prince Dante of Thedes."

"It's been a while," said Dante, shaking Cas's hand, while Matty shook with Jules, who winked.

"I'm the terrible middle child I'm sure you've heard about."

Wren blew a raspberry. "Please. Compared to me, Leo, and Ben, you're almost as much of a saint as Cas here."

Jules didn't challenge his younger brother. Instead, his eyes went wide and he looked back at Cas. "Did you hear?"

"Hear what?" Cas asked, sounding nervous.

Wren, however, was practically hopping in glee. "Ben *missed* his announcement."

"No!" gasped Cas.

"Luckily, Dante and I were ready to go, so they just sort of glossed over it. But Ben's a no-show. I don't even think he's back in the country."

Cas frowned at Wren. "No, we saw him yesterday."

"Shhh. He wanted it to be a surprise!" Wren scolded.

Jules tutted and looked out over the crowd. "Knowing him, he'll stagger in drunk and singing the national anthem."

Cas actually paled. "Not again," he rasped.

Matty loved how natural the banter was between them. It reminded him of his own sister. Matty had been able to talk to her on his new phone for a good hour between all his grooming today. It had been a huge relief to tell her the whole truth, and – when she'd gotten over her initial shock – of course she'd teased Matty about not being capable of a casual fling in the slightest. The teasing showed she cared, just like Cas and his brothers. It didn't matter that these guys were royals. They were still real people with family dramas, like anyone else.

But they were also still princes too, and this was their country's big night. So before long, they were interrupted by other dignitaries and diplomats and royals wanting their attention and pulling them in three different directions. Matty watched as Cas's conversations ranged from polite small talk to genuine-sounding catch-ups.

Matty was always surprised when someone spoke directly to him. He was content to just watch Cas and listen in, if he was honest. But the more people who said hello specifically to him, the better he got at his own limited patter of small talk. Most people were more interested in Cas anyway, but then they ran into a Princess Amirah who had once apparently been considered a good match as Prince Leo's potential bride. She didn't seem salty about the way things had turned out.

"Did you see Leo and his fiancé enter?" she said with a giggle before she sipped her Zasfer.

Cas and Matty nodded. They hadn't spoken with the heir to the throne yet, but Matty was sure they would before the night was through.

Princess Amirah's eyes glittered almost as much as her sari as she looked around the room, then back to Matty and Cas. "Leopold van Rosavia, in love with a man. Well, I never." And then she turned to Matty with a big, bright smile. "So, how did you two meet? You're American, aren't you, Matty?"

He swallowed. They hadn't actually discussed what he should and shouldn't say about that, but Cas didn't jump in to speak for him. In fact, he just beamed at Matty, waiting for him to answer. So Matty decided to just keep it simple, but tell the truth.

"My niece is in Alpina for an archery tournament. We happened to bump into His Royal Highness in a sporting goods store in the city. I'm afraid I didn't recognize him to start with – we don't exactly get a lot of Rosavian news in New York. But we just sort of hit it off."

Cas squeezed Matty to his side with a chuckle. "I tried to cook dinner for Matty, and it was a disaster."

"Well, no, it wasn't," Matty corrected playfully, "because I saved the day."

"Oh my god, you two are too adorable," said Princess

Amirah with a sigh. "How long are you in Rosavia for, Matty?"

That burst his bubble pretty quickly. "Oh, um, we fly home tomorrow, actually." It was amazing how the happy tingle in his belly from the wine and good company suddenly fizzled away.

"Actually," said Cas sincerely, "I was hoping to talk to you about that."

Matty blinked, and Amirah cleared her throat. "That sounds like my cue to leave," she said cheerfully. "Oh, look! There's the French ambassador's daughter. I wonder if she'll dance with me?" She winked at Cas and Matty. "Catch you later!"

She melted into the crowd, leaving Cas and Matty. They were hardly alone, but Cas steered Matty by the elbow to a sort of private corner by a huge Thedian vase that Matty could probably fit in, if he felt like climbing all over centuries-old art.

Cas smiled at him warmly and rubbed his arm. Matty tried not to nervously down his entire drink in one go. As confident as he was in his and Cas's relationship, this was still a problem for them. Matty lived four thousand miles away.

"Have you had any thoughts about what you'd like to do regarding the living situation?" Cas asked. "I know this is sudden, but the fact is you don't live in the city. I don't want you disappearing to another continent without at least some plan in place."

Matty smiled. "Me either. But all my relationships before were in New York, and they still failed, so-"

"So, those guys were assholes," Cas said firmly. But he was

still smiling, so Matty knew he wasn't actually mad or anything. "Distance isn't going to break us up, sweetheart. But I *do* want to keep seeing you as often as possible." He chuckled and kissed Matty's forehead. "I kind of like having my boyfriend close by."

Matty chewed his lip, Cas's words seeping through him like he was slipping into a hot bath. "I like that, too," he admitted. "What do you suggest?" This was definitely one of those problems he just wanted Cas to fix.

Cas nodded. "Well, to start with, how about I get an apartment in New York, and we can manage flying back and forth for a while? Just take one thing at a time. I'll pay for the flights, of course, but we might want to start thinking about what kind of role you'd like to take on in the royal household."

Relief made those pesky tears want to spring in Matty's eyes again. That all sounded perfect, exactly what he'd hoped for. A slight worry crossed his mind, wondering if that was greedy of him. But that was his awful parents and useless ex-boyfriends talking. Once and for all, he banished them from his mind.

Cas told him he was perfect, and Matty believed him. He was a good person who deserved good things. And he wanted so badly to do something that he felt mattered with his life.

"You mean like the charity work you mentioned?" he asked excitedly. He had to be honest, that sounded *way* better than ripping ticket stubs or waiting tables.

Cas nodded. "But I know you want to be close to your family, too, so we'll just start by dividing our time and see how it goes. Is that a good enough plan?"

Matty beamed and kissed Cas softly on the lips. "Absolutely."

"Well, look at you two, hiding away in the corner," a simpering voice floated above the thrum of the ball. "I suppose you're used to hiding, though." Von Tarr laughed her tinkling glass laugh that she obviously thought was adorable and had probably helped her get away with a great deal of shit in the past.

Matty kind of felt sorry for her. How sad to be so fake, reveling in other people's misfortune.

"Hello, Ms. von Tarr," he said pleasantly, relaxing into his most carefree smile. Cas automatically put his hand on the small of Matty's back, and Matty leaned against his side. "How are you this evening?"

Ida von Tarr blinked, her smile only faltering slightly. Her lumbering cameraman was hovering by her shoulder. Matty wondered if he had the right lens in tonight to capture all the gossip they would no doubt be publishing by morning. In fact, he wondered how they had even gained access to the royal event at all.

But he didn't care about that, not really. He wasn't here to control anything, aside from him and Cas having a good time, together representing the country that Cas was so proud of.

He raised his eyebrows, waiting for von Tarr to reply to his question. She didn't, of course. She cleared her throat and shook her head, doubling her effort on her fake smile. It stretched her red lips like a mad clown, her eyes narrow like glittering beetles in the twinkling chandelier light.

"Come on, guys," she said jovially. "You're not fooling

anyone. I thought Benedict and Leopold were the ones who kept things interesting around this place. Did you want your share of the limelight, Cassander, by bringing a commoner to dangle off your arm like a Christmas ornament?" She laughed, less like tinkling and more shattering glass. Her tone changed to faux concern. "This won't last more than a minute, Mr. Doyle. Don't you have any self-respect? He's just using you for a joke!"

Matty wondered if Cas was going to respond in the time it took for the smile to creep onto Matty's face. He was genuinely relieved when Cas appeared to leave the reply to Matty. In fact, he felt a thrill rush up his spine as he leaned slightly closer, looking von Tarr in the eye.

"Your Highness," he said softly.

Von Tarr blinked. "What?" she snapped.

"The correct term," Matty said slowly as he straightened up again, "when addressing any member of the royal family, is 'Your Highness.' Hopefully you'll remember that in the future." He turned and looked at the love of his life. "Like so. Would you care to dance, *Your Highness?*"

Matty was getting pretty good at reading every tiny flicker on Cas's face. And the adoration in his eyes in that moment could have fueled Matty all the way back to New York, it was so potent.

"I'd be delighted," Cas said back, then brushed his lips over Matty's ear. *"Your Highness,"* he whispered. Not that Matty cared if anyone else heard, let alone von Tarr. She could only hurt them if they allowed her to. The two of them knew exactly what it meant for Cas to call Matty that.

Matty didn't know for sure if one day he might have the honor of becoming a prince of Rosavia. But Cas's new little name for him confirmed he could step up to that challenge, if that was where fate brought them. They still had some bumps in the road ahead of them, but this was their start of forever, he was sure.

And as Cas led him to the dance floor and guided Matty through his first-ever waltz, Matty wasn't scared or unsure or intimidated.

This was his dream come true, his real life, as impossible as it might seem, and he was going to live for every moment of it.

Epilogue

"Stop pacing."

Cas threw a withering look at his valet, who was sitting at his dining room table, but she didn't shift her gaze even a millimeter from her phone to appreciate it. She just kept bouncing her foot where one leg was crossed over the other.

"I'm not pacing," he grumbled, shoving his hands in his pockets. That didn't help, as there was something in one of them that was the main reason behind his nerves. Instead, he yanked his hands back out of his pants and began walking across the room...until he remembered he wasn't pacing.

He gave up and flopped on the sofa with a huff, checking his watch for the hundredth time. "He's late."

"No, he's not," Valentina said calmly, again not looking up. "He's not due for another few minutes. I've been watching the traffic report and everything."

"Why did I let you in here again?" Cas bemoaned, looking

around his suite. He adjusted the framed selfie on the side table of him and Matty that they'd taken just before the ball, then moved it back to where it had been.

Valentina snorted. "You didn't. I forced my way in to stop you from driving yourself crazy." She finally looked up over her glasses and arched an eyebrow at him. "Also, from letting you meet darling Matty looking like you've been dragged through a hedge backwards. Go fix your hair and then sit on your hands."

Cas sighed, but for once, he didn't mind being bossed around. It was ridiculous how nervous he was, and he was grateful for the telling off. Why was he losing his shit? It was just Matty. They'd seen each other every two weeks since the Royal Ball, taking turns to fly and visit each other, and video calling every day. And what Cas had to ask today, he was pretty hopeful that he knew what the answer would be.

But it was just so *fast*. Normal people didn't do this, did they?

"Just because you're now pacing in the bathroom doesn't mean I can't hear you doing it," Valentina called out in a sing-song voice.

Cas huffed and finished re-taming his hair. Then he washed and dried his hands before marching back into the living room. "Okay, but *now* he's late."

Valentina opened her mouth…just as there was a knock at the door.

She gave Cas a triumphant look as she rose to her feet. Then she clip-clopped swiftly across the room in her pencil-thin heels. As she stopped, her hand on the door handle, she looked over her shoulder and fixed Cas with a firm stare. "Relax. *Breathe.* Everything is going to be fine."

Cas inhaled deeply, then nodded. Only then did she open the door.

Matty's face showed a moment of surprise at being confronted by Valentina, but then he broke into his usual friendly smile. "Hi, Valentina! How're you doing?"

Cas was just able to make out her wink. "I'm great, Matty. I'll leave you boys to it." She then turned and *definitely* winked at Cas. "Have fun," she said in that same sing-song voice. Then she and the footman who had escorted Matty disappeared down the corridor, and Matty was stepping inside Cas's suite.

He automatically locked the door. That was their custom. Shutting away the outside world so it was just the two of them.

Well, and Bella. But she was busy sunning herself by the window, squirming on her back as was normal.

As Matty abandoned his larger-than-usual suitcase by the door and rushed into Cas's arms, Cas inhaled his unique scent. He was generally tired and rumpled after his long flight, but to Cas, he was always heavenly.

"I have some news," Matty said. He was practically vibrating, he was so excited.

"Come here," Cas murmured, leading him by the hand to the sofa. He figured he couldn't keep it in any longer, so he held Matty's hands as they lowered onto the cushions. "Matty, before you say anything, I have something to ask you," he began…

…just as Matty blurted out, "Cas, I'm moving to Alpina."

For a second, they both just stared at one another.

"What?" Cas asked.

"What?" repeated Matty.

Cas shook his head. "Did you just say you're *moving to Alpina?*"

Matty chewed his lip as a smile warred with his lips. "Um, yes."

A laugh escaped Cas's throat as he threw his arms around Matty. Then he cupped his face. "What? How? I don't understand? What about your family?"

Matty beamed, his eyes full of happy tears. "That's why I'm moving. Finley got accepted by an elite archery coach from the training summer camp. She came with me on this flight, and is literally starting school right now." He sniffed and rubbed his eyes, clearly overflowing with pride. "She got into Elm Willows. Isn't that amazing?"

Cas was so full of emotion he couldn't say anything for a second, so he kissed Matty on the lips. Then he kissed him again and again before wiping away Matty's spilled tears with his thumbs. "That's incredible, sweetheart. She'll love it there, I'm sure. And huge congratulations to her on being signed by the coach."

Matty nodded and chuckled wetly. "I know. It's a dream. So Reghan and Lola have thrown everything to the wind, and are applying for work visas and looking at houses on the edge of the city. Reghan is doing pretty good, and should be well enough to travel soon. My friend Esosa is helping them. Her sister Shommie and her family are thinking of leaving the

UK and getting a place here too, so then we'll all be together! And best of all, it looks like Reghan and Lola can get a real *house* here for what they were paying for an apartment in Queens," he added in a scandalized tone.

Cas chuckled. He had been looking into buying his own apartment in New York, so he could well believe it. But... maybe he wouldn't have to now? "So there's nothing keeping you in America?" he asked tentatively.

Matty blew a raspberry. "Absolutely not. Especially as Reghan is doing so well on her treatment. In no small thanks to you," he added fondly.

Cas had insisted on covering all of her medical bills and getting her the best treatment available. Reghan had always had a good chance on this round of chemo, but she really seemed to be thriving. No doubt the mountain air would also do her a world of good.

"So they're getting a house, but you...?" he prompted. He wanted Matty to be bold and ask for what he wanted. He'd been getting so good at that in the time they'd been together. But this was a big one. Cas held his breath.

But not for long.

Matty grinned and bit his lip, bouncing slightly on the sofa. "I thought maybe we could move in together. If that's what you'd want?"

Cas let out a cry and threw his arms around Matty, kissing all over his cheeks as he dragged him down on the sofa. "I've wanted that since you first left me on that wretched plane back to New York. Three months has been enough!"

Matty laughed and managed to wrangle Cas in for a kiss on

the lips. "I packed everything I could into that case," he said, glancing toward the door. Cas *had* thought that was an extra-large bit of luggage compared to what Matty usually brought with him. "My sister can ship the rest, although there isn't much, really." He sighed and placed his hand above Cas's heart. "I've got everything I need right here."

Cas placed his hand over Matty's and squeezed it hard. "So you don't have to leave again?" His voice almost cracked with emotion.

Matty shook his head. "Nope. I'm all yours."

Cas's heart skipped a beat. He really hoped so. "Well, about that question I wanted to ask." He pulled Matty up so he was sitting...

...then Cas moved off the side of the sofa so he was kneeling on the floor. On one knee.

Matty's eye widened with a gasp. "Cas?" he asked, a smile playing on his lips as his eyes filled with tears. "Are you proposing?"

Cas swallowed, finally retrieving the small box from where it had been digging in his pants pocket. "Shush, let me ask my damn question first." Matty looked amused, sitting up straighter on the sofa. Cas held up the box and opened it to show the sapphire-encrusted band inside. "Um, yes. Matty Doyle, you changed my life. You helped me become the man I always wanted to be. I know it's soon, but I know how I feel. Will you marry me?"

Matty bit his lip, then slid off the couch to kneel in front of Cas. He tugged on Cas's pant leg, encouraging Cas to get on both knees as well. "Oh, Cas," he said with such deep fondness, choking back a sob. "Why are you nervous? I love you *so* much. I'm moving across the world for you. You're already my whole life. Yes, *yes*, of course it's a yes!"

Cas really had thought he'd be so cool in this moment. Instead, he gulped down his hiccup and threw his arms around Matty's neck again, hugging him for dear life. "I thought you'd be more surprised or something," he confessed with a laugh.

Matty leaned back and cupped his hands on either side of Cas's face with a happy sigh as tears traced down his face. "Don't get me wrong, hearing you actually ask me is a dream come true. But...look at what I'm wearing, Your Highness," he said pointedly.

Cas blinked. "A shirt and jeans?" he said uncertainly. "You look hot," he added, just for good measure.

Matty snorted and shook his head. "A double-*cuffed* shirt. Look." He twisted his wrist and showed Cas the rose cufflinks he'd given him. Cas's heart caught in his throat. "I knew it would be complicated. I knew it wasn't going to be simple for us. But that night, you earned my trust that when the stars were aligned, our lives would come together the way they were supposed to. Destiny has our backs, remember? And when Finley got signed by that coach..." Matty grinned and took a shuddery breath as more tears spilled down his cheeks. "I booked myself a one-way ticket and decided to really show you how serious I am about us." He kissed Cas again as Cas's heart ached with relief. "I'm sorry I'm not more surprised, but, baby...I was already a sure thing."

Cas remembered sharing those words after their first kiss, and he laughed even though his eyes were wet. "I hate to break it to you," he whispered conspiratorially. "But I was a sure thing, too."

"Aren't we hopeless?" Matty said as he laughed and wiped his face.

"Totally," Cas agreed, kissing his love through his impossibly happy smile. "God, I love you so much, Matty. I thought about proposing in the city apartment, but I haven't been back there really since our time there, and it felt…"

Matty gave him a slightly sad look and caressed the side of his face. "Fake? Yeah. This is home now."

He looked around Cas's suite, and Cas realized he was right. Matty had fit in so well here, conversing easily with family and staff alike. He'd blossomed here in Rosavia.

Then Matty turned back to Cas, a sudden look of excitement. "But how about we spend tonight at the cabin?" he asked eagerly. "Just us two, in the woods away from everything. Kind of like a honeymoon for our proposal night?"

Cas thought of that night. How everything had changed for them after the storm, only for the glorious sunshine to come back for them in the morning.

Matty was right. Cas couldn't believe he hadn't thought to propose there. *That* was where their real love had begun, and they hadn't been back there since that night.

But the rest of their lives were going to be in this palace. They could escape whenever they wanted to the cabin for a vacation, but the palace was going to be their real lives. So, no. Cas knew this was the perfect place to propose. They didn't need a fantasy. Real life was wonderful enough for them.

Besides, Matty was right, he had *kind* of proposed the night of the ball.

"Okay, sure thing," Cas said, waggling his eyebrows. "If you want to stay at the cabin tonight, that's what we'll do."

"But this time without getting lost in the pouring rain," Matty said with a laugh.

"I want to be with you, come rain *or* shine," Cas said firmly. Then, with a grin, he added, *"Your Highness."*

Matty inhaled sharply, his eyes shimmering with yet more tears as they widened and his mouth dropped open. *Holy fuck. That* was the surprise that Cas had been hoping for, deep down. He wanted this moment to be so special, so authentic for Matty.

"Oh…!" Matty said, fluttering his hands in front of his face. "Oh! You've said that so many times. But this makes it *real* now, doesn't it? I'm going to be a prince? *Your* prince!"

Cas sniffed, finally losing the battle with his own tears. He kissed Matty and held him so tightly. They were huddled on the floor by the sofa, just like after the first time they'd made love in the light, when Cas had realized that Matty had already captured his heart.

"You're my *everything,*" he said emphatically. "I just wanted to get you a shitload of precious stones to prove it." They laughed wetly as Cas slipped the ring over Matty's finger. "I know diamonds are worth more-"

"The sapphires are perfect," Matty insisted. "I want blue roses *everywhere* at our wedding. They've been my favorite since the start, and I'm obsessed." He waggled his fingers at Cas, showing off the band. "And now I'll match."

Cas caught his hand to kiss the palm. "Wren will be thrilled. But he'll be even more thrilled that he gets to select an American rose for you." Cas thought fondly of how much his brother had matured this year. "In fact, I'm pretty sure he's been working on that since the ball."

Matty winked. "See. I knew there was a reason he was your favorite brother."

"Shut up," said Cas, rolling Matty onto the floor as they kissed in a tangle of limbs. Then he sighed, knowing he had to be totally honest. They'd promised each other that. "Are you *sure* it's not too soon? Because I've had my moments of doubt, and who knows what the press and people will think-"

"Shh!" Matty pressed his finger to Cas's lips. "I'm supposed to be the adorable one, and you're supposed to look after me, remember?"

Cas sighed. "Yes," he said firmly.

"So stop second-guessing taking something for yourself that doesn't revolve around crown and country." Matty rolled them so they were side-by-side, their heads pillowed on their arms as they looked at each other. "Like Finley says, when you have something in your sights, you have to fire, or you might miss. A crazy set of circumstances brought us together, but *we're* the ones who control our own fates and are going to make sure we *stay* together, right?"

"Right," Cas agreed with a relieved exhale.

Matty looked at his sapphire ring, then gave Cas a leisurely kiss. "I told you I'd look after you as well," he said softly. "Just like you look after me."

Cas brushed back one of Matty's gorgeous wayward curls. "And when we do that, we're stronger than ever," he said.

"Exactly," Matty agreed. He entwined the hand that now wore Cas's ring with Cas's own. "Forever."

Cas looked into Matty's blue eyes that matched his new ring perfectly. Cas had been so resigned to fixing everyone else in this family for so long, he'd never truly expected to find his own happiness. But he had. All because Matty's luggage had gotten lost on his connecting flight. All because so many tiny little strands of destiny had been brought together by the universe, and Cas had walked into a sporting goods store at precisely the right time.

Fate was on their side, and Matty was right. Now it was up to them to do the rest.

"Forever," Cas promised.

Because that was how fairy tales ended for lucky princes.

With a happily ever after.

Also in Rosavia Royals

Welcome to the tiny European country of Rosavia, where roses ramble over alpine slopes and princes fall for the men of their dreams. Every Rosavia Royals book happens simultaneously, so books can be read on their own, or in any order... but keep an eye out for familiar faces around the palace!

Join the Rosavia Royal Fans and chat about your favorite parts in our Facebook group here: facebook.com/groups/RosaviaRoyals

If you loved Rosavia, check out Men of Hidden Creek! Sign up to our newsletter to hear about exciting new worlds: wheretheheartisbooks.com/subscribe

All Rosavia Royals Books:

Up for Heir (#1)

by Stella Starling

A playboy heir needs: a man to marry, right now.

After spending half his life dodging his duty to the crown, the rebel heir to the Rosavian throne has been told in no uncertain terms that it's time to settle down. Prince Leopold has one month and a vetted list of suitable princesses, and he *will* announce his engagement during Rosavia's Royal Ball. But Leo's got his own ideas about what really suits him…

Royal Librarian Edvin Blom is good at not attracting attention. Shy and self-conscious of his stutter, he's used to being overlooked and more than happy to stay in the background. At least, until the

Crown Prince with a wild reputation shows up at the library's new opening and decides to flirt with Edvin's sister…

Edvin isn't at all what Leo thought he wanted, but turns out to be everything he can't stay away from. Edvin's been burned by falling for someone out of his league before, though. And believing that Leo has really fallen for him? While Edvin's drowning in his own doubts and insecurities, that might prove impossible… unless love gives them both a reason to come up for air.

Reign or Shine (#2)

by HJ Welch

A secret prince needs: a lost tourist to save.

Prince Cassander is on vacation from his overdeveloped sense of duty. While hiding out as simply 'Cas' in the Rosavian capital, he rescues a gorgeous, distressed American tourist. Matty has no idea that Cas is second in line to the throne. And with only two weeks together to explore the sparks between them, he doesn't need to ever find out.

New Yorker Matty Doyle is a fish out of water, taking care of his niece and mending his broken heart. When Cas rescues him, the handsome stranger coaxes Matty out of his shell and he throws caution to the wind. Nobody knows him here. Would it hurt to live a little for once?

But a prince can't stay secret in his own country for long. Cas would give anything to protect Matty from reality, but how can this fantasy together continue when they belong in different worlds?

Throne Together (#3)

by Zoe Dawn

A pining prince needs: a second chance at love.

Prince Julius has only ever wanted one man. Raised alongside Prince Dante of Thedes, the two were inseparable until their unspoken mutual attraction ignited into a single passionate encounter. Convinced that it ruined their friendship, Julius retreated to his duties in Rosavia, where he daydreams of another chance to win Dante's heart.

After four years apart, fate brings Prince Julius back to Thedes. He offers Dante a coveted invitation: return to the Rosavian palace for ten days, and be his plus-one to the Royal Ball of the century. Before long, they realize one night of passion wasn't enough, and they can't imagine losing each other again.

As the clock ticks down to the ball, Julius catches wind of Dante's family meddling, and he must decide if their feelings are real or if they've both been played. Were they always meant for each other, or is it all an illusion that will melt away at midnight?

In His Court (#4)

by Max Rowan

A spy prince needs: a man who sees through his disguise.

Prince Benedict is not what he seems. His image as a lazy playboy is carefully constructed to hide the truth. Trained since childhood to become Rosavia's top spy, he spends his life in disguise—and danger—to protect his country. Nobody sees the loneliness in his heart.

Felix Wright is a genius with four degrees, no real-world experience, and a top-secret job... and he's never even been kissed.

A lifetime of being alienated for his most valuable assets has left him reluctant to trust the charming prince who thrusts him into fieldwork for the very first time.

When the Crown Jewels are stolen two weeks before the royal ball, it's their job to save the country's reputation. Benedict helps Felix believe in himself, while Felix slowly coaxes the real prince out of hiding. But can they find the jewels and rescue the most priceless treasures of all: each other?

Barely Regal (#5)

by E. Davies

A bratty boy prince needs: a firm but fair Daddy.

Prince Renford is a royal brat. Nineteen and last in line for the throne, Wren hates his made-up job: Commander of Roses. Good thing his long-time valet has a firm hand—if only Wren could tempt him to break all palace protocol and use it.

Thom Pierce is sixteen years older. Old enough to know he should ignore his prince's less-than-subtle flirtation. He's been burned by a higher-ranked boy before. His job and reputation are at stake if the palace catches a scandal unfolding under their noses.

Wren needs the part of Thom that he's kept locked away for years. If the young prince wants to be taken as seriously as his older brothers, he has to grow up fast. Thom's rules could help Wren become the man Thom knows he can be in time for the Royal Ball... or they could attract the very attention that forces them apart forever.

About the Author

HJ Welch is a contemporary MM romance author living in London with her husband and two balls of fluff that occasionally pretend to be cats. She began writing at an early age, later honing her craft online in the world of fanfiction on sites like Wattpad. Fifteen years and over a million words later, she sought out original MM novels to read. By the end of 2016 she had written her first book of her own, and in 2017 she fulfilled her lifelong dream of becoming a fulltime author.

She also writes contemporary British MM romance as Helen Juliet.

You can contact HJ Welch via social media:
Website – www.hjwelch.com
Newsletter (with FREE original stories)
Facebook Group – Helen's Jewels
Facebook Page – @HJWelchAuthor
Instagram – @helenjwrites
Twitter – @helenjwrites
Book Bub – @HJWelchAuthor
Email – helenjulietauthor@gmail.com

Robin Coal wonders if asking his straight housemate Dair to be his fake boyfriend for his high school reunion will be the worst thing he's ever done...or the best. But there's no way he's going home to face his abusive ex alone, and former Marine Dair is just the protection he needs. So long as he doesn't find out about Robin's secret crush, everything will be fine.

Mechanic Dair Epping never expected to spend a week sharing a bed with his adorable friend, however pretending to be bi is easier than he imagined. He knows he'll do anything to keep Robin safe from his ex-boyfriend, but as the chemistry between them grows, the line between fake and reality begins to blur.

Could Dair actually be bi? Even if he was, would an ex-Marine really be interested in a computer geek like Robin? When his ex's intentions turn dangerous, how far will Dair go to protect the man he's falling for?

Book One in Pine Cove. Safe Harbor is a steamy, standalone MM romance novel with a guaranteed HEA and absolutely no cliffhanger.

www.ingramcontent.com/pod-product-compliance
Lightning Source LLC
Chambersburg PA
CBHW020922110726
47900CB00001B/265